THE ELECTRIC SHEEP MASSACRE

A <u>LIQUID COOL</u> CYBERPUNK DETECTIVE NOVEL

Book Four

AUSTIN DRAGON

Published by Well-Tailored Books, California

The Electric Sheep Massacre
(Liquid Cool, Book 4)

978-1-946590-57-2 (paperback)
978-1-946590-51-0 (ebook)

http://www.austindragon.com

Book cover design by Whendell Souza

Printed in the United States of America

CONTENTS

Introduction

My posthumous mentor, Wilford G., worked the supercity of Metropolis as a freelance private detective for seventy years until he died at the ripe old age of 92. He said, in this city, you'd come across such an array of bad guys that it would make your head spin. Each would bring their own unique version of vice and violence to the table. In the short time in my new career, I could already attest to this reality.

But sometimes, it wasn't the ultra-violent or ultra-brainy bad guy that stuck with you. Sometimes, it would be a crazy maniac, who was just plain weird. To this day, I don't know what that blond-haired Japanese guy was all about. On this case, he was a stalking shadow that was always either just a few steps ahead of me or just a few steps behind.

I met him and many, many more in a case where illegal drugs and illegal VR (virtual reality) intersected. I encountered people and places so grimy and slimy, I felt like burning my clothes and wished I could shed my skin for a new one. Like most of my big cases, it started simply, but it was a facade for a much more sinister situation underneath.

Unlike my other cases in Metropolis, I solved this one by leaving my supercity. It was only "across the pond," across a Great Ocean, but UKT seemed far enough away to be in another galaxy and those Brits were as alien to me as space people Up-Top.

This case was a travelogue. I literally traveled to the far corners of Metropolis, other countries, and traveled to another place I never thought I'd ever see in my life, as black as any outer space void.

The blond Japanese maniac, the London Prime characters, the Road Courier, "The Shocker," the Far Escape mercenaries—none of them were the actual case. The case was an impossible event that took place in VR, and all its darkness and shadowy intrigue was as real as the mass-murder itself. It was my case of **The Electric Sheep Massacre**.

PART ONE

The Hinterlands

CHAPTER 1

China Doll

"Post-wedding bliss" was supposed to be my watch phrase for the next couple of months. We had fully settled into our new 150th floor apartment home in the Concrete Mama. Who said one couldn't live in style in Rabbit City? I'd married a famous full-time fashionista with mad interior design skills. The whole place looked like one of those photos out of an haute couture home magazine, featuring some gazillionaire in Silicon Dunes or Opus Fields, but it wasn't. It was Rabbit City, and it was all ours!

"Cruz, what's that?"

China Doll was my wife. Women called her China; men called her Doll. Only her parents and I called her by her first name, Dot. Her question pierced the air before I even knew she was in the room with me.

I was about to answer, but as had happened before, I was stuck for a pet name: "Honey?"—no way—I wasn't using that. To me, honey was bee goo, though it was supposed to be healthy and antiseptic. That was no way to address one's significant other, for me.

"Cruz, what's that in your hand?"

No, it wasn't anything crude. I had walked back into the bedroom and grabbed it from the back of the top drawer of my new dresser—we had matching his and hers dressers, another wedding gift from one of our million and one relatives. I had managed to keep it hidden for this long.

"Uh, nothing," I replied.

"Cruz, what's that in your hand?"

I had spun around to face her. As the consummate fashionista with every piece of clothing, every accessory, and every piece of jewelry being the trendiest and the most stylish, the color of the day was indigo. Her hair was tied back, with the ponytail carefully resting on one shoulder, with her pearl necklace and colored neck scarf. Her makeup was always perfect, but never overdone.

She was across the room with her hands on her hips—a pose any warm-blooded husband knew to fear like the bubonic plague. Every one of her fingers had a colored ring, and each wrist had multiple bracelets.

The "contraband" in my hand were my old-school electric hair clippers. I had one hand behind my back, so she couldn't see them. I was figuring out how I could hide them, but before I could put my plan into action, Dot had marched across the room, grabbing the hand behind my back.

"Cruz!"

I admit that trying to drop the clippers to the floor and kick them under the bed was childish. She bent down and reached underneath for them.

"Cruz!" She stood up with the hair clippers in her hand. She had a scrunched-up nose expression of disapproval. "How could you? You're married to one of the top beauty and image stylists in Metropolis, but you cut your own hair!"

"I was getting rid of them."

"Cruz, this is totally unacceptable. You're a famous detective, and no famous detective cuts his own hair. How old is this?"

Now she was holding them from the very tip of the handle as if they were radioactive.

"They're not that old."

"Cruz, this thing is ancient. It's spoiling the *feng shui* of our home."

She and my long-time hair clippers were gone from the room.

"Dot, what are you doing with my clippers?"

She reappeared at the doorway, smiling.

"What clippers." she said. It wasn't a question; it was declaration.

I knew they were plummeting 150 stories to the bottom of the Concrete Mama trash chute.

Husbands of Earth unite! Hide your stuff from sticky-finger wives!

The routine was simple. Dot and I always left the apartment together. The only thing I had to ensure was that I had my tan fedora on my head, my tan slicker on my back, keys and wallet in the pocket. I had my guns locked in the vehicle, so I didn't worry about them. Dot, on the other hand, had her purse and at least three bags. Sometimes, she had her big easel portfolio from working on some fashion designs for a client. Obviously, all *she* had to carry was the purse. *I* was the one loaded up with all her baggage. Baggage was supposed to be what you had when you were going to Metro International for a two-week vacation to some exotic man-made island resort, not to your work place every day.

I was still getting used to living on the 150th floor. Before getting married, I was on the 100th floor in apartment 9732. All floors below the 101th floor had to go all the way to the main lobby to catch the separate elevators to the parking sections. Now we were big time, having switched with other tenants in the building, who wanted to have a smaller place. I kept my room number—for mail purposes—but now had three times the space with the wife.

Dot drove a dark silver Bee. It was just the kind of hovercar speedster bug a booshy fashionista would drive. It was small and speedy, which was perfect for her. I loaded up the trunk with her work baggage and sent her on her way with a kiss. She jetted out of the parking bay like a rocket as she always did.

My vehicle was a classic vintage red Ford Pony. My baby! Built from scratch as a kid and still driving strong. It had been in mint condition until my last case, but I was never going to sell it, so it didn't matter. To all that saw it, it was the perfect, original muscle vehicle—bright red to stand out in a sea of dreary blacks, grays, and silvers.

The Pony was ten times faster than my wife's Bee, but I flew out of the parking bay in a way that was smooth and cool. My destination was my own detective agency office—Liquid Cool.

CHAPTER 2

Punch Judy

Morning sky traffic in Metropolis was always a mess. If it happened to be raining, it was worse than a mess. Heavy rain, and suddenly, people couldn't drive. I couldn't imagine what human life was like when there were cars rolling around on the ground on cheap rubber tires. How did people get around without killing each other all the time? Sky traffic meant the madness was all around you—above, below, either side. But for the experienced hovervehicle driver, this was as normal as breathing. Danger was part of driving.

As I flew out of Rabbit City to Buzz Town, where my offices were located, I reflected on my wife's exceptional stint as fixer in my last major case. Without her quick thinking and clever planning, I would have been a permanent piece of the pavement at the foot of my Liquid Cool building tower—the tower didn't belong to me; I just had an office in it—but I wasn't going to leave the danger behind to become a fancy stylist, even if I ever learned how to cut hair without clippers, and she was never going to become a private eye. She didn't say anything about it anymore because she knew it was the job, my job.

I was smart enough not to tell her about all the times I'd gotten shot or just "how bad bad could be" in this world. Wilford G. said it best in his book, *How to be a Great Detective with 100 Rules*. "When it comes to the day in the life of the street detective, in regards to your spouse, keep your mouth shut!"

Liquid Cool was on Circuit Circle in Buzz Town, not a high-end part of the supercity, by no means, but it was not the dumps. It was that in-between section of the city, and I felt my firm classed up the neighborhood.

Many didn't know it, but we'd dramatically increased the secret surveillance of the building. The main lobby doors, the parking bay, the elevators, and hallway to my offices were all under the watchful eye of visible and hidden cameras. All those cameras fed to a bank of monitors at the desk area of my secretary, office manager, or whatever extra title she had given herself for the week—Punch Judy.

Some called her Punch. I called her PJ. She had nicely toned-looking bionic arms that she liked to show off. When she'd first started, they had their au-natural silver shell. Now that she had a steady paycheck, she had gotten the spray skin treatment. With the hard edges and lines, they were obviously bionic, but her arms did look good on her.

In I came through the main door, and there were a couple of people waiting in the lobby. PJ also lived in my same Concrete Mama building, which I always seemed to forget and remember all over again when I saw her first thing in the morning. My ex-felon, cyborg secretary was respectable nowadays, always getting in and opening the office doors before her boss arrived.

"Ah, you decided to work today," she said to me as her bionic fingers typed away at super-speed at her desk.

"What are you typing all the time?" I asked.

"Um, is your office out here?" She stopped typing.

"I know where my office is."

"Out here is my domain. In there," she said, pointing to my personal office door, "is yours. Don't you worry about what I do out here. You take care of the clients; I take care of the business."

I began laughing. "Okay, boss." My door was already open and I strolled in.

As normal, on my desk were stacks of messages arranged the PJ way: solid paying clients first, strong potentials, possibles, and "garbage." She had a new stack category—"Phishy foolishness."

"Is Phishy coming in today?" I asked.

"No," she yelled back from her desk. "He said he'll call you later."

I felt the PJ presence at my doorway and glanced over. There she was smiling at me. I hadn't even walked around my desk to sit down.

"Clients?" I asked.

"*Paying* clients," she said. "Oh, wait." She disappeared and then reappeared. "Wrong ones. They're next."

"Who are these?"

"*Poubelle.*"

"I heard that," said a male voice of one of the waiting clients.

PJ always acted as if I knew French, which I didn't, but she was getting me up to speed on her favorite words and phrases. Non-paying clients she referred to as *poubelle*—trash. She seemed to forget, in a multi-ethnic, multi-lingual supercity like Metropolis that she wasn't the only person who spoke or understood French.

"Hey! No eavesdropping." I saw her head turn, shouting at the waiting clients.

CHAPTER 3

The Firm

I had been getting unsolicited offers for partners on a steady basis, and large private investigation firms wanting to buy me out to work for them were relentless. I wasn't interested in either, but they kept coming. Now, they were resorting to pretending to be clients, to get face-time with me.

I wanted to remain a one-man shop. That gave me the most freedom and the least headaches. Why would I sell my own company to work in a cubicle at one of the megacorporate detective firms? I'd be back to nothing.

"Mr. Cruz, it would be the opposite of nothing." The man who understood French was a big man with a big mustache, broad shoulders and had a shiny ring on each of his fingers, except his thumbs.

The other man with him was some toady who probably was there to open doors and push elevator buttons for him.

"I'm not selling Liquid Cool," I said.

"We're not buying, Mr. Cruz," he said. "My firm wants you to work for us. We're a solid firm. One hundred years in business. Five hundred full-time detectives. We'd make you a partner right from the start. You'd have your own team under you, your own secretarial staff, even your own driver."

"What would be the cut?"

It was going to be a firm "no" on my part, but I was curious to know what this megacorp thought I was worth, to make money off my reputation, which I had built on my own, without any help from them.

"With the full resources of my firm behind you, your cut would be one percent of profit—the company's profit." He said it smiling and wiggling his eyebrows at me.

"Mr.—"

"Dean."

"Mr. Dean, I'm flattered that your firm wants to hire me, but I need to try this solo thing for a while, and see how it goes—see where it takes me. My needs are few at this stage in my life. The only team I need is me, myself, and I. My cyborg secretary is quite adequate for me at the moment. I like to drive myself to and from where I'm going, especially when that ride is a classic Ford Pony. So, let's leave it there. I'll keep your card, and as things change in life, I'll know where to go."

"Fair enough, Mr. Cruz. Remember that we were here first."

Actually, he wasn't the first one to want to hire me, more like the 50th, but I wasn't going to tell him that.

"You bet, Mr. Dean. It's a deal."

The two men stood, and we shook hands. I walked them out of my office. Yep, PJ was right. They were clients from the *poubelle* pile.

CHAPTER 4

The Far Escape Crew

I did not like shifty people—people who couldn't look you in the eye, people who were always fidgeting with their hands. I had four of them sitting in my office. Well, one of them wasn't shifty; she was annoying. Her eyes were locked on me, and she was not blinking.

"A private detective," she said. She had fair skin and long jet-black hair, wearing a matching black slicker outfit.

"That's me," I replied.

"I never met a real detective before. I read about them in books. Don't think that I ever read a detective book, though. I always thought they were sleazy little men who peeped through dirty keyholes to get the incriminating evidence from grimy little clients."

"What brings you down to my sleazy little office, Ms.—"

"Black."

"Ms. Black," I repeated.

"Yes, and this is Ms. Blue and Ms. Green and Mr. Pink."

"Mr. Pink?" the one male among them asked. "Why do I have to be Mr. Pink?"

"Because that's what we agreed upon," Ms. Black snapped back.

"There are more colors in the rainbow than pink."

"Pink's not a color in the rainbow," I added.

"There! It's not even a real color of the rainbow," he said.

"We're not changing names again," Black said.

They had no problem revealing to me that they were using aliases, but I ran background checks on all clients, so they'd probably decided they were being charitable by saving me the trouble.

Ms. Blue was petite, with short blond hair, in a dark top and white bell bottoms. The only thing blue about her were her eyes. Ms. Green was this tall brunette in a one-piece brown slicker. I felt as if she were one of those karate-chop fighters. I couldn't tell if her eyes were green.

"Pink is not the name for a man."

"We are not changing names again!"

"Do you all want me to come back some other time, when you know your own names?" I asked.

"No, that will not be necessary, Mr. Cruz."

"Are you sure?"

"We're sure," she answered.

"Actually, I don't think I'll be able to help you."

"You don't even know what we want to hire you for, Mr. Cruz."

"The last time a woman came into this office with a fake British accent to hire me, things didn't go my way. I'm sure you can find another sleazy little detective to hire."

"Did I hurt your feelings, Mr. Cruz? Also, my accent isn't fake, and it isn't British, by the way. We could play 'Name the Country' for 500 bucks, and maybe you can guess."

"Oh, it sounds British to me, but I admit, I've always been terrible at foreign accents."

I stood from my desk.

"Good luck with your detective search. I hope you find the right person you need."

The four of them didn't know how to react. That last sentence was genuine. I had reached a comfortable point in my new career. I could turn down any case or client I wanted and still pay the bills. Being a famous detective was starting to reap benefits.

They did leave, but PJ gave me a look. We both knew we had not seen the last of them. They came to see me for a reason. They didn't just randomly pick me off the Net. They weren't going to go away so easily, at least until they'd presented their case to me.

CHAPTER 5

Phishy

Australia. Ms. Black had an Australian accent. British—Australian—whatever. She had a non-American English accent, and she wanted to hire me. Speaking other languages was fine; I couldn't understand the person, but speaking English with accents—I was going to be very cautious about that forever, after my previous NeuroDancer case.

Ms. Black had called me a sleazy little detective, which I took no offense to at all. Yet here I was in the heavy rain, parked in my vehicle at a rest stop diner, doing another cheating spouse case. I hated them, but there were so many of them, and it was quick money. All I had to do was screen the clients, so the people and places I was dealing with weren't too low-end; then, it was like automatic money. Get the case, solve the case—all in a day. Originally, I wasn't going to take such cases, but I had to remember I was a private detective. There was always going to be a bit of sleaze, a bit of violence and vice. Every one of my cases was not going to be some high-profile, high-intrigue major case. The average case was going to be little ones just like this one.

The idiot mark I was following met his girlfriend right in public. I preferred to take pictures with a separate camera device, rather than my mobile phone—more versatility, more features, and all I used the camera for was for this kind of work, so I left it in the glove compartment of my vehicle. I had plenty of pictures for his wife, so another easy paycheck.

I was flying away when my car video-phone rang, and I picked it up.

"Cruz!"

Phishy was a street hustler. Nothing dangerous or too illegal, nothing more than misdemeanor situations—pay the fine and be on his way, not even a blot on the record. Cops and courts couldn't be bothered with street hustlers working non-violent, low money scams. With the vile crime of Metropolis, one had to set priorities properly.

"Phishy, where are you?"

My work associate was known for his long-sleeved shirts with fish all over them. He also had procured my two favorite weapons—my pop-gun and my Up-Top omega-gun.

"I'm working the streets, Cruz, hustling my deals and making money."

"What about the project?"

"Oh yeah!"

You had to keep Phishy's rat brain focused.

"Is it ready?"

"It's almost ready, Cruz."

"When?"

"Give me until the end of the week."

"Phishy—"

"Don't worry, Cruz. I'll have it ready. You've got a whole network of sidewalk johnnies and sallies out there for you."

"But I don't want them—"

"No, no, Cruz. No one will know that it's you. People will be working for Cruz, but they won't know they're working for Cruz. I love it!"

"Tell me when it's ready. I want to be able to test the network."

"Don't worry, Cruz. It'll be ready."

"Okay."

"Oh, I wanted to show you something, Cruz."

"What?"

On the video screen, a black fedora appeared in front of his face. "Ta da!"

"What's that, Phishy?"

"It's my new hat."

"Phishy, you can't be wearing a fedora. I have one. The Sidewalk Johnny Brigade wears them. You have to be Phishy. You're different from anyone else."

I saw his rat brain spinning. "Yeah, Cruz. You're right. I have to be different."

"If you start wearing a fedora, then everyone's going to start saying you're part of the Cruz crew. Without it, you'll be Phishy, the independent operator. That's what we want. That's what you want."

"Yeah, Cruz. You're right."

I loved when my random non-logic made logical sense. I just didn't want him copying me.

"But I'll keep the hat anyway," he added, to my annoyance.

CHAPTER 6

The Sniff

PJ frantically called me on the video-phone. A "really important VIP" was waiting for me at the office. I had no idea what the heck that meant, but I was finished with the job, so returning to the office it was. Usually, once I left the office, I didn't go back until the end of the day. I stayed out working case after case, or hitting different business districts in search of new clients. I didn't need to do the latter anymore, but I did it anyway. This was still a supercity of 50 million people and even though Liquid Cool was the center of some high-profile cases, even businesses on my very own floor had no idea who I was or what I did. "Famous detective" was a phrase, not a reality. PJ would say, "Who cares about the Average John and Jane; you have to be famous to the people who can pay their bills."

As soon as I entered the office and saw the dapper little man sitting in the waiting area, I recognized him—"The Sniff". Anyone who was anyone in the classic hovercar world knew him. I had restored classic hovercars for a living and had managed to build my own from scratch, but he found, bought, and sold them for a living. I'd met him for the first time at the first hovercar show I'd ever attended. I was just learning about hovercars in general, but classic ones in particular. The center of the stadium was this same man, as dapper then as he was now. The hovercars he'd had on display were jaw-dropping. He even had a paleo-classic model that was over 600 years old, but its engine purred when it started as if it had come off the factory assembly line that same day. Hovercar freaks buzzed around the vehicles; hovercar collectors talked business with him. I actually wanted to be him, but the schmoozing (literally) was a bit too physical for my germophobic sensibilities. Handshaking is one thing, but I don't need all the hugging, cheek kissing, and butt slapping. I decided I would restore hovercars, and that's what I'd done, very successfully, until becoming a "famous" detective.

"I remember you," I said.

The Sniff walked over to greet me. "Mr. Cruz, good to see you again, young man."

"I hope you're not in trouble."

"Oh, no." He laughed. "Nothing as exciting as that. May we sit for a chat?"

"Sure."

I led him to my private office, and we sat in my personal lounge area. He had in his hand a leather black portfolio. I don't think I'd ever seen him in person or in a photo without it.

"Do you want anything to drink?"

"Your very nice secretary made me a lovely cup of lemon tea."

That was news to me. I didn't know we had tea, but PJ had told me she ran the business. I just did the client thing.

"How can I help?"

"No, Mr. Cruz. I want to help you. I want to buy your Ford Pony."

I laughed.

"Buy my vehicle?"

"It is a classic."

"Yes, but it's not at the level that you buy and sell, Mr. S."

"Oh, Mr. Cruz. You are far too modest about your vehicle. I don't think even I could build a hovercar from scratch, let alone a high-tech classic, such as the model Ford Pony you built."

"True, but I'm picking up on something more, Mr. S."

"Because, in this case, what makes your vehicle unique and a commodity is—you."

"Me?"

"Mr. Cruz, your vehicle is very desirable in certain circles at the moment. Owned by a private detective of some note."

"Mr. S., please, don't B.S. me. No one cares who I am, unless they're hiring me for a case, and then all they care about is me solving a case. No one cares about the vehicle I drive."

"Mr. Cruz, your vehicle is a celebrity curiosity."

"Oh," I realized. "You mean the dead Movie-Town actors."

"I mean the dead Movie-Town superstar actors that you killed in your vehicle."

I wasn't quite sure how to react.

"Who wants to buy it?"

"Mr. Cruz, my clients, like yours, insist on remaining anonymous. I have two buyers, and once officially listed, I believe we'd get nibbles from at least a hundred more. This is my scouting mission to let you know that there are eager buyers out there who'd gladly take the vehicle off your hands for a fair price—a price that you'd be more than pleased with. Besides, with your skill, you could simply build another."

"It took me eighteen months to build my Pony."

"I'm sure you could build the next one even faster."

I couldn't believe I was seriously considering his offer.

"I've been made offers for the Pony before—"

"Yes, and you have always said 'No,' but we both know that an offer from my clientele is significantly different than the rabble on the street."

"I can't argue with that."

He stood from his seat. "I have left my card with your nice secretary. Think about it. Talk it over with your wife. Call me with a decision. My firm is about selling the dream. I expect both the buyer and the seller of my transactions to be fully satisfied with their piece of that dream—no regrets."

"Yes."

"It was nice seeing you again, Mr. Cruz. Hopefully, we can do some good business together. Oh, before I leave, here's another card for you, personally. I wrote on the back an estimate of what I think we could sell your vehicle for."

The Sniff was good. I'd gotten so many explanations as to how he got his nickname. He could sniff out a classic hovercar anywhere on the planet. He could inspect a vehicle and by sniffing alone tell what kind of condition it was in. When his firm delivered a vehicle to you, you'd sit inside all day sniffing yourself silly, inhaling that "new car smell."

He thanked PJ for his "lovely" cup of tea as he left the office. I looked at the back of the card, and my eyeballs almost fell to the ground.

I didn't have time for that. The call I was expecting came through, and I was in the Pony again, flying out of Buzz Town.

CHAPTER 7

Ms. Black

I had heard of the place before. It was a dimly-lit diner, bar, dance club all in one. The Sketchy Squirrel. The name said it all—it was for sketchy people doing sketchy things—meaning criminal things. While Dot and I wouldn't be caught dead in such a place, it was far from empty. It figured my fidgety group would know of the place and would want to meet there.

I decided to enter through the diner section first. It was so dark that I couldn't see anyone's face. A hand grabbed my forearm as I walked by, and there was Ms. Black sitting in a booth with some neon drink in front of her with a big straw. There was a door between sections, and whenever someone passed through it, the dance music would blare.

"You'd rather meet here than in a quiet office where you can actually see and hear people," I said as I sat down across from her. I noticed the rest of her crew in the booth right behind her peeking at me.

"You said I reminded you of a previous bad client with a non-American English accent, so I thought it would make you more comfortable to meet here."

"Here? Do you know how shady this place is?"

"Yes, drugs and more in the back restrooms."

"Why did you call me again? I thought you wanted your detectives sleazy."

"That is definitely not you, Mr. Cruz. You're kind of on the square side."

"No, I'm an isosceles trapezoid." I drew a picture in the air.

She was amused. "I'm not sure if you can help us, but everyone says you're resourceful, and you have quite the reputation for someone in the detective business for such a short time. I don't see it myself, yet."

"I'm a quick learner."

"What do you know about the Hinterlands?"

Now, I knew why she wanted to hire me and gave her a look. "I never did that race."

"I was told that you did. There and back."

"It's not true."

"You never raced hovercars."

"I did hovercar racing but never there. I don't know who started that rumor, but I never did. You know why?"

"Why?"

"I was a big chicken. I'm still a big chicken."

"We need to get to the Hinterlands. That's what we need. If not you, then who?"

"Why do you want to go there?"

"Are you going to get us there?"

"I'm still thinking."

"When you finish thinking, tell me, and I'll tell you."

"Do you know anything about the Hinterlands? Not rumors. The real stuff."

"I know it's dangerous, but with the right driver, we can manage."

I almost laughed. "You're expecting me to drive you there?"

"We have the money."

"Money? You can't spend money when you're dead. The driver would have to get you there and then drive back. That's insanity!"

"My guess is your thinking is over and the big chicken says 'No'."

I looked at her for a moment.

"When would you need to leave?" I asked.

"This week. The sooner, the better."

"I'll do some checking. Call me tomorrow morning, and I'll let you know if I can help you."

"You mean really help us?"

"I don't know yet, but tomorrow morning, I'll tell you for sure. If it's a yes, then we'll meet again—and it won't be in any Sketchy Squirrel."

She began laughing. "You're more offended by its name, aren't you?"

"Yes. Grown people don't go to any place named Sketchy Squirrel." I stood up. "Tomorrow."

"Okay, Mr. Cruz. Tomorrow. No Sketchy Squirrels." Now she was a laughing fool. I wasn't sure if it was the alcohol she was drinking or me.

CHAPTER 8

Scorpion Racer

There were not many red hovercars in Metropolis. I think I knew most of the ones in and around Rabbit City and Buzz Town. I was a man of my routine. I had noticed the Scorpion hoverspeedster when I left my offices. I was paranoid by nature, so if I thought I was being followed, I would try to lose the tail. I did so before flying to the Sketchy Squirrel.

I was back on the sky lane to my office. It was the red Scorpion behind me. I had a few case files with me, so I didn't have to go back, but I wasn't about to do any detective work with a possible tail. I slipped on my open-knuckle driving gloves, and I was ready. Most people thought Scorpions were fast, but they just looked fast; they were junk. My Pony could outrace one driving backwards.

My finger was about to shift into high gear when I saw flashing police lights—lights that must have popped out of the body of the vehicle, or I would have seen them. The damn Scorpion was an undercover cop car! Metro Police didn't have a Scorpion in their motor pool, so who was this guy? I was suspicious, and as I pulled off the sky lane traffic to set down onto a pit stop, I did what any good citizen did. I called the police.

My driver's side window was only down halfway, which was not what I usually did, but I needed to know if this guy was legit first. Both the Scorpion's driver and passenger door opened, and two men exited and started walking to me. I was tempted to pull my gun from its holster and rest it inside my jacket, but I couldn't do that now.

The man on the driver's side knocked on my half-down driver's window. I pushed the button to have it go down all the way.

"Yes?" I said.

"Are you Mr. Cruz?"

"I don't mean to be rude, but are you a police officer?"

He leaned down to peer inside my vehicle. "That's what cops do." He spoke with an accent! What was with all the accents? And, why didn't he answer my question?

"What do cops do?" The voice came from my dashboard video-phone.

"Oh, sorry, officer," I said. "This is Officer Riker. We were chattin' when you pulled me over."

"What's your unit number?" she yelled at him.

His mean face turned white, and he was already a very white Caucasian guy. "Uh, unit number?"

"Who are you?" she yelled. "Impersonating a Metro PD office is a felony and I'm—"

"Excuse me, ma'am." The other guy was leaning in my vehicle. He had darker skin, a ponytail, and a big smile. He too had an accent. "My name's Detective Rais and this is my partner Detective Pius."

"You're not Metro PD!" she said.

"Yes, ma'am, that is correct. We are from Euro—"

"I don't care where you two are from! Get your asses to Police One and register before I send real cops to arrest you both and throw you in jail. You can't pull over any Metro citizens. This is America. This is not

Euro-wherever-you're-from. I am going to wait for you two in the main lobby! How long am I going to have to wait?"

"We're leaving now, ma'am," Rais said.

"Don't call me 'ma'am'! My name's Officer Riker, but if your asses are not here pronto, you'll be calling me something else when I put my foot up your backside."

"Leaving now."

The two of them were out of my window, back in their hovercar, and streaking away.

"Thanks, Riker. A detective can't be too careful these days. There are all kinds of crazy people out there."

"Don't you know it. Crazy people impersonating cops is the surest way to get yourself shot!"

"That's what I'm saying," I said.

"I'll see you."

She was off my video-phone, and it was my time to laugh.

Who knew what those two clowns wanted? I was sure I'd find out soon enough. What was it with all these non-American accents around me? PJ was more than enough.

CHAPTER 9

Sidewalk Johnnies

When I was a kid making a name for myself on the classic hovercar restoration scene, I got involved for a short time in the hovercar street racing scene. The two went hand-in-hand, because no real hovercar collector would race their vintage "baby," but street racers had to have their speedsters restored too. Fast hovercars and expensive hovercars—classics everywhere.

I didn't last long on the racing scene, because I had no real interest in it. I wanted to restore classic hovercars, not race them at insane speeds, risking life, limb, or felonies if caught. Hovercar racing was illegal, so promoters were always finding new places to race, keeping just ahead of the police. That meant more out of the way places, and that meant more dangerous places. I had been to quite a few of them—all seedy parts of the supercity, mostly on the "mean streets" and some in places not even on the map. There were places so scary you were afraid that rodents would jump you to take all your money or shank you just for fun.

The Hinterlands was, on the scale of dangerous hovercar racing throughways, the Mount Everest of them all. To get there, you had to fly through the River, which wasn't a river. It was a corridor between

Metropolis and the next outer city thousands of miles away. The Hinterlands were what everyone called the region at the end of the River, the empty region between supercities. There were no hovercar sky lanes, no buildings, no life, nothing—except for "them." It was where the feral hoverracer gangs roamed.

I knew these gangs existed, but I didn't know what was urban myth and what was truth. There was one major hoverrace that I was supposed to ride shotgun on, but I conveniently disappeared. I ran away as fast as I could. I was not getting eaten by any cannibal gangs. No one got killed on that race, as had frequently happened in years before, hovercars crashing into the corridor walls or crashing to the ground at hundreds of miles an hour. Still, everyone said they'd heard the gangs coming, which is why the hoverrace was immediately cut short.

That was a long time ago. I had to find out what was actually out there on the River. Once I knew that, I would know why these accent-speaking people wanted me to drive them there or find someone who could.

One of the things that always made me feel like a real-life detective was working the streets for information. I was putting together a network to make the information come to me, but until then, I didn't mind making the rounds, chatting it up with the local sidewalk johnnies—street hustlers who spanned the walkways of Metropolis.

There were some people who went from their tower to their hovercar or public hoverrail and knew nothing of the world below on the streets. For the johnnies here on the streets, there was no world outside of here—the action and hustle of the streets. No rain, no matter how heavy, would ever dampen the life on the streets.

The River was a remnant of the past when the supercities pumped out their backwash and sewage. Back then, the River was always filled with water, just not the clean kind. Now, it was pumped through gigantic underground tunnels, which I was far too familiar with. Now dirty gangs had replaced the dirty water.

No one I talked to could tell me much about the gangs. Everyone said they knew someone who had heard them or had even glimpsed them, but it was never any kind of description I could use. I quickly realized that the sidewalk johnnies couldn't help, any more than my police contacts could. The River and the Hinterlands were outside of Metropolis. They knew inside, but outside the city was as foreign to them as the dark side of Pluto. I was wasting my time.

I needed new direction. Who could I ask who would know? After a few hours on the streets, back alleys, and a few bars, I'd learned more about the illegal courier business than I wanted to know. I knew a bit about the biz myself, as there was the legal hovercar market—like The Sniff—and the illegal one. Both sides used couriers to transport vehicles from seller to buyer. One, in particular, I had heard the name of before. I didn't think he was even a real person.

"Be careful, Cruz. He's dangerous," one sidewalk johnny told me.

"I just want to hire him."

"Then you'll be okay. Money keeps him in a good mood, but don't get on his bad mood side."

"Where can I find him?"

CHAPTER 10

The Far Escape Crew

I was in my office working the phones for a good two hours. I had come in early, beating PJ in for a rare occasion. She came in, wearing a bubble coat, and peeked in my private office.

"Good. Call those clients," she said and went to her desk.

I was clearing up the back log. Most of the people I spoke with didn't even really have a case. Others should have been wasting the time of the police, the local psychologist, or Metro Asylum. Others had cases too convoluted for me to have any interest. A few were outright criminal. All these calls I had to go through, to whittle them down to a few legit cases. I scheduled them myself.

"Make sure to copy me on the calendar when you schedule the clients," PJ reminded me, even though I always did.

Ms. Black had called me right at 9 o'clock, as I knew she would. It took her and her comrades a half hour to walk through the door.

PJ did her thing and led them in. We already had the chairs set up in front of my desk.

"Mr. Cruz," Ms. Black said and sat in the middle.

Again, Green and Blue were fidgety, and Pink was constantly shaking his head around like some hyperactive kid who couldn't sit still.

"Can you help us?"

"I can."

"Will you help us?"

"Depends."

"Depends on what?"

"Depends on whether you tell me the truth to my next question."

"Let me guess. You ran into two men."

"Yes. They also have funny accents."

"Funny accents?" Ms. Blue asked. "My accent isn't funny. Your accent is funny."

"I don't have an accent."

They all smiled and started laughing.

"Whatever," Mr. Pink said.

"Tell me about the two men."

"I would think that was obvious," Ms. Black said to me. "They're after us, and we're running from them."

"Why are they after you?"

"I don't think that's important, Mr. Cruz."

"They're police."

"Not in Metropolis, they're not," Ms. Green said.

They all started laughing again.

"No jurisdiction," Mr. Pink sang.

I had clients running from the foreign police.

"They can get Metro PD to arrest you for them. Whatever you all did."

"No interdiction," Mr. Pink sang.

"Meaning what?" I asked.

"Meaning they're criminals," Ms. Black answered.

"They're criminals, too?"

"They can't do anything," Mr. Pink said, "and we're not criminals. We're clients." He smiled.

Ms. Black, with a smirk, said, "You look like a man who doesn't like to get entangled in things. We'll pay you to introduce us to the courier you've found, and that will conclude our business."

"I couldn't find you on any active warrant databases. I even checked Interpol."

Ms. Black was amused. Her comrades weren't.

"Why did you do that?" Ms. Green asked.

"Did you really think I wouldn't?"

"Is this where we pay you?" Ms. Black asked.

"Not me." I pointed to the door. "Pay my secretary. She's the one with the bionic fingers to count the cash at the speed of light."

"You do know how to count, don't you?" Ms. Blue asked, mockingly.

I stood. "Say 'sorry.'"

"Why do I have to say 'sorry?'"

"He's going to charge us more if you don't," Ms. Black told her.

"Sorry."

I looked at Ms. Black. "You need to keep your posse well-behaved."

"Posse?" Mr. Pink said. "Posse comatatus," he sang. "I ain't no posse."

"You Americans talk weird," Ms. Blue said. "I feel as if I'm on a spaceship with a bunch of aliens."

"You all are the only aliens in this office."

"Americans talk so funny. Say these two words for me," Mr. Pink said, half-laughing. "Say 'car'. Then say 'water.'"

"Are you going to ask me to pull your finger next?"

They all burst out laughing. Pink was playfully thinking about it. I pointed to my front door again.

"Pay the secretary and let's go. I want you all out of my city."

CHAPTER 11

The Road Courier

As you worked the streets of Metropolis as a detective, you either physically or mentally created a list of places. There were places you wanted to go, places that would be nice to live, places to avoid, places you were scared of. I went to Mad Heights in my first case and almost didn't come back. They called it Mad City for good reason. The place we were going was even more dangerous.

A good rule of thumb was that the further you were from the center of the city, the worst things got. Way past Mad City there was Thieves' Point. That was not the real name of the town; in fact, it was three different sections of the supercity, but no one even remembered those names. It was known as Thieves' Point, and it didn't matter what its original name was or how the City had its name listed in the database.

I sat in my hovercar waiting for my clients to return. They did, in a beat-up hovervan. In this part of the supercity, there were no parking lots or fancy parking bays. You parked down on the street with the rodents and garbage on the curb. Yes, I was in a used hovercar—not my Pony. There was no way I was bringing my vehicle to this place and no mobile hovercar security guy would ever fly here, not even the regular guy I used.

In the time I'd been waiting, I heard at least a dozen hovercar alarms go off. I was surprised I hadn't heard any gunshots or blasts yet, but the night was young.

My clients walked to me, and I watched them like a hawk. My clients weren't criminals. They were soldiers! Green watched the left flank, Blue, the other. I could see Pink and Black approach with guns in both hands. The way they walked, as a unit, scanning their surroundings high and low, I knew these were professionals. I could tell law enforcement, and I could tell military—it was in how they walked into perceived danger.

I got out of the hovercar.

"Where's your sex-mobile?" Black asked.

"If you're referring to my classic Ford Pony, it's where it should be. Safe and sound at home."

"You definitely are a hovercar person. More concerned for the vehicle than yourself," she said.

"Hovercar people are just like pet people," Pink added. "You ever see a pet person? They'd dive off a building to save their fluffy critter. Jump in front of a bullet or laser pulse. Get run over—"

"I'd like to get out of here sooner rather than later," I interrupted. "I see you're all properly armed. It's good to know that you haven't lost all your military training."

I could see all them stop a beat. Blue and Green glanced back at me. They didn't like that I'd figured out they were military.

"The place we're about to go into is dangerous. No. It's extremely dangerous, but you can't shoot anyone. If that happens, then all hell will break loose. Be tough and fearless. It's okay to show the weapons you have."

"How do you know this place, Mr. Cruz? It doesn't look like the kind of place you'd frequent," Black asked.

"I've never been here before, but my sources are good. Let's go."

"Where's your—"

Mr. Pink stopped his question when he saw me pull my omega-gun from my jacket.

"I don't think that gun is from Earth," Pink continued.

What was the name of the bar? I had no idea. I had its GPS coordinates, and that was it. I was told most places in Thieves' Point didn't have any kind of neon signage. They were right. This unneighborly neighborhood had very little in the way of outside lighting at all.

It was a black block-like building of no more than ten stories—tiny. As we walked to what appeared to be the front entrance, I'm sure we all had the same thought. Did anyone that entered this place ever come back out?

The front door was locked. We pulled and pulled, knocked; there was no bell.

"Is this place open?" Pink asked.

"Are you sure you have the right place, Mr. Cruz?" Ms. Black asked.

I ignored them all and took out my mobile. I re-read the message on the display. I dialed. We heard the door unlock.

I took the lead and opened it.

Oh my God! The head-banger music from inside almost blasted me back. I literally almost fell back. That was only the first wave. The second wave of near-toxic smoke almost put me on my back again.

"Mr. Cruz, let's soldier on," Ms. Black said and walked around me. Her comrades followed, leaving me at the door.

I forced myself in. Inside the dimly lit bar and club was a clientele of mohawked, pierced, cyborg-looking, hoverbiker-looking, bodybuilder-looking freaks—both male and female. Of course, they were all staring at us. We were not 'regulars.'

I took back the lead, ignored all the bar ruffians, brushed past the serial-killer-looking waitresses to scan the place. I saw who I wanted.

The little man in the corner with glowing spectacles and a flapper hat puffed on his drug cigarette in a silver holder.

"Mr. Cruz, I assume," he said.

"Yes." I sat down on a nasty stool at his tiny circular table. My clients sat or pulled up stools to sit around us, too.

"Oh, Mr. Cruz. I didn't know we were having a party," he said.

"I heard you like to shoot people," I said. "So, I decided to bring my friends along to the party."

The man had rotting teeth in his mouth. You'd think that living in a time when we actually had Martian colonies, people could invest in basic dental care.

"The only people I've ever shot were people who didn't pay me. What can I do for you, Mr. Cruz? Our mutual acquaintance said you wanted to hire some courier work."

"Yes, to the Hinterlands."

"Why would you want to go there?"

"Never you mind that. I want to hire him."

"Him." He exhaled some smoke. "Hiring him is expensive. Going there is expensive. Plus my fee. Very, very expensive all around, Mr. Cruz. I don't think I ever did business with a person who could afford all three at the same time."

"Are you finished?" I asked.

"I am."

"I also brought my friends here in case we needed to shoot you."

He laughed with those rotten teeth. "Why would you do that, Mr. Cruz? I'm so friendly."

"I may not be wise to Thieves' Point. But I am wise to not getting cheated, and knowing what things actually cost."

"It's not about what it costs, Mr. Cruz. It's what the market will bear. No one alive in Metropolis or anywhere else can get you to where you're going. He knows the River, everything that lives and crawls there, better than anyone else. If you think you can find better, by all means, find them. He will only be in town for a short time, and then he's gone."

The man was right. He had us. We'd have to pay, and pay a lot.

"Can he be ready for early tomorrow morning?" I asked.

"If the money is right, he can do anything."

I looked at Ms. Black. "This is going to be very, very expensive."

"Who is he?" she asked. "And then you want us to pay your fee too, Mr. Cruz?"

"The price I quoted, cut it in half," I said. "I made the connection and I'm done. This is the only courier who can get you there alive."

"Excuse me." The man said the words in a creepy way. "You will be with them?"

"No," I said. "My friends are going. I'm remaining behind."

"No, Mr. Cruz. I don't know them. I know you. You don't go, he won't take them anywhere."

"Why do I have to go? You don't know me. We've never met before."

He smiled. "I know when you're so famous, you forget the 'little people' like me. I'll give you a clue. We shared a cell together."

My clients looked at me.

"Do tell, Mr. Cruz," Ms. Black said.

"You had a friend there, too. That man was a comedian. I never laughed so hard in my life."

"Okay, okay." He was talking about my future father-in-law at the time. My future mother-in-law at the time, him, and me had been all temporarily arrested. "I'm not going."

"You're not going, Mr. Cruz. That's fine, because we're not paying."

I sat at the table looking at the man. Ms. Black sat on her stool staring at the man.

"What do you recommend on tap?" Mr. Pink asked him as he stood up.

"The beer tastes like piss, so go for the hard liquor. I'm a vodka man, but the Japanese whiskey is very tasty," he said.

Mr. Pink got up. Blue and Green followed him to the bar. That left Black and me to sit with the man who was now blowing circles of smoke at us.

"When they pay, I ride shotgun," I said to the man. "That's the only way I'll go."

"I don't care where you sit, because we're not paying," Black said again, but the man smiled. Her resolve was already wavering.

The River was a truly intimidating place. It was a concrete river corridor that was over 200 stories deep and 10 miles wide. What was scary about it was that it was so pristine and quiet. The mind could go wild imagining what it had been like decades and centuries ago when it was a real river of filth one moment, super-heated backwash the next, to clean it out. They said gangsters would use it to dispose of dead bodies, too.

We stood along the side, waiting. My clients were not happy. No, they were angry.

"Mr. Cruz, I hope you know that we don't have a penny left to our names because of this."

"If you had money to pay for this, then you'll have no problems getting more," I said. "Stop whining. It's done. You've hired the best, and that's what you need. Look at it."

I looked over the edge to the bottom. It was so far down that your eyes got confused, so you had to put a hand out, so they could focus again.

"I don't know what the big deal is," Black said. "We could have saved all that money and hired a hovertruck and driven ourselves."

"Then why didn't you?" I asked.

She kept her arms folded and looked away.

"Because you would never have been seen again."

"Why couldn't you have driven us?" Blue yelled at me.

"I'm a detective, not a courier."

"Some detective you are. All you've done so far is cost us all our money. Why are we still waiting here? It's time, isn't it. I bet no one shows up."

"Then you'd lose that bet." I pointed behind them.

A hovertruck glided low, about ten feet up, in the distance. It was pure black and was completely silent. I'd never come across a silent hovertruck of its size before. It drifted to a stop in front of us and then descended to a few inches off the ground.

I placed my ear near the engine. The purr was mesmerizing. I heard the passenger door open.

My clients had picked up their duffel bags, but they were waiting for me to go in first. I opened the door and climbed up the foot ladder into the huge cab. In the driver's seat was the Road Courier. Black climbed up first, and when she saw that he was wearing—a silver face-plate mask, she stopped.

"It's okay," I said.

She moved into the back seats of the cab. Her comrades all climbed up into the backseats, and I planted myself in the passenger seat, closing the door. My eyes lit up as I scanned the dashboard of the cab. This was a hovercar restorer's dream. It wasn't vintage; it was customized. I knew what every indicator, dial, switch, and button did. If the end of the world ever came, this hovertruck was where I would want to be.

The Road Courier saw me holding back a smile. His face was behind his mask, but his graying black hair was visible. His whole outfit was a thick leather jacket, corduroy jeans, and combat boots.

I handed him a note. "Broken Hill is where we're going," I said.

He took it from my hand, put it in his jacket pocket and then grabbed the high-tech binoculars in his lap. He scanned down the River.

"Have you met this driver too, Mr. Cruz?" Black asked.

"No, we've never met, but I know about him."

"Is he famous like you?"

"No, I'm not famous. Not like him. In the courier business, he's a legend."

"Legend how?"

"He gets you from point A to point B."

"That sounds like a skill anyone can do."

"Not like he can."

I had barely finished my sentence when the hovertruck hopped up and dived down the River corridor. We were all screaming, until he stopped it to hover right at the bottom.

"What was that?" Mr. Pink yelled. "Pardon me, while I allow my stomach and intestines to slide back down out of my mouth."

The Road Courier ignored us. All he was doing was watching down the River with his binoculars. I could see the tips of them extend. He might have been seeing miles in the distance at those settings.

"Are we there yet?" Ms. Blue asked.

I turned in my seat to look back at them. "You all need to behave," I said.

"Behave?" The look Ms. Black gave me was as if I had spit in her face. "We've paid this man all our money."

"If you annoy him, he'll throw us out and refund your money."

"Refund?" Ms. Black asked. "You have to be joking. Who refunds money when you're doing something illegal?"

"He does."

"How do you know all about him, if you've never met him?" Black asked.

"You know I was in the hovercar racing scene. People there knew him and hired him. They told me."

"All I know is that we're not there yet," Ms. Blue said.

"He'll start when he starts. When he starts, he doesn't stop until he gets to the destination—and nothing stops him."

"Nothing?" Black asked.

"Nothing."

"What's out there?" Ms. Green asked. "You hear all the stories. I don't believe any of them, but there is something out there. The stories have to be based on something truthful."

"Gangs," I answered. "What else?"

"What kind of gangs?" Green asked.

"Gangs like you've never seen before."

"Have you seen them?" Black asked.

"An acquaintance of mine, when I was on the scene, heard them. I was too chicken to go along, but he recorded it. He recorded it as they were driving back as fast as they could to get away."

"Why is everyone scared of something they've never seen?" Pink asked.

I looked at him. "Today, you'll see them, and then you'll know why."

Pink liked to play around. He had a face for it, but he had a deadly serious expression now. They all did.

The Road Courier tapped me on the shoulder. I pulled myself back into my seat. He had an old electric notebook. I looked at it: INSTRUCTIONS.

I'd heard that the Road Courier didn't talk at all on a job. He gave you his instructions typed on an electric notebook to read. Once you'd acknowledged you understood, then the job started.

"What's that you're reading?" Black asked.

"His instructions," I answered, while I read. I finished and tapped the check box with my finger.

"Why are you reading them? We're the ones who paid him."

"I'm the one riding shotgun."

"Then maybe we should switch places."

"It's too late for that." I looked at him and nodded.

The Road Courier took the electric notebook from me. He then flipped a switch, and it seemed as if clawed hands came up from the bottom of our seats across our chests. They were heavy duty seat-belts, and they clicked into place. Our seats moved; we realized that they were actually hoverchairs.

The purr of the engine turned into a roar, and the hovertruck took off.

"Mr. Cruz," Black called, but I was busy watching the scene off to my side. We had been driving for about an hour when the right-side wall of the River changed. It was half as tall and you could see past it into the distance. I saw what looked like a giant mound of something at the bottom of a gigantic tunnel opening. I was squinting my eyes because I thought I could see movement.

"Can I borrow your binoculars?" I asked the Road Courier.

He handed them to me, without ever taking his eyes off the road.

"What do you see?" Blue asked.

I peered through the binoculars and could see two men walking up the hill of dirt and garbage. Both men looked dusty and dirty, but they weren't bums. Their clothes actually looked nice and trendy. What the heck were they doing out here?

I gave the binoculars back to the Road Courier. The right wall returned to its normal design, which meant no more view.

"What did you see?" Blue asked again.

"Nothing," I answered. I didn't know at the time, but I would learn far more about those two men in the very near future.

"Mr. Cruz," Black repeated.

"Yes, Ms. Black."

"How do you know this driver? I feel you know a lot more, but are not sharing."

"Of course I know more, but detectives have trade secrets, so we don't share. You have your secrets. You don't see me all broken up about the fact that I'll never know what you mercenaries are up to in the Hinterlands and why two crooked cops are after you."

"Somehow, I get the feeling that you already know," Black said.

"Maybe I do. But the driver isn't a driver. He's the Road Courier."

"He's a legend," Mr. Pink said sarcastically.

"Yes, he is."

"We're going to find out for ourselves on this ride," Pink added.

"Yes, you are." I looked to make sure the passenger door indicator said: Locked. "Maybe a lot sooner than you think."

The four of them looked out of the front window too.

When you live in the universe in these times, you come across things you've never seen before—funny, weird, or scary. We were all staring at the hovercar wrecker in front of us, because we were trying to figure out if what we were seeing out the back window was a guy in a tiger mask or an actual tiger.

Wreckers were hovercars made to crash into other hovercars. The one in front of us was purposely trying to slow us down to block us. The Road Courier never took his eyes off the road and looked as cool as a cucumber from my vantage point. He swerved a couple of times, but the wrecker moved with him.

"That can't be a tiger," Blue said.

"Is that a tiger?" Pink asked.

We were still not sure. The Road Courier gunned the engine, hitting the rear corner of the wrecker, violently spinning it around. As we passed it, we were able to see it.

"That's a tiger!" Blue and Pink shouted.

The tiger was in the back seat of the wrecker, and the driver looked at us, wearing goggles, a leather cap, and the bottom of his face wrapped up in cloth. He lowered his window.

"Gun!" I yelled.

The Road Courier crushed that wrecker into the side of the River in a second.

We watched the wrecker crash to the ground and explode. Surprisingly, we saw the tiger land and run down the River in the other direction.

"Wow," Pink said. "Cruz, you're cold blooded. I didn't see any gun. You wanted Road Courier to kill that guy."

I turned my head. "Listen up, Pink. I don't know what kind of Mickey Mouse military outfit you all were in, but if someone is driving around in a hovercar made to crush other vehicles, and it appears in front of you and slows down to stop you, has a wild jungle cat in the vehicle, and he's rolling down his window with only one hand on the steering wheel, you don't wait for him to pop something out of the window at you. You shoot first and don't bother with questions later. I already told you that the only people around here are gangs. I'm not even supposed to be here, but I am because of you. I intend to get you all out of my city to your destination, and I intend to get back home to the wife and the Pony, all without getting dead. Is that all right with you?"

I turned back around. I was mad. It was as if they refused to get how dangerous this trip was and we weren't even a quarter way to the Hinterlands.

"Remind me never to get on Cruz's bad side," Ms. Green said.

"Yeah, Cruz'll kick you out of his fancy red hovercar from twenty stories up if you don't behave yourself," Ms. Black added, "like he did with that American movie star. What was his name?—Tuck Rogers or something."

"It was the jokes," Pink said. "Cruz didn't like his jokes—but he likes mine fine."

I hated people calling my Pony a hovercar. It was a vehicle, not a hovercar.

"Now what do we have up here?" I said.

Three more hovercar wreckers were racing at us. They each had one or more poles sticking up from their trunk area. I had no idea what they were for. As we got closer—

"Are they insane?" I yelled.

A passenger crawled out of the window of the center wrecker onto the roof. He reached back to grab a pole. He had it in his hand. The Road Courier dived below the hovertruck suddenly, but kept moving forward, increasing speed. We heard a bump.

"What was that?" Blue asked.

We were all looking behind and to the roof.

"Did he jump on the truck?" Pink asked.

"That's impossible. He'd fall off," Black said.

I pulled my omega-gun from my jacket. It had a new tip, and I had my laser pointer on it.

"He has magnetic boots on," I said.

"How do you know that?" Blue asked.

We heard footsteps on top of the hovertruck.

I turned to the Road Courier. "Do you want us to shoot too?"

He pointed to a bumper sticker on the top of the dashboard that, for some reason, I hadn't noticed before: Only the Driver Is Permitted to Fire Deadly Weapons Inside the Vehicle.

The roof walker appeared and jumped on top of the front of the hovertruck, startling all of us—except for the Road Courier. We could now read the words on his T-shirt: Feral Marauders. He had goggles, a dirty white scarf around his neck, spiky hair, and yellowish fanged teeth. He punched through the windshield with a robotic fist. He was a cyborg, and he yanked the windshield out.

The Road Courier extended his arm holding a shotgun and blew the marauder off the hovertruck. All we heard was his scream as he fell. Another wrecker dived down to smash right into the passenger side of the truck. I almost jumped right out of my safety belt. A second wrecker slammed into the driver's side. The Road Courier pressed a button and a new windshield rose up and auto-sealed with the opening as if it had always been there. Something bumped us from behind.

We could see shadows appearing above us; more and more wreckers came into view. Some of them had people standing on top of the hovercars, each with long poles in hand.

The hovertruck dove and the Road Courier slammed on the air brakes. The vehicle behind us was another hovertruck, and it flew past us and crashed into two wreckers, sending them all crashing to the ground. But two of their roof-walkers jumped onto that hovertruck with their poles.

The airspace all around us was filled with wreckers. I had to admit I was as scared now as my clients in the backseat. There were so many of them. I had to look at the Road Courier. He was unfazed, but I wasn't. I was scared out of my mind. There were too many wreckers. We'd never get away from all of them.

The Road Courier leaned back in his seat and put both hands on the steering wheel. His silver mask opened and retracted back. I don't know where it went—into the chair, down the back of his shirt, but it was gone. The Road Courier looked like a regular guy with a weather-worn face. He grabbed the dark shades from the middle container, put them on, and reached down.

A large red button rose from the middle of that container. I knew exactly what it was, because I'd thought of installing one in the Pony many times before. I caught a glimpse of Ms. Black's face from the corner of my eye and looked back. She knew, too. She yelled and tried to grab at it with her arms. "No!" The Road Courier pounded that Nitro button.

The hovertruck jumped to a speed so fast that time seemed to go in slow motion. I was slammed back into my seat. I had to grit my teeth with tremendous force because I felt like my skin was being pushed into my skull.

Those Feral Maurauders never had time to think, let alone react. Our hovertruck blew through all of them, their wreckers, and anything else in front of us with such force that they weren't blown to bits; they were atomized.

My clients were screaming at the top of their lungs as we rocketed through the River and saw what the Marauders had in store for us: a multi-layer wall of wreckers with roof walkers, dozens of hovercars deep. We blasted through the center—bodies, vehicle pieces, and poles everywhere.

We finally started to slow down and return to normal speed. The Road Courier coasted to a full stop. The River was long behind us. We were on some kind of open dirt field, in the distance a thick fog, but we could make out grid towers with flashing lights on the roofs. We were at the Hinterlands.

The passenger door opened. My clients scrambled out and each fell to the ground. Ms. Green was the toughest of the four, because she stayed on her feet; the other were on their knees, but all of them were throwing up the previous day's meal.

I simply sat in my seat with a sense of calm. I didn't expect to see one live Marauder or wrecker in sight on the way back. Oh, we'd see plenty of wreckage and corpses, though.

I pulled my mobile from my jacket and flipped to the display. There was the smiling picture of my wife, but I swiped to another picture and leaned over to the Road Courier.

"Here's my baby," I said "a classic Ford Pony. I built it from scratch."

"You built that from scratch?" he asked.

"When I was in high school."

"No way."

"It's been featured in a bunch of magazines. Do you think I should customize it with a nitro, too?"

"Oh no," he answered. "Too much stress and you'd have to replace the whole engine. It wouldn't look right. They never made that kind of hoverengine for a Pony."

"Maybe I could build a special tricked-out engine."

"No," he answered. "It might look okay, but then you'd run the risk of blowing the body apart, not to mention that you'd lose any stability and handling using the nitro."

My clients finished their throwing up, having gotten to the Hinterlands safe and sound. The outpost of Broken Hill would be a simple half-mile walk for them. The Road Courier and I talked hovercars and engines on our way back.

The Marauders were good at clean-up. There wasn't a body part or part of anything the whole way back. I was glad that it started to rain hard again. The Road Courier flew past in the shadow zone of the River, which made his jet-black hovertruck practically invisible.

PART TWO

Gokiburi

CHAPTER 12

Cyberpunk

A woman screamed, but it was barely audible in the downpour.

Cyberpunks came in all varieties. Some loved the dark and vampiric look, others loved their silver outfits, others wore so many bright colors that they blinded you when they walked by. What they all had in common were sex, drugs, and virtual reality (VR). One of them meandered down the grimy street; the rain ran down his matted hair, and his mouth began to foam. He stopped and reached around as if he were blind.

Under a building rain shield, a few nearby sidewalk johnnies were drinking and chatting it up when they noticed him.

"Looks like we got a walking OD," the johnny said.

They walked to the kid. "You all right? Need an ambulance?"

When he turned to look at them, they jumped back. A tiny image, like a TV screen, was flickering on the cornea of his eyes. "I—need to—count the electric sheep."

The cyberpunk closed his eyes and then dropped to his knees. The sidewalk johnnies grabbed him before he fell face-first into the pavement. His body started to convulse, and the foam flowed out of his mouth. The sidewalk johnnies set him down and moved back from him. His eyes were audibly popping like a piece of electronics short-circuiting.

"What the—!" a johnny said. "Does he have bionic eyeballs or something?"

CHAPTER 13

Silk

Where did the trendy get their clothes? Goodwill Clothiers. I never understood it myself, but in the fashionista world, buying used clothing was the rage. In fact, no one bought clothes new. Dot told me that even the rich—not to be confused with the uber-rich—and celebrities bought their clothes used. Goodwill was a massive retail chain in Metropolis. I'd never known they even existed until I met Dot. Watching her go from rack to rack, aisle to aisle, I found amusing. They were all old clothes to me, but to Dot's sophisticated eye, she was an artist creating a masterpiece of fashion for herself. Looking around the multi-level store for all ages, there was not a bum in sight. Everyone shopping was well-dressed, and some were obviously wealthy, based on the jewelry and necklaces I saw. The saying was that the rich were rich because they didn't spend any money. I believed it.

Dot dragged me along on her monthly shopping binges. I hated it, but it's what I had to do. I dragged her along to hovercar shows. She hated it. It's what you had to do in life as married Homo sapiens. I would be here a while, because she had only started in on the clothes, then she'd have to go for shoes, and finally "accessories." Thank God for the mobile phone. At least I could get some work done.

My wife was as well-known in this store, as I was at the Good Kosher store. She had her own personal attendant. Silk was a tall, thin, brunette with straight, black hair down to her knees. People always thought Dot was Japanese, rather than Chinese. Silk was Korean, Japanese, and Chinese, or the term I preferred to use—Asian. She was a nice woman, but all I saw her as was a shark in women's clothing trying to get my wife to spend as much money as possible. Dot didn't need any help with that as far as shopping went. It was all her own money, but a husband had to be careful, because once she was done with 'her' money, then she'd do the snapping crab routine to get 'your' money. Yeah, I had my eye on Silk as I made my calls.

I told PJ that I probably would not get back to the office for the day. She was not pleased.

"Reschedule them," I said. "You did say they were walk-ins."

"Yes, I'll do that, but the two men who came in were very pushy."

"What did they look like?"

PJ described those foreign cops with the accents. I knew I'd be seeing them again.

"Good. I finally get to find out why they're bothering me."

"They're cops?"

"Not in Metropolis, they aren't."

"Oh, good," PJ said. "Then I can punch them when they're rude to me again."

While she had me on the phone, she gave me a rundown of the appointments for tomorrow. With my office work by phone done, it was back to aimlessly wandering the retail aisles of the store.

"Mr. Cruz." It was Silk.

I turned, and she had a small black box in her hand.

"This is a complimentary congratulatory present for you from Goodwill Clothiers International management on your marriage to China Doll."

She handed it to me with a genuine smile.

"Thank you."

Silk gave me one of those bows, and I attempted to reciprocate. She left me there to wonder what was in the box. Dot was out of sight somewhere in the store, but I knew Silk knew exactly where she was and was heading back to her.

"Hmm," I said to myself.

I opened the box. "Is this a Rolex? It can't be." I stared at the black metal watch with a big display face. "It can't be."

CHAPTER 14

The Scorpion Cops

It was. Goodwill gave me a genuine Rolex watch and gave one to Dot too. That meant that Dot spent a *lot* of money in that store. Silk had three juvenile attendants carrying our shopping bags to the Pony—that's how much shopping Dot had done. Half the bags were shoes.

In the past, I had unwisely commented on "How many shoes can one woman wear?" "This is way too many clothes for one person to buy," "Are you a shop-o-holic and have you sought treatment?" I was a quick learner and had made such comments once, but after severe punishment by my then-girlfriend, Dot, that mistake was never repeated. I kept my mouth shut as my Pony was filled to the top with her shopping bags.

The day was over, though. Dot would spend the whole night sorting her new fashion acquisitions and clearing out those items that were no long acceptable to be donated back to Goodwill. What a racket! You donate your stuff to them for free, and then they sell that stuff to your neighbor for a profit. Dot warned me that I was getting close to the 'severe punishment zone' with my comments.

"Cruz, they donate their money to worthy charities all over the planet," she scolded.

Worthy charities? Ha! Swiss bank accounts were what I was figuring.

The next day at the office, my two foreign cop "friends" with accents were waiting for me in the lobby. They must have only arrived, because they were just sitting down when I came through the door.

I stopped in mid-stride. They stopped in mid-sit. I pointed to my office. They followed. PJ laughed.

I sat down in my chair.

"How did it go with Metro PD?" I asked.

They sat down, and the one with the mustache and ponytail spoke first. "Very well, actually. We cleared up any misunderstandings that you might have, mistakenly, given them."

"Chief Hub said to tell you 'hello,'" the bald one said to me.

"Did he, now? What do you two want, and why were you following me in that overpriced Scorpion?"

They both smiled.

The ponytailed one placed a set of photos on my desk. It consisted of all my Far Escape clients. The photos were mugshots.

"Are you two military police?" I asked.

"Why?" the bald one asked.

"Never mind. Let me save you two some time. They came in to hire me, but didn't tell me what it was about, and they were all fidgety. I don't like clients who don't look you in the eye. I told them to find another detective to hire. They came back a second time to try again. I didn't reconsider. That was it. I haven't heard from them or seen them again."

"Did they tell you where they were going?" the ponytailed one asked.

"What did they do?"

"We're not at liberty to disclose that," the bald one answered.

"There are no arrest warrants out on them."

"You check to see if potential clients have arrest warrants?" he asked.

"I do full background checks on potential clients before I accept their cases. This is Metropolis. I'm picky about who I work for. Okay, you won't tell me what they did, so there's nothing more to talk about."

"We are military police," the ponytailed one said. "They're AWOL, and we need to get to them before unofficial becomes official."

"I see. Why are they in Metropolis?"

"We were hoping you could tell us," the bald one said. "They have no family or acquaintances here. They've never been here in the Americas before as far as we can tell. However, they did seem to know you."

"Yeah. I'm famous."

"If you do hear from them, we would appreciate a call. We've been tracking them for weeks. We do need to catch up with them sooner, rather than later."

"You have a card?"

They both stood, and each one them handed me a business card. Australian Defense Force.

"I will call if I have something to call about."

"Very good, Mr. Cruz," baldy said to me.

"Sorry about the other night," the pony-tailed one said. "We meant nothing by it. Sometimes, you fall into a routine, and you don't even realize it."

"It would be fascinating to see which one of our vehicles is faster," baldy said with a wide smile.

We were at my office door and I opened it.

"Scorpions are more dangerous than ponies," he continued.

"No, they're not. Scorpions are a few inches in the dirt. A pony is a horse. A horse that can kick either one of us across the room or stomp a scorpion into nothingness. All you need to know is that a Scorpion speedster is a hovercar with lots of show and noise. A Ford Pony is a hovervehicle, classic, and superior in every way. In the time you'd take to circle one block in this city, I could fly around your entire continent in a full rain storm. I never have to brag about my Pony, only state the facts. My Pops told me as a kid, 'If you have to brag to everyone about all the power you have, then you have none.' Enjoy your stay in Metropolis, gentlemen."

CHAPTER 15

The Surf Brothers

I had lied to them; they were lying to me. I expected that they'd watch me for a few days, but their prey was long gone. I got paid, didn't get shot, and that's all I cared about. They weren't government military. No government law enforcement on the planet gave its personnel bright red Scorpion speedsters as their undercover vehicle. The only military they were, probably, was freelance for some megacorporation over there, the kind of 'freelance' that meant you were a full-time employee. Again, I didn't care. The Road Courier case was closed out successfully.

I was just about to see my next client—a man in a suit—when the front door burst open. I could see that PJ was sitting behind her desk, but had her shotgun in hand underneath. It was the Surf Brothers.

"Cruz!" the younger one said. "We need your help."

I'd met the two Dominican brothers on the hovercar racing scene. They worked for Metropolis Trash Services as long-time trash collectors and had on their standard uniforms—white jumpsuits with the word "TRASH" on the back and front. The younger brother had slicked-back black hair and the makings of a goatee, while the older brother looked almost the same, only heavier, a bit taller, with a slim mustache. The men were both five-feet-two, but had seriously muscular builds.

"Sir, I'm sorry," I said to the man in the suit. "I need you to wait."

PJ did her thing and offered the man refreshments, while I took the brothers into my office and closed the door. Neither of them sat down in the chairs in front of my desk, so I didn't sit either.

"What's wrong?"

"You have to come with us, Cruz," the older one said.

"Come where?"

"We need to take you there. Please, Cruz, we're in trouble."

"Okay."

I opened the door again and led them out.

"PJ, I have to leave. Reschedule my appointments."

"But I have an appointment," the man in the suit said, standing up from my waiting room chair.

"I'm so sorry, sir. It's an emergency. PJ, get his contact information and I'll get it from you on the road. Sir, when I'm finished, I'll come to you. Just give my secretary all the details."

Salvage was a big side-business for the trash men in Metropolis. It was actually against union policy, meaning you could get fired, but no one listened, because it would never happen. Workers could make almost a second salary from what they found in people's garbage.

It had been some time since I had seen inside a hovertrash truck. I sat behind them in the back seats. One would expect them to be dirty on the outside, but they were always shiny and clean. Inside was even better; it had the quality of a booshy hoverlimo. They had the works, anything you'd want. For the Surf Brothers, that meant all their fancy exotic foods. They liked to eat.

However, they were not their normal smiling and joking selves this time. Both were very serious and scared.

"What happened?" I asked.

"We have to show you," the younger brother said.

Hovertrash trucks were classified the same as police, fire, and medical services, so they didn't have to follow normal sky traffic laws. They could fly anywhere, and did. We'd been following the normal traffic, but then the older brother pulled away to create his own fast-lane, faster than the fast-lane. I was watching out of the passenger window, but settled back in a bit since we were flying so fast.

After a while, we'd flown beyond the traffic.

"What do you call all this out here again?" I asked.

"We call it all kinds of things," the younger brother said. "Salvage Land when management isn't around. Or we call it the Sprawl."

"It's good salvage territory?"

"Normally, it's good salvage territory."

"Cruz, we're going to have to go out by the River."

The River? I leaned to the middle to get a better a look at him.

"You two salvage that far out?"

"Yeah. You either have to get to the good places first, or you have to find places no one else is going."

"There's nothing near the River," I said.

"There is. You have to know how to get there."

The supercity's garbage, to the brothers, and the tens of thousands like them, was virgin soil to dig for lost treasures and precious minerals. I looked out the window again, and the surroundings were quite familiar. We were getting close to the River again. In fact, I could see Thieves' Point in the distance. Once we flew over that, we'd be close. I couldn't believe that I'd be there again.

"Are we going in the River?" I asked.

"Oh, no," the older brother said. "That's crazy. We'll be flying along it. On the other side of the wall."

Good. So at least I wouldn't have to meet up with any Feral Marauders again.

We'd been driving for hours. I'd forgotten how big Metropolis really was and how long it took to get to its edge, even flying as fast as we were. My eye immediately recognized the spot. A mound of dirt and garbage underneath a massive tunnel opening, coming out of the side of the earth.

"What's that?" I asked.

"We call it the Valves," the older brother said.

It was the exact spot I'd seen those two men climbing up when I was sitting in the Road Courier's hovertruck. Then, I'd been watching it from binoculars many miles away. Today, I was about to be on top of it and walking exactly where those two men had been.

We walked up the hill. It was definitely dirt and garbage, but the garbage was more like particulants—garbage that had been processed, but tiny pieces of it remained.

"What is this? Is the River still used?" We'd reached the top of the hill, and I looked up at the large opening.

"The city doesn't use the River anymore, but all these Valves," the older brother began, "are still active."

I stopped and turned to him. He smiled. It was the first time I'd seen either of them show any positive emotion today.

"Don't worry," he said. "We're not going to get washed away. It's only active once a week and late at night."

"Follow us," the younger brother said, and we walked over the hill which now leveled off. We walked under the Valve. There were a couple of steps and an old, rusty looking door on the side. The younger brother kicked the door open hard. "The hinges are terrible. You have to kick it open and closed."

Before I could even say it, both brothers had flashlights in their hands, and they led me in. I was not eager to be in a deep, dark tunnel after one of my previous cases, but I trusted the brothers.

"How do you find any salvage here?"

The older brother answered, "You have to go down a bit, and there's a shallow river of garbage that accumulates before processing. It's from all over the city. We help search through it at least once a week with our gear. We've got nice metal detectors and matter readers."

Matter readers? I thought. I remembered: 'Organic' matter detectors.

"Cruz, you'd be shocked to see what we find, what people throw away in the garbage."

"I don't think anything shocks me any more these days."

"Cruz, I'm sorry, but do you still have that germ thing, phobia thing?" the younger brother asked.

We had been walking awhile, but I stopped. For him to ask me that meant we were coming up on something that I didn't need to be seeing.

"What are you about to show me? You know I don't want anything to do with nastiness."

They pointed. I turned my head to where their flashlights were pointing. There was a mound of something, and it was infested with giant roaches.

"Gokiburi," they said, almost at the same time.

I didn't know much Japanese, but I knew the word for roaches. I ran—not to them, but back the way we'd come. I kicked that door open as I was running. Outside, I checked myself thoroughly to make sure there wasn't one of those nasty insects on me of any size. Unfortunately, I got caught in an "OCD loop," and I would keep doing the same thing over and over again.

"Cruz, none of them are on you," the younger brother said. Both brothers were standing next to me now, near the door.

"Are you sure?"

"Yes. You can stop now."

"I won't tolerate roaches."

"They aren't roaches," the older brother said. "They're cadaver roaches, but not the same."

"Cadaver roaches are not roaches?"

"Well, they are," he said, "but they're mutated. The government created them and put them in the garbage."

At first, I was wondering if my friends were telling me some kind of crazy conspiracy theory urban myth.

"It's true," he said, "but don't tell anyone. How do you think the cops can find bodies dumped into the garbage? They look for the gokiburi, not the body or body parts. They were genetically engineered to swarm any human organic matter."

I remembered. "Yes, gokiburi. One of the CSI instructors mentioned it when I was interning in one of the classes at Police Central as a kid."

"Yes."

"Genetically modified roaches to eat people." I checked my body again.

Both the brothers held up their hands to calm me "No!" They were in government-bureaucrat, damage-control mode.

"Cruz, don't ever say that," the younger brother said, "even to joke."

"We have enough science fiction writers with stories of roaches and insects taking over the planet, and being able to survive a nuclear blast," his brother said.

"Well, they can," I said.

"No, they can't."

"If you had a nuke blast in a city, and we went to that city in your radioactive protection suit and left a whole bunch of food scraps all over the place, leave for a few weeks, come back, there'd be roaches playing with the food."

"That is not—"

The brothers were smiling, realizing I was playing with them.

"Cruz, the point is that they eat corpses, not live tissue. You don't want to start a citywide panic—and you can't tell anybody the cops use them to find bodies. If you weren't friends with the cops, we wouldn't have told you, but we know you know how to keep secrets."

Metro Trash Services and the Metro Police worked together on cases far more than anyone could imagine, which was why the Director of Trash Services had dotted line reporting to the Chief of Police. If you were a criminal and wanted to get rid of the evidence, don't throw it in the trash. It would be found.

"Why are we here?" I asked.

The brothers looked at each other. They were hesitating.

"We wanted to know what we should do," the older brother answered.

"Do? Call the police. That's what you do."

"If we do that, then everyone will know our spot," the younger brother said.

I couldn't believe them. "You have a dead body there, but won't call the police, because you're worried about that? Call the police right now, so they can get down here to identify the body before your roaches eat it all away. What's wrong with you? What are you not telling me? I ask because I've never known either one of you to be morally challenged. What's going on?"

"We—we—"

"Tell me."

"We were the ones who dropped him off here," the big brother said.

"He paid us. It's against company rules, but there was nothing illegal about it. Well, not technically," the little brother said.

"Two," I said.

The brothers looked at me.

"What?" the younger one asked.

"You dropped two people here."

The brothers had those shocked expressions I'm sure many a police officer has seen when a perp was caught red-handed doing whatever crime they were doing.

"How could you know that?" the older brother asked.

"I saw them. Never mind how, but I saw them climbing up the hill." I shook my head. "What are the odds of my seeing two guys that two of my friends dropped off in a part of Metropolis none of us are supposed to be in." I pointed at them. "The term is called trespassing, and it's illegal. Now, we have one dead person and possibly a second. I'm like a cosmic magnet for this stuff."

"Then we shouldn't call the cops." The younger brother was still trying.

"Yes, we'll call the police. What we need to do is get our stories straight. Since I'm such a lucky guy, I bet those two who got themselves killed by who-knows-who were up to something criminal, too. My whole day is shot now," I said, throwing up my hands, "and you two aren't even paying clients. I had a paying client in my office, and I threw him out to help you two."

"If it makes you feel better, Cruz, we can give you a couple of good items from our last salvage," the younger brother said. "It'd be like a wedding gift."

"Yes, yes," the other said. "Congratulations on the wedding, Cruz."

CHAPTER 16

Officers Break and Caps

"**O**fficer, it was like this. My brother and I were just exploring—" the older brother began.

"The tunnels?" Officer Break asked.

"Yes, those tunnels."

"The tunnels that are illegal to go into."

"Sorry, Officer."

"Do you know why it's illegal to trespass into them?"

"You can get caught up in a backwash."

"Bingo! You'd be caught up in a backwash, sucked right up in the tunnel so fast it would rip your body apart, or maybe you'd drown while getting sucked through the tunnel, or maybe your body would make it to processing to be pounded and pushed through a commercial sieve into a million pieces."

"Sorry, Officer."

"However, you know that as a government employee of Metro Trash Services."

"Sorry, Officer. We hadn't been here before, so we must have forgotten where we were. We were just exploring."

"Exploring for what?"

"Well—"

"Salvage."

"Is salvage more important than living, more important than following municipal and union regs?"

"Sorry, Officer."

"What happened?"

"My brother and I saw them. The Gokiburi, and we knew right away that it was something bad, that it was a dead body."

"Then what did you do?"

"We—we called the police."

"You called the police?"

"Yes, that's why you're here. We called the police."

"How long after you found the dead body with roaches did you call the police?"

"Umm. Right away. We were scared, yes, and we ran out of there, but we came out and called the police. Cruz can tell you."

"Yeah, I bet he can. So, Cruz was doing a ride-along with you?"

"Um. Oh, yes."

"So, trash men do ride-alongs, like police and firefighters?"

"Yes, of course we do. Why shouldn't we?"

"You know I interviewed your brother."

"Yes."

"Before you."

"Yes."

"He told me the same story you did."

"Yes."

"Exactly the way you told me."

The older Surf Brother said nothing this time.

"Who coached you two on what to say?" Officer Break asked.

He remained quiet, but his eyes darted in my direction.

I was not too far away, watching the White Shoes arrive. I only saw them briefly in my last case when we uncovered the Gangster's Graveyard, but this time I got to see them arrive. They were like CSI, but for external crime scenes. They didn't wear those white booties like for indoor jobs. They wore high-tech white hovershoes. Technically, they were walking six inches above the ground on air. It looked so cool. People said this or that looked like something out of the future, which was nonsense, but these White Shoes looked as if they came from the future. Their hovershoes were so delicate that nothing underneath their feet would be disturbed, not a strand of hair, a speck of dirt, nothing. The calibration was that amazing.

"Mr. Cruz," I heard Officer Break's voice.

It was Officer Break and Officer Caps. Metropolis Police wore full silver-and-black body-armored uniforms with visored half-helmets. Despite PEACE in big bold white letters on their chests, they could kill you in an instant. They were the government's soldiers in the never-ending war on crime. You couldn't stop the criminals we had with anything less than a police force that was nothing short of hell on earth.

Officer Break, the Black policeman, had been on the Force for some twelve years. Officer Caps, the White policeman, had joined the Metropolis Police Department ten years ago. The senior officers had been partners for over seven years now and walked over to me. I knew Metro PD had put a flag on me in the database so that any call that came in that involved me, they were the unit to respond. I called them Ebony and Ivory, but never aloud.

"You're coaching witnesses, now?"

"What do you mean?" I said with fake indignation.

"One day, Cruz, you're going to be so clever that you'll clever your way into the Metropolis prison system."

"What did I do now?"

"We know how much you love the games, I'll give you—"

"If we skip the games, will you let us go, and not have me come down to Police Central?"

"Cruz." Break was shaking his head.

"If we have to go downtown for questioning, my whole day will be shot. I'm married now. I have responsibilities."

They burst out laughing.

"Aww," Caps mocked. "We're married men too. If we have to go downtown, why shouldn't you go, too?"

"Because we don't know anything."

"Says who?" Break asked. "You did a good job of coaching your friends. In the future, there's a difference between telling the same story and telling the *exact* same story."

"Yeah, I warned them about that."

"You're a piece of work, Cruz. You're going down to the station, all three of you. We'll even let you call your wife to tell her that you won't be taking care of any responsibilities today, but maybe tonight; there's a 50-50 chance, if you're lucky."

The two members of the Metropolis Police Force were laughing at me again. Yep, the Surf Brothers and I would be spending the rest of the day at Metro PD being questioned, while the White Shoes processed the scene.

CHAPTER 17

Japanese Blond

When I'd left my Liquid Cool office with the Surf Brothers, it wasn't even lunch time yet, but here I was walking out of Metropolis Police Central, and it was almost 9pm. I was told that they'd let the Surf Brothers go at around 6pm, so the extra hours they kept me was for spite.

I tried to find out who the body was, but they weren't talking. Officer Break and Caps weren't even the primary interrogators. They dropped me off, and then I never saw them again for the rest of the time I was there. It was a marathon of questions, waiting, eating snacks, and watching TV while waiting. This was how it was done: now, centuries before I was born, and would be done centuries after I was dust, so there was no reason to get upset over it.

Since I'd hitched a ride with the Surf Brothers, it meant my Pony was still at the office parking bay, which was not acceptable. The officers did allow me to make a few calls at around 5pm, and I had PJ call Let It Ride Enterprises to get a mobile security guard to watch it; my normal guy was on vacation. I walked outside from a side entrance to the public area, where I could catch public transportation (Hell no!) or get a hovercab.

"Hey, hey!" I heard the shouting and someone approaching me.

It was an Asian man coming towards me, wearing a yellow jacket over a black turtleneck. He had blond hair, but I was almost positive it was a wig. He seemed to have no facial hair at all, including no eyebrows.

"Are you Mr. Cruz?" he asked in his Japanese accent.

"Who wants to know?" I asked.

He stopped in front of me, pulled his silver business card holder from his jacket and pulled out a card. When he handed it over, he waited until I started to read it, when he said, "Ichi Jumper."

"Ichi Jumper?"

"Yes."

"What's that?"

"That is me. I am Ichi Jumper."

"What do you want?"

"You were at the River, with the police, and the dead men."

First, he knew where I'd been, and who I'd been with. Second, he knew there was more than one person dead.

"Who are you? I've got your name, but who are you?" I asked.

He had a mean expression on his face, and he poked his index finger into my chest as he talked. "Stay out of this, Mr. Cruz. It does not concern you."

"Stop that." I attempted to slap his hand away, but he'd already pulled back. "What doesn't concern me?"

"Stay away. Ichi Jumper has warned you. There will be most severe consequences next time."

"Don't you threaten me, you blond-wigged mutt!"

He wasn't even listening to me.

"Ichi Jumper has spoken!"

He jumped into a waiting hovercab and it flew away.

CHAPTER 18

Holly Live

I was pissed. I sat in my hovercab on the way home to the Concrete Mama, thinking about that guy. Staring at the card he'd given me was useless. All that was on it was his name, some crazy icon, and that's it—no phone number, no contact email, address, or company name. Ichi Jumper poking me in my chest, threatening me. Who did he think he was?

My mood didn't improve when I walked through the door. Oh course, Dot wanted to know what was wrong. What was I going to say? A Japanese guy in a blond wig poked me in my chest. That sounded silly. So, I just said it was sitting in the police station going over the same story over and over again from my Surf Brothers incident.

I didn't care much for the media. However, I knew the game and how to use them for my benefit. I had done so before and would do so again in the future, if I ever needed to. The next day, I arrived at my Liquid Cool office building before opening hours to get my Pony. The guy who was watching it overnight wasn't new to me; he had done work for me before. I gave him a healthy tip and sent him on his way.

That's when the jackals descended.

I'm not sure they realized how close they came to getting shot because they startled me. The reporter and her camera man jumped out from the shadows like psycho child snatchers.

"What's wrong with you?" I yelled at them.

"Ladies and gentlemen, we're here with famous Metropolis detective Cruz, outside his Liquid Cool agency office." It was Holly Live, the famous Metro reporter who'd actually used me in my first case to catapult herself to the top, and hadn't stopped climbing. She was smart—no inside-the-studio desk job for her. She stayed on the streets, and ambush interviews were her favorite. "Mr. Cruz, you were at Metro PD last night. Can you comment on the two dead bodies found near the River? Are they the two missing children?"

If I told the truth, namely that I didn't know what the hell she was talking about, I'd look like a fool on national TV.

"Sorry, I can't comment until I get that authority directly from Metro PD."

Now that was a smooth response!

I walked to the elevators with her following closely behind.

"When do you think that will be, Mr. Cruz?"

"When they feel it's appropriate to do so. There is still an ongoing investigation." I sounded as if I worked for Metro PD.

"With such a high-profile case, can the Metropolis Police afford to keep the people in the dark?"

"They're not doing that. They're doing their jobs and being sensitive to the family. Imagine if it were you, and the police went off half-cocked saying things publicly, only to learn later that they were false. Imagine the pain that would cause the family."

"I agree, Mr. Cruz."

No, you don't, you heartless media jackal!

"Mr. Cruz, is Metropolis safe for foreign tourists? Can foreign tourists expect to visit our great supercity with the assurance of the police and our political leaders that they will be safe?"

"That's a loaded question. I will defer again to the Metro PD, but let me just say that the safety of this city is in the best hands under the leadership of the police chief. Thank you."

I got in the elevator and made sure they didn't follow me in as the doors closed.

CHAPTER 19

Madam Personna

When I came through the door, I could hear that PJ had her TV on at her desk. She got up to give me a standing ovation. There were three people sitting in the waiting area, and they stood up to applaud too.

"Great performance," one of them said.

"You're a natural on TV," another said.

"Now, that's what you should be doing," PJ said, "building the Liquid Cool brand like that."

Brand? I had no idea what my cyborg secretary was talking about. "If you say so," I said. "Come into my office to debrief me. I know you like the fancy words like 'debrief.'"

"Oh, yes. Debrief is a French word."

"No, it's not." I just walked into my office with her following. The phone rang.

"Oh, I need to get that," she said.

We did have an answering machine, a rather expensive one, but PJ insisted on the human touch.

I went into my private office and sat down at my desk. I scanned the stacks of messages.

"Cruz, it's for you on line one," she yelled.

She loved saying that line. I picked up the phone.

"Mr. Cruz." I recognized the voice immediately before I even got in front of the video-phone display.

"Chief Hub."

"You are both a source of constant surprise and annoyance all in one."

"You saw my performance, then. I think I should be able to get at least three 'Get out of a ride down to the police station for questioning' cards for that. Your ears must be ringing with all the city saying, 'Oh yeah, Police Chief Hub has our city in safe hands.'"

"Funny, but do you even know what the hell you were talking about?"

"Not in least, but my secretary was about to brief me when you interrupted us."

"Isn't your secretary a felon?"

"Ex-felon, but it gives my firm street cred."

"Well, when you're done amusing yourself, you might skip the briefings from the felon and get the information straight from the horse's mouth."

"Who would that be?"

"Missing Persons."

"Oh, great," I said with annoyance.

"Yes. Mr. Cruz. You'll have to come back in to Police Central. I'm sure we can get you out of here sooner than last night. We should start charging you rent for all the times you've been here."

PJ gave me the initial rundown. A very wealthy family visiting Metropolis on vacation arrived one night and woke up the next day to find their two teenage children had never returned from the hotel's recreation center. Video released to the public showed that the two of them went outside the main entrance and never returned. It was a high-profile missing persons case, and the media, already spinning it as crime in the supercity, had turned its attention to innocent tourists. The tourism and travel industry was as frantic for the police to find the kids as the parents.

When I arrived at Police Central, I found myself escorted to a room. I was a civilian, and no matter how friendly we were, they were never going to co-work a case with me. It was one of the press briefing rooms, and it was filled with people. I should have smelled the stench from down the hall. It was filled with Metropolis's detectives. They all noticed me as soon as I came through the door. Some looked at me with contempt, others smirked, there were a couple of astonished faces. I recognized the guys who had recently tried to get me to work for them. All the main ones were in this room, from the one-man shops, like mine, to the major firms that had their own building towers.

Now I was burdened with where to sit. It was politics now. Whoever I sat next to, everyone would immediately believe there was some kind of meaning behind it—so, I just moved to the back wall and stood.

Then the jackals flooded in. Reporters galore came in. There was Holly Live, but this time she had all her competitors with her. Then, from the front of the room, the parents entered. They came in, holding hands, and stood behind the podium to the side. Chief Hub entered from the front of the room entrance too, flanked by two other senior officers. He walked right to the podium.

"Good afternoon, everyone." He had notes with him, but he dropped them down on the top of the podium. He didn't need any notes. "Recently, a story was leaked that the bodies of two young tourists here in Metropolis from London, United Kingdom Territories, were found near the area known as the River. We can conclusively say that those two bodies found were *not* the bodies of Mr. and Mrs. Goodstar's teenage children, which means they are still missing, and our police need the help of the public to find them."

He turned to the parents and stepped aside to give them the podium.

"Good afternoon, people of Metropolis. My wife and I know that this will be broadcast city-wide. We desperately need your help to find our children. Your police chief has graciously assembled your city's best private investigators to help in the search. We don't care who it is. We will pay any amount to find them. If the police find them, we will donate a sizable amount to your city. Now, I understand, Police Chief, you can't even seem to be taking money for doing your job, but we'll do that, whatever it takes, offer whatever amount for a reward."

"If you offer an amount in the sum of one million dollars, I will find your children!"

What an uproar there was as the woman in the sparkling turquoise top, within a black slicker coat down to her knees, and stylish black boots up to her knees, with bright red hair, spoke.

She had the stage and the attention, courtesy of the world. She strolled up to the front, I felt not for the parents to see her clearly, but so that the media camera people could film her with an unobstructed view.

"My name is Personna. I have been gifted with the sixth sense since I was a child and have used those psychic powers to find many missing people all over the world. Even Metropolis's police will admit that I have been successful in every case that parents have brought me into.

"Mr. and Mrs. Goodstar, I do not seek to take advantage of you at this terrible time. My fee is my fee."

She noticed that the parents were looking to the back of the room.

"There's a man at the back with his hand up," Mr. Goodstar said. "Do you have something to say?"

"Yes," I answered.

I could see Chief Hub's mouth drop to the floor, and a look of shock on the faces of his senior officers. Once again, all eyes were on me, and Madam Personna was giving me the evil eye.

"You can hire me to do the same thing as her for a lot less than that. The only question for you to ask yourself is do you want a mumbo-jumbo, 'psychic,' or do you want to stay in the real world with the adults and find your kids with a real-life detective, who gets results. Even if you don't want to hire me, at least hire one of the real detectives here in this room. The clock is ticking for your children, and you need serious people for this serious situation, not a sixth sense, third eye, or magic rabbit feet. Let's get real. That's what your kids need in this time of urgency."

PART THREE

The Psychic Case

CHAPTER 20

Shocker

I enjoyed belittling a charlatan hustler and, more importantly, putting the focus where it belonged, not on Madam Personna, but on the missing kids. Dot and I were going to have kids one day, so that was where I was coming from—the greatest horror of any parent, something happening to your kids. One of my first major cases was about a missing girl, and I still remembered that look of desperation in the mother's eyes. She was slowly going mad with the fear that she might never see her kidnapped child alive.

Well, Mr. and Mrs. Goodstar listened and then left the room. If Personna had possessed laser beam eyes, she would have vaporized me to dust as she marched out of the room, but my fellow detectives all gave me thumbs up and pats on the back. In their eyes, I'd kept all of them in play to be hired by the couple. The media jackals, of course, didn't want to let me leave until they'd interviewed me to death.

When I'd finally left Police Central, I checked the newsfeed on my mobile several times. I was surprised that the Goodstars hadn't made any decision yet. I'd asked, and a couple of the officers said that they had already left to return to their hotel. Maybe they felt they had to talk it through more or sleep on it before deciding on their final course of action. Maybe. All I knew was that, if it were Dot and me, we would have made the decision right there. Five minutes and done. I'm sure Missing Persons had told them all the grimy statistics about missing kids. In any supercity, if you don't find them in the first 72 hours, the odds plummet by the hour on the chances of you ever finding them again—alive or dead.

I remembered another statistic. They were kids, but not children. They were teenagers. When a teenager was missing, the overwhelmingly odds were that they'd run away. But for now, the media craze was telling the public that crazy gangs had snatched them.

I was back at the office.

"Did you get them to hire you?" PJ asked as soon as I came through the door.

I shook my head.

"What happened?"

"I don't know."

I walked into my private office to my desk.

"Do you think they're fakers, the parents?"

I glanced at her standing at the doorway. "Did you see their press conference?"

"Yes, it's playing everywhere on the news," she replied.

"Do you believe them?"

"Do you think it's a publicity stunt?"

"They're super rich. They don't need publicity. I don't know."

"That means you don't believe them. Fakers!"

She disappeared to go back to her desk.

"Oh, that client you had to reschedule from when your garbage friends came by—"

"Garbage friends?" I laughed. "They're trash men with advanced degrees."

She appeared at my doorway again. "Advanced degrees to pick up garbage? Get ready for this man. He's a paying client, and he really wants to see you. He's famous too."

"Famous?"

"He's 'The Shocker!'"

I'd known his face looked familiar when I passed by him with the Surf Brothers. He returned to the office later that afternoon looking as dapper as he had the previous day. His slicker outfit was all gray, and he wore a black cap on his balding head. His hair on the sides was silver gray.

PJ was right. He was anxious to meet with me and seated himself in my private office.

"Thank you for meeting me, Mr. Cruz."

"I'm sorry about the other day."

"No need. It's totally understandable. When you provide high-quality services, you have lots of people who want them. I'm sure you know who I am."

"Why don't you tell me your story in the way you want? The media loves to give nicknames to people, but they never consult with them to see if it's okay."

"Thank you, sir. I despise the name, 'The Shocker.' No, Mr. Cruz. I'm a businessman of 50 years, who got tired of the crime and the refusal of the city to deal with it, because I don't happen to live in the right sections.

"My store has been in the family for two hundred and fifty years. I'm the eighth generation to carry on the business. We've been selling bestselling consumer electronics in this city from the first day we opened. Always quality merchandise.

"The area has always had more than a fair share of crime, but we coped. But in recent years, it got really bad. One month they broke into my store every weekend, four weekends in a row. I did everything. I hired security guards and the criminals shot at them, almost killed one. I got robots; they shot them to pieces. Alarms worked, but they didn't care. The police wouldn't come. I did everything. One time, I called the police and they didn't come until six hours later. My councilman was useless. He's a carpetbagger who really lives in Paisley Parish. I was at my wit's end.

"I'm an electrician myself, building and fixing things since I was a child, so I rigged a system to shock them when they crossed the threshold of the store. It worked. Burglaries dropped off to nothing, but I always knew they'd try to find another way in. My wife and I went on vacation one weekend. We were woken up at 1am in the morning. We were out of the city at a resort hotel. We hadn't had any kind of vacation in five years. We had to come back and they charged me with multiple counts of murder. Twenty seven burglars rammed a hovercar into my store, demolished a whole wall, and they stormed in with weaponry I've never seen before. It was all caught on video. They killed themselves, not me. They damaged the shocking system I had rigged up and got themselves electrocuted. Police showed up for them, but never for me or my family!"

Mr. Manifold was fuming mad and closed his eyes briefly to collect himself. This was the real "Shocker." He was just an Average Joe in Metropolis with a business and a family, trying to get by in life without bothering anyone. The media would never show this side of the man to the public.

"Take your time," I said.

"Thank you. The police and the city have been nothing but a disaster for me, and my family. They shut down my business. That's what they did. At least, the people of Metropolis are on my side. The good news is, my attorney says no jury will convict me. The bad news is, my attorney says that I'll be bankrupt long before then."

"How can I help?" I asked.

"My attorney is very expensive, and he has detectives that he hires to build our defense case. I told him that I want to hire you."

"Me? I've never done any kind of legal case before."

"You never did detective work either until you did it. Look where you are now. You're friends with the police, so they wouldn't interfere with you, but you look out for the little guy. Also, you get results. I need results. I need this case to go away before I lose everything my family has worked for in over two centuries."

I didn't need any time to think. "I'll take your case."

Defense attorneys. I didn't like them, but besides criminals, they also worked for innocent people, and the railroaded. Mr. Manifold had gotten a raw deal, and I didn't like that. I cleared my calendar and was determined to wrap his case up in a day or two.

His attorney's office was in Neon Blues, a decent part of the city, and I came in ready to be briefed and go to work. It was almost lunch time, and I had been sitting in the lobby for almost an hour.

I stood up from my chair and walked calmly to the reception desk where two college-aged receptionists sat answering calls. Both looked as if they were dressed for clubbing, rather than work.

One put her calls on pause and said to me, "Mr. Suret knows you're here. He'll be right out."

I nodded, but instead of going back to my seat, I walked past their reception desk area and around the corner. I could hear them panicking and calling after me. I moved down the hall, saw his office, turned the knob, and threw open the door.

A tubby man sat at his desk eating with his hands as if he were born in a barn and stuffing his face with some meat-like glob of something.

"Who are you?" he asked.

"You little punk," I yelled. "You have me waiting in the lobby, while you're eating your slop. Why did you tell me to arrive at a specific time and then have me wait? Is this how you defense attorneys do business? I'm going to tell Mr. Manifold to fire your ass!"

I turned around as that slob jumped up from his desk.

"Mr. Cruz, please."

"Oh, so you do know who I am, you mutt!"

One of the receptionists, wearing heels as long as her legs, was stumbling her way down the hall. I brushed past her with the slob attorney calling after me.

"Please, calm yourself, Mr. Cruz. I was on a call and was grabbing a few quick bites before I brought you in."

I left in a huff.

CHAPTER 21

Run-Time

I was on my way to Let It Ride Enterprises, but I already had its CEO on the video-phone.

Run-time was my best friend, the best man at my wedding, and I had known him since we were little kids. Run-Time was a big deal in Metropolis. A middle-school drop-out at 11 years old, body shop go-fer at 12, hovercar mechanic at 13, valet attendant at 14, hovertaxi driver at 17, hovertaxicab owner at 19, millionaire at 22, started Let It Ride Enterprises at 25, mega-multi-millionaire by 30. He was listed in the "Who's Who" of the supercity's business elite, and he wasn't even 40. He owned all the top car washes, hovercar body shops, hovercar rental shops, hovercycle rental shops, hovertaxicab, and hoverlimousine services in the city. Anything that had to do with private transportation, Run-Time had his hands in it.

"Run-Time, can you recommend a good attorney?"

"Do you want fancy or good?"

"He doesn't have a lot of money. I hesitate to use the name, but it's The Shocker."

Run-Time smiled. "You're working that side of the fence, too? He must have an attorney already."

"The guy he has is a bum. He needs much better. I'm going to handle the field investigation work, but he needs a decent attorney."

"I'll make a couple of calls, and I'll have a name or two for you within the hour."

"Thanks, Run-Time."

Run-Time was a busy man, so I'd planned to wait at his office if he'd been in a meeting, but since I'd gotten him on the phone, it was back to Liquid Cool.

In the door, I came to hear from PJ that the British couple was going to hold another press conference about their missing kids.

"Maybe they'll announce they're hiring you," she said.

"It's not me. If it were me, I'd be there at Police One with them. I really hope they're not going with the psychic."

"No, they can't be that stupid."

Run-Time called, and he had ten minutes to go. He always came through. He told me his top choice, but he gave me a couple of others. Of course, the only one I was going to call was the top choice—but it wasn't for me to say.

I called Mr. Manifold and told him about my experience with his attorney of record.

"You think I should dump him?" he asked me. He looked worn on the video display of my office video-phone. The weight of the world was on his shoulders.

"If you have a chance of getting out of this, it won't be with him. I already made some calls, and I got a top recommendation for you—same level of money, but he gets results. And he's from a police family, so he'll guide you as a true legal advocate, not some shady, pseudo-criminal defense attorney."

"Yes, I like that. I'll get rid of the other one."

I gave him the number, and he thanked me.
The press conference was in five minutes.

CHAPTER 22

The Brits

Mr. and Mrs. Goodstar appeared at the podium. They were holding hands again, before the husband took the lead to take center stage. PJ and I watched on the bigger TV in my private office on the wall. This time, there were no police in sight.

"Thank you, people of Metropolis for...helping us through this ordeal that my wife and I find ourselves in. We have consulted with the best and we have decided on the best person to help us locate our two children."

Madam Personna appeared next to them. PJ made a disgusted sound and I almost walked away.

"They are stupid," PJ said. "They're definitely British. If they were French, they would have made the right decision."

I couldn't believe what I was watching. Mentally, I was not interested in anything else he had to say. The psychic took to the podium to speak.

"As with so many parents that have sought my gift, I take the trust that the Goodstars have placed in me seriously. We will work together to find their children as quickly as possible and bring the wrongdoers to justice."

"So, your third eye on your third foot already told you they were snatched by *wrongdoers*," I yelled at the TV. I looked at PJ, shaking my head. "What kind of word is that? I'm going back to work."

"So am I." PJ returned to her desk as I turned off the TV.

CHAPTER 23

The Surf Brothers

There would be no case with the Goodstars, after all. Mr. Manifold's new lawyer hadn't called yet. I had wrapped up some quick cases earlier in the week, and my next client appointment wasn't until tomorrow. My only plan for the day was to get through all my messages.

In the meantime, I was back with my Dominican friends in their hovertrash truck.

"What do you think they were doing?" I asked.

"Cruz, we have no idea," the older brother replied. "We dropped them off near the Valves and left."

"They were looking for something," the younger one said.

"What?"

"We don't know," he answered. "It was like one of those scavenger hunts, where you're told to find something, and you go around the city to find it. You know where to go, even though you've never been there before, but you know what you're looking for is there."

"That's a good analogy, little brother," the older one added as he drove us back to the Valves. Any police or White Shoes would be long gone.

The Surf Brothers had already given me a good description of them. My police sources still hadn't identified them, which only meant they weren't in the system: arrests, warrants, convictions, persons of interest in any case, in the Federal crime database, or Interpol database.

When we landed, I got out and walked around the outside of the Valves to see what I could see. CSI would have scanned and bagged any possible piece of evidence inside of the Valves, so that would have been a waste of time. I kicked around outside.

I remember when I'd seen them through the binoculars of the Road Courier, two guys just walking up the hill. They'd looked as if they knew where they were going—no sign of distress. I felt if we could simply identify them, then we'd have our answers.

"I wish you knew who they were," I said. "How did they know to contact you?"

"It was totally random, Cruz. They walked up to us on the street—ran to us. We'd never seen them before. They wanted us to drop them here, and they were willing to pay. They said only trashmen would know the area by the River, which is true. It was quick money."

"You weren't suspicious?"

"Cruz, suspicious about what? Two guys asked us to take them to the River, drop them at the Valves, and they paid us a bunch of money."

"We need to find out who they were," I said.

"Are you working a case?"

"No, I'm just curious," I answered.

"It's not good to be curious when no one is paying you," the older brother said.

"I'm just passing the time until my next paying client. We can go."

CHAPTER 24

Ichi Jumper

The lawyer called. This time, I wasn't waiting in a lobby for an hour. The new lawyer was waiting in the lobby for me when I walked through the doors of his Buzz Town offices. They were on Circuit Circle too, but across the street and at the other end of Liquid Cool's building. That was nice. It was only a two-minute hop away in the Pony.

Our task was simple. We had to gather evidence that showed that The Shocker hadn't turned his store into an electrocution room. I agreed with the new lawyer that no jury would convict him, but any jury trial was always a gamble. We had to get the prosecution to drop the case altogether.

I got the files on a data disk, and I was off to work. I didn't need to visit Mr. Manifold's store. The disk had detailed pictures and schematics of the shocking system he'd rigged and all the photos of the crime scene, bodies, store layout, wiring, etc. If it were not all on a disk, the file of paper might well have been the height of an average monolith tower.

Personna was on the newsfeed again. She seemed to be doing more interviews than using the third eye of her third foot to find these kids. The more I saw her face, the more I disliked her. I'd told the parents I could do the case for a fraction of the cost, but instead, they'd decided to give a million dollars to the Madam. The parents were not on my favorites list, either, at the moment.

I called Phishy from the Pony—quick call, then a quick drive back to the office.

As I pulled into the parking lot, instead of parking, I went all the way through and then flew back out. That blond-haired Japanese guy was waiting by the elevators. I could see him watching me go from my rear window. I had a contingency plan for these kinds of situations when I needed to park secretly. I flew around to the delivery bay, which most people didn't know about, and parked there. The plan was to get to my office as fast as possible—my secure office.

I came out of the office, my omega-gun already in hand. I peeked out and there was a figure, but it was an old lady. She was hobbling down the hall. I kept an eye on her as I walked out to my office. I had seen her before—one of the tenants on the floor.

When I pushed the door open, I breathed a sigh of relief, but PJ wasn't at her desk. I walked to my private office and was about to unlock the door, when I instinctively glanced back. I ducked. The laser-light bladed knife buried itself in the door where my head had been.

I bolted after him; the main office door hadn't even swung closed. Not taking any chances, I grabbed a few magazines from the lobby table and threw them out the door ahead of me—in case, he was waiting to shoot the first thing that appeared—before jumping into the hall. Ichi Jumper was down the hall waiting for the elevator—waiting? I aimed and fired. I missed! The blond-haired Japanese maniac jumped into the elevator. I ran after him, but the elevator closed.

"I missed him!" I yelled. "I never miss."

I kicked the hallway wall and then slammed my fist against it. The omega-gun flew from my hand. All this time, that old woman was standing there like a statue, but suddenly she came to life to bend down and grab my gun.

"Give me back my gun!" I yelled.

"Mine!"

I grabbed at my gun in her hand, but she wouldn't let go.

"Give me back my gun!"

"No, it's mine now. Finders keepers!"

Here I was playing games with this old lady, and Mr. Ichi Jumper was getting away. I knew I'd never catch him now.

PJ appeared from around the corner.

"What's happening here?" she yelled.

"This crazy woman won't give me back my gun."

"Mine! I'll call the cops on you!" she yelled.

That was exactly what I didn't want to hear. I had a gun permit and a concealed carry permit, but my favorite gun from Up-Top was illegal, and if the police got a hold of it, I would never see it again.

"Hey you!" PJ yelled at the woman. "See those biceps." She flexed her bionic arms at the woman.

"So," the old lady said. "You have metal arms."

PJ—Punch Judy—punched the wall right next to the woman's head. I had forgotten the raw power of her punches. The sound was unnerving, and the hole in the wall now was substantial. "Go away before I punch you in the head! Leave the gun!"

The old woman let go of my omega-gun. She gave both of us dirty looks. "There was a time when a better class of people used to be in this building." She walked off to wherever she was going.

"Yes, before you moved in," PJ snapped.

We looked at the damage. PJ and I decided we wouldn't tell the building landlord about the hole in the wall.

"What's that?" PJ saw the knife embedded in the center of my door as soon as we walked back into the office.

"Where were you?" I asked.

"I was in the restroom. Look."

Now, I noticed the "Back in 5 minutes. Have a seat." sign on her desk. She pulled the knife from the door.

"This is a serious weapon. You found this in the door?"

"Someone threw it at me."

"What? Are we calling the cops?"

"No police."

"Why? You call the police all the time."

"Do you want to spend all day at Police Central being questioned? Then the building landlord will find out about that hole you punched in the wall out there."

"Yes, no cops. We don't want all that hassle. Oh."

She ran to her desk, unlocked the enclosure, and opened it all back up. With her bionic fingers typing like crazy on her mobile keyboard, she pulled up the video recording feed of the office and hallway. She paused it and rewound it to where she wanted. There was me, coming into the office, and there was Ichi Jumper, coming around the corner, ninja-like, after I'd walked through the door, with his knife in hand.

"What? You missed!" she said, pausing the recording when Ichi jumped into the elevator and it closed.

"I know that," I said with annoyance.

"You never miss straight, close shots."

"I know that."

"When was the last time you were in the VR range?"

"I can't remember."

"Probably before your wedding. See what happens when you neglect practice." She held Ichi's knife in her hand and started to slice the air with it. "When I was in my gang back in France, we'd practice our knifing moves and shooting every day. That's how you get and stay good. Look at you now. You're a detective who can't shoot. You should have given your gun to that old woman. She probably can shoot better than you can."

I didn't need any of this. I walked to my private office door, unlocked it, and went in.

"I have work to do. I don't want to be bothered for anything or anyone. Except Phishy. He's coming."

"Oh, great. Stupid man is coming."

CHAPTER 25

Phishy

PJ had taken it upon herself to further 'fortify' our office security. It was one thing I wouldn't have to do, so I appreciated it. She had the whole client service (magazines for the waiting area, the pictures on the wall, types of refreshments to offer) and physical security measures (hidden metal detectors, placement of video surveillance, easy-access shotgun under the desk) down to a science.

I was behind closed doors poring through the documents on my computer screen from Mr. Manifold's new lawyer, taking notes as I went along. I could hear a voice outside my private office.

There was a knock.

"Come in, Phishy," I called out.

The door swung open, and there he was in the flesh. He always wore a dark colored vest and pants, with some off-white colored, long-sleeved shirt extravaganza with colored fish all over it. He said he had his street name to maintain. Today's color was powder blue.

Phishy was still spinning around, doing his chicken dance. This was how he greeted me, with some dance jig. I had to wait until he had sufficiently amused and tired himself out. There was no point in yelling at him to get serious. Phishy had to be Phishy first, before his brain could interact with others.

He always did this when he first met me for the day.

"Cruz!" he yelled.

It would take a few moments for him to stop being dancing Phishy, so I continued looking at the page on my screen. When he stopped, he walked over to my desk.

"What's the case?"

I switched off the screen with a button and covered up my notes.

"I have a job for you."

He jumped with a smile.

"Actually, for our Sidewalk Johnny Brigade."

"Cruz, the network isn't done yet."

"This is not for the network. This is for the Sidewalk Johnny Brigade."

He planted himself in the chair in front of the desk.

"Do I need to take notes, Cruz?"

"No. Just listen. Do you know Madam Personna?"

"Personna, you mean?"

"Isn't she Madam Personna?"

"No, she doesn't use Madam anymore. That's when she first had her little psychic parlor. She's big time now."

"Doesn't she own all those psychic parlors in Metropolis?"

"Maybe, but she's not Madam anymore."

"Well, that's the job. I want the Sidewalk Johnny Brigade to watch her. I want to know what she's up to from today going forward."

Phishy smiled again. "You're working the missing British kids case!"

"No. I'm getting you to get our Brigade to observe Madam Personna and report back to me."

"Daily?"

"No. When you have something interesting to report. If that's daily, yes. If not, don't bother me."

"Good. You think she's up to no good. Yeah, I think so, too. I bet she already knows where those Brit kids are and is just milking all the free publicity she can get. Maybe she's trying to squeeze more money out of the parents!"

Phishy said the last sentence with wide eyes as if he'd figured out a big, dark conspiracy all by himself sitting in my office.

"Okay, Phishy. Time for you to go and get to work. Get me the scoop on this psychic."

"You've got it, Cruz!"

Phishy's smile never left his face as he jumped up and was gone out the door.

CHAPTER 26

The Landlord

When I came into the office the next day, there were half a dozen men in suits waiting in the reception area, standing, frowns on their faces. PJ was behind her desk in her timid mode, almost hiding. The lead man was, of course, the building landlord. He lived in booshy Elysian Heights, and it was rare he ventured into the lower, working-class areas of the supercity to be in close proximity to us "peons." He somehow always made exceptions for me. He hated me and had once told me to my face that he didn't care how many friends in the city or on the police force I had, or how famous I got. He told me I was trouble and that the second he found a loophole to get me out of the building, he would do it.

"Good morning, sir." I gave him a smile as fake as the sincerity of my greeting.

"Good morning, Mr. Cruz."

"How can I help you, Mr. Shiro."

"Mr. Cruz, I'd like to hire you to find out who punched a hole in the wall outside there." He gave a mean glance at PJ. "Maybe you have a few theories as to who it might have been."

"Sorry, Mr. Shiro, we can't help you. You know we have video surveillance of the hallway but, somehow, that part of the tape got deleted. That's the funny thing about technology. You never know when it will decide not to work."

"Yes, funny."

His face was getting redder by the minute.

"Mr. Cruz, the beauty of the Legacy laws is that as the owner of the building, I may not be able to do anything about legacy occupants—or what I call vermin living in another man's property rent-free for life— but I also have no obligation to fix a thing. That responsibility falls to the vermin. I get the tax write-off. I'm listed as the owner. Let's see how long that hole in the wall will remain there. In fact, I'll let all the tenants on this floor know about that hole in the wall near the Liquid Cool office, where gun battles and visits from police are a common occurrence."

"Mr. Shiro, I can see that you're mad, but I don't know why. I've been investing in this building since I got here. I'm not going to leave a hole in the wall near my place of business. I also know that, if I don't have it fixed, even though we had nothing to do with it, it won't get done. I have pride in my place of business and its surroundings. You don't have anything to concern yourself with."

"You are a menace to Metropolis, Mr. Cruz."

I turned to PJ. "Did you hear what he said?"

"What?" PJ asked. She stood up and then started to realize. "Yes, it would be perfect!"

"Thank you, Mr. Shiro. My secretary was asking me for new quotes, because she wanted to add more Liquid Cool T-shirts to our virtual store."

"Let's get out of here!" the landlord stormed out of the front door with his men.

"'You are a menace to Metropolis, Mr. Cruz.' Thanks for helping, Mr. Shiro. Please come back soon," I yelled.

CHAPTER 27

Captain Monitor

When we arrived at Police One—the official tower headquarters of the Metropolis Police Department, it was through all the security checkpoints and then to sign in at the front desk. Police officers who recognized Mr. Manifold, or The Shocker, gave us mean looks, but most gave us secretive thumbs up as they walked past us.

I had all my work done and Mr. Manifold, his new lawyer, and I were waiting for the police chief. As we quietly waited in the clean inside-the-station lobby (not to be confused with the open bay general lobby of chaos), I noticed that there was a lot of commotion down the hall. Police officers were gathered, overflowing from some conference room. You could feel the tension in the air, and we could almost hear the voice of someone, probably a commanding officer, talking to troops. I knew a Red Ball when I saw one—those high-priority, media-storm, all-detectives-and-police-brass on-deck investigations—but there were no high-profile cases or situations that I was aware of.

Captain Monitor came around the corner and immediately saw me looking at the gathered officers. He walked to them, whispered to a few of them, and within moments, they crammed into the room and closed the door. When I'd first met Monitor, he was a police officer, then a detective. Now, he was a captain! In a short time, because of his family connections, he was already a member of the brass. Another man in a suit appeared and caught up with him. The two of them reached us.

"The Chief isn't here today, so you're stuck with me," Monitor said.

They took us to his spacious office. Monitor sat, and his man stood at the back and closed the door. We all took our seats in three small chairs in front of his desk. I always felt that it was part of some secret psychology class given to government bureaucrats. "Make sure the chair that you have your visitor sit in is small, close to the ground, and uncomfortable. That will maintain your superiority in the communications relationship. Make sure your chair is big, high above the ground, and imposing."

I laid the file in my hand on the top of the desk right under his nose.

"I did investigations of all 27 criminals, and one, in particular, was of interest. He was an electronics expert, who specialized in hacking into electrical systems. I'm going to say that this skell hacked into Mr. Manifold's electric shock system, which only used the same levels used by the stun-sticks of the Metropolis Police Department, by the way, and amplified the juice. *He* actually was the cause of the electrocution deaths, not Mr. Manifold. Here are all my findings."

"Mr. Cruz, do you have any evidence to prove what you just said to me?" Monitor asked.

"Captain, we don't have to prove anything. All we have to do is say it. If the case were to reach the courts, the judge would open my file folder there and read my findings and say, 'Why the heck is this case in my courts? Dismissed.'"

The captain smirked. He opened the file and flipped through the pages. He looked up at the officer in the suit standing behind us.

"You can issue the lift to allow Mr. Manifold to open up his business again."

"Yes, sir." The officer reached into his pocket to grab his mobile phone. He was going to email someone.

"Mr. Manifold, you can expect the charges to be officially dropped sometime today."

Manifold was ecstatic, and his new lawyer was all smiles. Manifold shook his hand and then mine. Monitor just watched us, and after a few moments, we all quieted back down. We all sat there without a word, looking at him.

"Mr. Manifold, I can understand your position completely, but I'm to say to you what Chief Hub would say if he were here. You feel the police weren't on your side, that the criminals are running wild—not true, but I can understand your position. Metropolis has over 50 million people living in it. We don't and never will have enough police for the supercity. We can't be everywhere, even though we might want to be. In a free society, Mr. Manifold, there will never be enough police. Would you or anyone else really want a police state with a cop on every corner 24 hours a day, 7 days a week? Then the public would complain we had too many police. Law enforcement is in a perpetual no-win situation. We do what we can. We prioritize. That's how it is and must be."

Monitor reached in his desk drawer and took out a photo. He placed it in front of us. We looked at a disgusting photo of what looked to be two charred little bodies on the sidewalk.

"Do you know why we had to do what we did, Mr. Manifold? What do you think would happen in this city if every store owner started booby-trapping their place of business to 'get the criminals'? We have enough murders and mayhem in this city on a daily basis. We don't need any more. You think you're the first person in this city to do what you did? A few years back, another retail owner wanted to 'get the criminals,' stop the burglars breaking into his store. He rigged a fancy shocking system too, but not as fancy or professional as yours. The only thing he did was electrocute a ten-year-old boy walking to school with his six-year-old brother. He'd hold his little brother's hand, and while he was walking that fateful day, his other hand touched the metal grating of this store. The poor kids were electrocuted to a crisp—as you can see from the photo.

"Mr. Manifold, you can safely rig an anti-burglary intrusion system for your store. Your detective here could build a high-tech hovercar in his apartment, while in high school no less, but the reality is that most of the people out there in the public are not very smart. They can't do what you two can do. When they try to do what you two can do, we get electrocuted, charred little bodies on the sidewalk.

"Are you understanding me, Mr. Manifold?"

"Yes," is all Mr. Manifold said.

Monitor stood up from his desk. He didn't need to say any more. We got up and walked to the door.

I turned back, but he cut me off.

"No, Mr. Cruz. We will not give you access to the autopsy files for the two bodies at the River. The Metropolis Police Department is not your personal resource. Only legitimate parties are authorized for those files. Good day, gentlemen."

As we left, I glanced down the hall to the autopsy files room. Monitor was smart. Outside the door were four uniformed police standing guard outside the door. They saw me and waved in unison—not a good sign when the police were able to predict your sneakiness.

"Mr. Cruz," Manifold said, shaking my hand again. "Thank you, thank you. Hiring you was the best business decision I ever made. You saved my life."

"You're very welcome, Mr. Manifold."

The lawyer patted me on the back and shook my hand again. "Mr. Cruz, it was a pleasure working with you again. I hope we can work together again in the future. Don't be a stranger. We work on the same street."

It was a good day for me, case closed and a win for an Average Joe in the world. I drove home in the Pony from Police Central with a big smile—but what my mind really was interested in was what was going on in that Red Ball meeting.

CHAPTER 28

The Sniff

He was back—not the blond Japanese guy. The Sniff was standing in my offices again, well-dressed as always, with that black leather portfolio in hand.

"No, Mr. Cruz. I'm not here to pressure you or plant any kind of sweet reminders in your ear. I'm here on another matter. I am in need of your services."

That's what I liked to hear. PJ had scheduled my day lightly, so a paying walk-in customer from the moment I walked into my offices was welcome. I led him in and closed the door. He sat in his chair and I sat behind my desk.

"Mr. S., you want to hire me?"

"Yes, I do Mr. Cruz. It's a very delicate matter, but you have always been a man of discretion."

He opened his portfolio and out came a large photo. I took it when he reached forward with it. As a hovercar restorer, I recognized it immediately. A Rolls-Royce Spectre. It was so expensive a vehicle that all of them were Up-Top as far as I knew.

"I didn't think there were any on Earth," I said.

"You keep abreast of the industry, Mr. Cruz. There's only one. It's the model in the photo. That's why I'm here. It's been stolen."

My head popped up. "Stolen?"

"Yes."

"You have to call the police right away. While we're sitting here, it could be chopped up in a million pieces."

He shook his head. "This wasn't street thieves, and there are no chop-shops involved here. This was a sophisticated heist."

"Tell me you have it tagged."

"Of course. That's standard, but the signal has been cut. They know what they're doing. However, I do have a lead."

I leaned forward. He didn't even have to ask. I was taking this case. This was a matter of pride for the entire brotherhood of classic hovervehicle connoisseurs in the world.

"I have an address of one of the possible thieves. Fortunately, I have my fair share of contacts on the street, nothing as extensive as you may have, but fair. In this case, the tip is from a member of our sister industry of hoverbikes. They said they saw the act in progress and followed them to the address."

"How recent is the information?"

"As of five minutes ago."

"Pay my secretary. I'm leaving now."

"I thought you might."

CHAPTER 29

Repo Man

I was in Tokyo Town, and it was not a nice place. It was always easy to tell what kind of neighborhood you were in by its neon signs. Assuming they were in English, just read the signs. What I was reading was not for the family-friendly crowd, ruffs and half-naked women all around, walking in the rain. It was a "forever the nightlife" kind of place.

I wasn't in my normal tan fedora and tan slicker outfit. This time, I was in ninja-mode with a black hoodie slicker and my snazzy aqua-shoes for running on the slick, wet ground. I had reached the address pretty quickly and was walking around to get the lay of the land. My search was for some kind of back alley or private secluded garage parking lot. If this were the work of high-end hovercar thieves, a Rolls Spectre wouldn't be left anywhere on the public street where it could be gotten to.

I was moving quickly, because I had a lot of ground to cover. Going through strange back alleys was not a wise thing to do ever, but I did it. There was always someone there up to something sleazy or illegal. I ignored them as I continued my street search.

Was the lead bogus? Maybe instead of really secluded places, I needed to do the opposite—look at public places. The Sniff said these were not some low-level car thieves. If that was the case, then that meant a buyer or buyers who were not going to be to stepping into dark alleys filled with pimps, prostitutes, and dope daddies.

I was back to the main streets nearby, and looking at every major establishment. I figured that the best place would have to be an outdoor bar or diner, a place where all concerned could see each other coming and going.

I found myself at a diner with large neon red letters in Japanese and Cantonese. Decent and rich neighborhoods had their parking lots a few stories up, at the very least. Poor and dangerous ones—and government institutions—had their parking lots on the ground. The diner had a large one right in front of its open window design. Hoverbikes were crowded near the front, and the hovercars, row after row, took up the rest of the lot. What caught my eye was the one covered completely with a car cover.

It had the right length and shape. I briskly moved to it, keeping my eyes open. When I was about ten feet away, I ducked down and ran to it. If it was being watched, my little move wasn't going to fool them. When I reached it, I peeked under the cover. It was the Rolls Spectre. It also had a big bright orange anti-hovering device on the back.

I heard a noise and spun around. My omega-gun was pointed at him, and the man had an equally deadly gun pointed at me.

"How did you get this vehicle here with that big anti-hovering lock on it?" I yelled.

"What?"

"You heard the question."

"'Cause I was the one who put it on," he snapped back.

"What?"

"You heard what I said."

"You work for Parking Services?"

"Parking Services? I'm a repo man."

"Repo? What are you talking about? This vehicle belongs to my client."

"That vehicle belongs to my client!"

I couldn't believe what I was hearing, but he was telling the truth. I put my gun back into my jacket and produced my detective license. He did the same and produced his hovercar repossession badge.

I threw up my hands. "My client is a liar!"

The repo man began laughing. "Welcome to my world."

The Sniff was waiting for me at the Liquid Cool offices when I returned. He was smiling, with his leather portfolio in hand.

"Mr. Cruz, did you really find it so fast?"

"I found it, all right."

"Please tell me it's not damaged."

"Does a big bright orange anti-hover lock on the back count as damage?"

"I don't understand."

I opened the main door, and the repo man walked in.

"This, Mr. S., is Sid, the Repo Man. Sid took your vehicle because your vehicle is not your vehicle. It belongs to Classic Hovercar Dreams LLC, which you rented it from two years ago, but conveniently stopped making payments on six months ago. Is that why you came to my office the other day to buy my Pony?"

"Mr. Cruz, let me explain."

"You're a liar! You wasted my time, and you could have gotten me shot—or Sid. You want your Rolls? Pay your bills on time!"

The Sniff looked as if he were going to faint.

"Sid," I turned to the repo man and said, "Sorry for all the trouble." I gave him a forearm handshake and fist bump. His whole right arm was bionic.

"No problem, Cruz. Like I said, welcome to my world."

"PJ."

"Yes, boss."

"Escort this liar out of the office. If he gives you any lip, you can punch a hole in him."

PJ stood up from her desk. "Oh yes, he knows about holes in walls. He told me he saw that big hole out there when he came in."

I walked past him in a huff. I wasn't ever going to sell my Pony to the liar anyway.

CHAPTER 30

Phishy and The Network

Being a detective, no, being a business owner, was about juggling a lot of things in the air at the same time. This was no different from any other time for me in the private investigation business.

Phishy returned with a new shirt with fishes, his same craziness, and the smile. With him were a bunch of sidewalk johnnies. PJ actually knew all of them, so that meant they were all from the Concrete Mama. Phishy and the johnnies piled into my private office for our meeting.

"Should I update you on that other matter?" Phishy asked.

"Not now," I replied. "After, but don't forget."

"Okay." I knew he was going to forget.

In my last major case, it was the sidewalk sallies of the Brigade that had literally kept me alive despite the villain who was my arch-nemesis. Too bad she had gotten herself shot dead—by me. This time, I needed a group on the streets for a far more expansive role.

"What's the word on the street about these missing British teenagers?" I asked when we all settled in my private office's lobby area, some sitting, most standing.

The sidewalk johnnies looked at each other.

Phishy started first. "People are saying that they're not even in Metropolis."

"Why are they saying that?"

"There's a lot of money out there on the street, Mr. Cruz, for any tips leading to their whereabouts. No one I know has even heard of a sighting of those kids," one of the johnnies said.

"What about children traffickers?" I asked.

The sidewalk johnnies and Phishy looked at each other.

"Do you believe that's what happened, Mr. Cruz? The kids walked out of the hotel on their own, child traffickers were waiting for them, and kidnapped them out of the country?"

"No, I don't believe that at all. What about Madam Personna?"

The men laughed.

"You don't like her at all, Mr. Cruz."

"No, I don't. What about her? How come her third eye on her third foot hasn't told her where they are yet? How does she justify herself to the media?"

"We don't know, Mr. Cruz."

"Okay, this is what I want you all to do."

They all leaned forward.

"I want to create a street network all over Metropolis."

"Not all sidewalk hustlers are good people, like us sidewalk johnnies, Mr. Cruz."

"Don't think of it as you're doing it for this case," I said. "Think of it as we're building a network for the next case, eyes and ears on the street that we can put into action fast. It's going to take time to build, and we've really been focused around here and the Concrete Mama. Let's reach out further."

"That's a big task, Mr. Cruz."

"That's why we have to start building it now. I'm working on a way to incentivize it too. We only want good leads. How much money is the reward from the parents on the street?"

"We heard it was up to two million dollars, Mr. Cruz."

Even I was visibly surprised.

"Are you sure you don't want the Network to look for the kids too, Mr. Cruz?"

"Maybe we should after all." They laughed. I was still thinking about the money.

"We'll get on it, Cruz," Phishy said and jumped up from his chair.

"Okay, you guys get to work. Phishy, you stay here."

The sidewalk johnnies said their goodbyes and left the office, closing the door behind them.

Phishy sat back down. "You have another job for me, Cruz?"

"Phishy, what's the scoop from the Brigade?"

"Oh, yeah. I forgot."

"I knew you would. You didn't forget the information, did you?"

"No." He reached into his jacket. "I wrote it down for you."

"I can't read your Phishy writing."

Phishy laughed. "Phishy writing."

"What do you have on Madam Personna for me?"

"We followed her and watched her."

"And?"

"Nothing."

"What does that mean?"

"I don't know how psychics do what they do, but she doesn't seem to be doing anything to find them. She's doing media interviews, visiting her psychic parlors, shopping for new clothes, shopping for a new hovercar, shopping for house furniture. Nothing. You'd think she'd already found the kids. Is that the information you wanted?"

"It's exactly what I wanted. Thanks, Phishy. Keep the Brigade on the job, watching her. Tell me if anything changes in her routine."

"You've got it, Cruz."

Phishy was genuinely happy when he could help me. He gave me his Phishy handshake, and I sent him on his way.

CHAPTER 31

More Ichi

There I was, in the field, when Dot called me on my mobile. I was on the streets on Circuit Circle. In my tan fedora and slicker, I always stood out. I'd grabbed a couple of Coney Islands from a hoverfood truck—the biggest and best hot dogs on Earth—and had finished them off before she called.

"Dot," I answered.

"Cruz, what are you doing?"

"Eating the lunch of champions."

"Eating off a hover-food truck again. How does eating mystery meat off a hoverfood truck fit into the whole logic of your germophobia?"

"It builds up my immune system to fend off the germs."

She laughed. "Whatever. I was calling so you wouldn't worry."

"Worry?"

"You'll see it on the newsfeed soon. Some drug addict went crazy in the streets close to the salon. He went berserk and tried to kill people with his bare hands. He was a cyborg, so that wasn't too difficult for him. Police shot him, but people said he was dead already, as if his brain was frying—just weird."

"Brain frying?"

"Yeah, and people said his eyes were glowing."

"That is weird."

"No one was killed, luckily, but a ton of people that he attacked had to go to the hospital."

"This was near Eye Candy?"

"Right down the street."

"I hope you all have guns in the salon."

"Cruz, this is a high-end beauty salon. Of course we do."

Now she made me laugh.

"As long as you're safe. I'll see you tonight. Love."

"Love. Bye."

While I was talking on my mobile, I had been walking. When I'd hung up with the wife, I was where I wanted to be. I turned into an alley, crouched down, and waited.

I wanted him badly. I was now dreaming of shooting that Japanese blond mutt. I didn't see him, but then I never saw him. I was making an educated guess that he was tailing me now.

It had only been a few minutes before a shadow appeared around the corner. I had gotten in serious trouble in a previous case when I'd shot an unarmed person. Luckily for me, that person was a crime boss that had planned to blow up the entire Concrete Mama residential tower just to get me, so the police gave me a pass. Otherwise, I would have needed my own defense attorney and still would have ended up in Metro Penitentiary. I wanted to shoot Ichi Jumper point-blank badly.

I did it. I shot at him and blew that stupid blond wig off his head. The shock of it made him girly-scream, and he ran away. I jumped up from my position, and he appeared again to grab the wig from the ground. I couldn't believe it. I shot again—this time to hit him—but missed!

This guy was a jinx. That's what he was. My proximity to this mutt was adversely affecting my mojo. This was the second time I'd missed a shot.

The foot race was on. He was running, and I was right on his heels. He was really bald, so all I had to follow was the shine from his dome. He darted around a corner into a bigger street and then slowed down. I was prepared to unload my clip on him if he had any weapon, gun or knife.

Instead, he turned around and took a martial arts side stance, facing me with his hands up.

"Seriously, you want to play karate with me?" I asked. "I have the gun."

He was unfazed as I walked toward him.

"Hi!" he yelled, and sliced the air back and forth with karate chops.

I was about to break out laughing. He had the blond wig tucked in the front of his pants, giving his male area a distinct bulge.

I never saw it. It flew past my head; only a last-minute jerk saved me. What was it with this guy and knives? There was a scream behind me, and I looked. A man was holding his leg, the knife sticking out from it. The woman with him was frantic. I turned around and shot at that mutt again. He hopped and then began running again. What had happened to my bullet?

I flipped the switch on my omega-gun to laser. Enough was enough!

Ichi Jumper did a complete vertical leap, as if his legs were powered by jets, and landed on top of a hovercar that was rising up into the sky traffic. I stood there; we all stood there, the entire crowd in the street. People even had their mobiles out with the cameras turned on. We all were waiting for him to fall. We all wanted him to fall so badly, me especially. We wanted to see the splat.

The hovercar kept ascending. Ichi Jumper put the stupid blond wig back on his head and raised his hands in the air and screamed at us.

"Ichi Jumper is better than Cruz!"

I could have shot myself right there. I was so demoralized; he got away again.

123

CHAPTER 32

The Brits

I was depressed. I didn't know who this guy was. He was following me, and I couldn't manage to kill him or even shoot him. I had killed quite a lot of bad guys or caused their demise, courtesy of Metro, Federal, or Up-Top law enforcement. I had gotten three chances and blew them. He was standing on hovercars, flying into the sunset with his stupid blond wig, laughing at me.

I took a deep sigh to calm myself. That's what Dot had told me to do. Breathe it out; don't let it back in.

I arrived at the Crystal Camelot Hotel—a favorite of the Euro-elite traveling class. It was another fancy establishment, where people paid more in one night for a room than the average Metropolitan made all year. When I came out of the elevator, a man in a suit was waiting.

"Mr. Cruz?"

"Yes."

"This way."

I followed him into the room—the door was opposite the private elevator. I waited for him to close the door behind us and he led me in.

The room looked like a museum to me with its marble animals and gold plated furniture.

He took me into another room, and there they were—the Goodstars.

The room was equally luxurious and spacious. Mrs. Goodstar sat on a chair facing me. On the side was a large desk; her husband sat behind it. I had been brushing shoulders with the wealthy a lot since becoming a detective and I found it fascinating how they lived. Their little hotel room had more rooms and was many times bigger than the entire Concrete Mama apartment home Dot and I lived in. Well, the Goodstars could keep their hotel room.

"Can our servant get you anything to drink, Mr. Cruz?" the wife asked.

"No, thank you."

The servant had me sit in the chair in front of the desk. It was as if I were a kid being brought to the principal's office for shooting spitballs at the teacher.

"Mr. Cruz," the wife said. "I didn't expect to see you again."

"Mr. Cruz, I hope this visit is not to try to—" the husband began.

I held up my hand. "Let me stop you. I'm here simply to ask you to get the police to give me access to the autopsy reports of the two bodies found near the River."

"But the police told us that they were not our children," the wife said. There was a bit of panic in her voice.

"I'm not suggesting anything contrary to that. It's actually a separate case I'm working. It would be easier if I could simply have you call on my behalf to get access to those reports. I'm trying to identify them. That's all. It would help tremendously and save me a lot of time."

"You don't approve of our decision to hire the psychic, do you Mr. Cruz?" Mrs. Goodstar asked.

"I'm in no position to approve or disapprove of any decision you and your husband make. They're not my children. I don't even have children. It just seems odd to me."

"Odd how, Mr. Cruz? There are many things in the universe that science can't explain. It doesn't mean that they don't exist or are any less valid."

"I agree. I believe in a lot of things science can't explain or won't. Now that humans are living on other planets and in space, I'm sure that list will grow. No, Mrs. Goodstar, what I find odd is that you and your husband picked only one choice, when you have so many available to you. But again, since they're not my children, it's not my place to say.

"Can you please help me with the police?" I asked.

"I don't see any issue with that request, Mr. Cruz," Mr. Goodstar said. "We can do that for you."

I had thought the decision to hire Madam Personna was the wife's idea, but based on the way she was not looking at him, and their body language, it seemed that he was the dumb monkey in this show.

The servant returned, and this time, they shook my hand to wish me good luck. I was led to the front door by the manservant and off on my way.

CHAPTER 33

Punch Judy

I stood at PJ's desk, looking at her main display screen connected to her mobile computer.

"What is this?" I asked. "Dot told me about another incident yesterday."

"I thought it was a fake story, but it's legit: people's eyes glowing, people being attacked and people dying."

"How are they dying?"

PJ scanned the news story. "O.D."

"Overdose? What kind of overdose does that?"

"There are lots of drugs out there. They're making new ones all the time."

"I've never heard of this—not like this."

"Lots of drugs make you crazy and violent."

"Glowing eyes?"

"Yes. That's different."

A video-call came in. It was Phishy. I went into my private office to talk to him.

"Phishy, what's up?"

"Cruz!" Phishy's face was all smiles on my display screen. "I got the scoop!"

"What scoop?"

"That British couple. They flew back to Europe."

"The British couple? Why was the Sidewalk Johnny Brigade watching them?"

"They weren't. They were watching Personna. She was on the same flight with them."

"When did they leave?"

"The flight's leaving now. They're in the air."

"Thanks, Phishy."

"Cruz, did that help?"

"It did. Thanks."

I hung up.

I came out of my office.

"PJ."

She looked at me as I stopped at her desk.

"Book me a flight to the London Prime."

"What?"

"The British couple with the missing kids and the psychic just got on a jet plane to there.

"*C'est incroyable!*"

"I'm assuming they're going back to UKT, so that's where I'm going."

"Why?"

"This whole case is wrong. It was wrong from the start."

"But you have no client."

"Don't worry. I'll have a paying client before this is all done."

"Maybe the psychic found the kids."

"Madam Personna? The only thing she knows how to find is a fat paycheck. No, they're not going there to find those kids. They're sneaking out of Metropolis."

"Sneaking? What about the kids?"

"I wouldn't worry about those kids. I think they're fine. I think those kids walked out of that hotel, got into a hovercab, went to Metro International, and flew back home that very night. They were running from the parents."

"C'est incroyable!" PJ said again.

Yes, it was incredible. But there was more. I had never been to Europe. Like most Metropolitans, I had never been out of the Americas; the majority had never even been outside of the supercity. I would be in London Prime across the Great Ocean within 48 hours.

PART FOUR

London Prime, UKT

CHAPTER 34

The Goodstars

I had been on a few domestic flights, but never an international one. This was a triple-decker jet, and each person had their own pod. The chair could recline to be a bed. You had all your entertainment covered—music, TV, movies, VR. The flight attendants kept the food and beverages coming. I had forgotten I was even on a jet; I was having so much fun. I even got a chance to practice some marksmanship in a VR shooting range game!

There was a reason most people didn't do international flights. It was so expensive. The flight and hotel were going to set the Liquid Cool bank account back a good few months of income. I had better make good on finding a paying client.

London International and Space Port was as huge as Metro International. If you didn't know where you were going, you had to use a hovercart. I noticed that they had domies here too—street punks who lived in the dome city of the airport. I gave them the evil eye, so they knew I was watching them. They gave me the finger.

Unlike Dot, who would have taken up half the cargo hold with her luggage, I had only two bags, which meant I was able to carry my bags on and take them off. I wasn't going to have to mess with luggage pickup. If I needed anything not in these bags, I would buy it here.

When I got outside the airport, I realized something. It was cold and rainy. I could deal with rainy—in fact, I loved it—but I wasn't happy with the cold. The other thing I noticed was there was no hovertraffic. It was weird. I stood there looking up at the sky. What I did see were hoverbuses and trucks. There were also high wired guides where hovertrains whipped by.

"Where are all the hovercars?" I asked.

"Everyone's on public transportation here, chap," a man standing next to me said.

"No hovercars?"

"This is Europe. No private transportation here. Who needs it?" He walked away to catch a hoverbus that had descended to the ground. People filed in.

"No hovercars," I said again. "What kind of backwards place did I come to?"

They did, however, have hovertaxis. So that was going to be my mode of transportation. London was like a megacity of domes. You couldn't see anything, either. It was cold, rainy, and bleak. With the polar ice cap to the North, I was obligated to shop for warm clothes.

"Where're you from, Yank?" the hovertaxi driver asked.

"Metropolis."

"You're from across the Pond. That's a big city. We're only a big island compared to you. How long are you visiting?"

"Maybe a week. I've never been here before."

"You'll love it. The best pubs in the world."

As we approached my hotel, the driver descended and went under the dome. Inside, I couldn't believe what I was seeing. People in short sleeved shirts, kids in shorts, the dome lights were like direct sunlight.

You'd never see this much skin in public in Metropolis walking around. Some were even wearing clear plastic coats. Every place had to have its version of useless fashion.

London Prime was not as huge as Metropolis—no other city was— but it was just as cosmopolitan. People and ethnicities of every kind were to be found, and at the airport, I heard foreign languages that I was not familiar with. I assumed they were Arabic and Middle Eastern. I couldn't speak anything besides English, but I could almost always pick out what the language was.

I gave my driver a good tip and asked for his card. It seemed as if I were doing something very American, because he didn't have a card, but I keyed his number into my mobile. I guess here it wasn't common for a person to call a favorite hovertaxi driver again. The American Hotel (it was affordable) was a ten-story tower. I noticed that, from what I'd seen of London so far, they didn't have the two-hundred story monolith towers like Metropolis.

I checked in at the desk. The man at the counter was very friendly and gave me a handful of brochures of local sites, especially the pubs, along with my key.

"What's this?" I asked. One of the brochures had animals. "London has some great animal habitats. Real animals in bio-domes that are exactly like they were in the past. Tourists also seem to like our natural farms—sheep, cattle, cows, goats, llamas, horses, chickens, and even those noisy roosters. Very popular."

"Barnyard animals. Oh, that sounds like fun." I hid my sarcasm well.

I'd thought I was going to freeze to death, but in the dome it was nice and warm—warmer than Metropolis. Outside the domes, you would freeze to death unless you were a polar bear. I had my big camera, because Dot wouldn't let me leave, and I wouldn't be allowed back in the house, unless I took a ton of pictures like any good tourist. In fact, she'd instructed me to email them to her daily.

I had called the number that the hovertaxi guy gave me but it was a wrong number. Did I type it wrong or he tell it to me wrong? Or did he not want me to call him while he was at the pub or taking a nap? I called another one, who came in five minutes.

This hovertaxi driver looked like a teenager and drove like one. He didn't look as if he were the type who could talk and drive safely at the same time, so I was glad he stuck to the driving. He definitely could use a defensive driving class or two.

I was wrong. London did have monolith towers like Metropolis, and we were driving to a bunch of them. It figured that the Goodstars would live in one. What did I expect? He landed and was off on his way after I'd paid and tipped him.

"Hello, sir," the doorman said to me.

"Yes."

"Don't let these drivers rip you off. Here in Europe, the gratuity is *included* in the fare—twenty percent."

"What!" I shook my head. "Bastards."

He grinned. "Drivers in Europe think Americans are stupid; drivers in America think Europeans are cheap—all just a simple lack of communication."

"And Europeans and Americans think off-worlders are tossers."

The doorman laughed and opened the door for me. "Very true, sir."

It was that same manservant as before who answered the door. "Mr. Cruz," he said.

The way he said it meant the Goodstars were expecting me.

The Metropolis hotel where they were staying was a flophouse compared to their palatial apartment home. We walked down the hallway and the left side was a glass wall. On the other side was a full holo-tennis court where two couples, dressed in white gear, were playing a match against each other. Their rackets glowed yellow and the holo-ball was purple. People loved to use the prefix 'holo,' though there was no true holography involved. It meant that something was covered with fancy mini-projectors to fool your eyes into thinking the object or background was changing into something else.

The man took me to the sitting room—the rooms actually had names above the door—where the Goodstars were sitting on the thick carpeted floor, legs crossed at a black table, eating their food with chopsticks.

They were looking up at the door when I was led in, but were very unemotional by my appearance in their own country.

The servant left me standing in front of them.

"You don't seem surprised to see me," I said.

"Why would we be?" Mr. Goodstar asked. "Our psychic said you'd be here."

I looked to the side, and there was Madam Personna eating her food out of a bowl with chopsticks.

I smiled. "So, did Madam Personna find your children?"

Personna hated that I added her old title to her name.

"Mr. Cruz, why are you here?" Mrs. Goodstar asked.

"Didn't your psychic tell you?" I asked.

"We can have our manservant show you back out," she said. "We didn't have to let you in here."

"Yes, that's true. So, the psychic didn't tell you that part. Where are your children?"

"That is none of your business," Mr. Goodstar answered.

"You two come to Metropolis, run a scam on the people and police."

He jumped up. Mrs. Goodstar threw her chopsticks down on the table.

"I'll ask again; where are your children?"

"You are a bloody nuisance, sir," Mr. Goodstar said. "What scam?"

"Do you think, once I tell the Metropolis Police Department that you ran a scam on them and the public, they won't do something?"

"Do what?" Mrs. Goodstar asked.

"You have heard of fraud, have you?"

"Mr. Cruz, I've been an attorney all my adult life, and fraud involves an exchange of money. We have not gotten a dime from anyone."

"But the Metropolis Police has shelled out considerable money for your scam."

"Stop using that word," Mrs. Goodstar yelled.

"If Metro PD shelled out one dime on your behalf for your false story, then that's fraud."

The husband walked to me and jumped into a martial arts stance with his hands up.

"Why is everyone wanting to play karate with me these days?"

"I don't 'play' karate, Mr. Cruz. I'm a third-degree black belt. Also, I know they don't allow Americans to bring their guns into Europe."

"You'd better sit back down and eat your Asian tortillas with your booshy choppy-sticks."

"Hi!" The husband actually charged at me.

I knew something that he didn't. I karate kicked him in the chest and punched him in the face. He fell to the ground. The women ran to his aide.

"Too bad your psychic didn't tell you that was going to happen, either. Black belt, huh? I know how to fight for real, against real people, and not holographic ones, you tosser."

"Get out of here!" the wife yelled.

"Look at the three of you," I said. "Thick as thieves. Your kids weren't kidnapped and rescued by the great Madam Personna. They walked out of that hotel to get away from Mommy and Daddy Dearest."

"You don't know anything!" the husband yelled. "You're making things up."

"I'm going to make a call to Chief of Police Hub, then I'm going to go to the London police station to report you, then I'm going to call the Metropolis media and get them to call the London media. We'll find out how much I'm making things ups."

"Is everything okay in here?"

Standing at the now open door were those two tennis-playing couples. The women were as buff as the men, and they were all giving me dirty looks. One of the men was holding his racket like a weapon.

The servant ran into the room, and his eyes widened, seeing Mr. Goodstar on the floor.

"Are you okay, sir?"

"Get him out of here!" Mr. Goodstar answered.

"Where are the two kids?" I asked.

The servant's face went white.

I looked at the tennis-playing couples.

"Where are the two kids?"

Their expressions turned from menacing, wanting to beat me up, to frightened and looking for someplace to crawl away and hide.

I was done with them.

"I'll show myself out."

I stormed out as the tennis couples moved out of my way.

CHAPTER 35

Personna

In Metropolis, if you wanted to look at the criminal database, you had to be in law enforcement or any of the complimentary services, like criminal prosecution or treasury. Here, there were no pesky privacy laws to deal with; just go to your local library community center. I sat at a table by myself in front of a desktop flat screen. There were a good number of people here at tables reading, studying, or getting files for research. It was either elderly patrons or kids, maybe secondary school age to college. That's what all libraries of the world were—quiet study centers, but without the food and drinks.

I had been poring over them for hours. None of the faces I was looking for were there, but the day was young, and there were a lot more photo galleries to review. Then I felt I was being watched. I never could figure out how you could 'feel' being watched, but humans always forgot that they were at the core animals. Animals had that survival instinct, even the human ones. It was as if we had some kind of radar. Maybe we were all latent psychics, like Madam Personna. Speak of the devil.

She was standing about ten tables away watching me.

I paused the page I was on—no one would bother it—and I walked to her.

She didn't even wait for me. She went out the door to the enclosed park area and sat on a bench. I came out and sat on the park bench across from her. There was a lot of green in the park, which is why I didn't like it. Metropolitans were afraid of green. Plants attracted bugs, critters, and my personal least-favorite, isopods. I made sure my body wasn't touching any plant, flower, or bush.

Personna found my discomfort amusing.

"I thought I left Metropolis, you, and your street friends behind," she said. "Did you think I wouldn't notice all those sidewalk johnnies you had following me all over town? Pathetic. Is that how private detectives work these days, or only you? I guess that's what you have to resort to when you have no money to pay for professional operators."

She saw that I was getting impatient.

"How much would I have to pay you to go back to Metropolis? Right now."

"Nothing," I answered.

"You'll go."

"There's no amount you can pay, because I'm not going."

"Why are you here? You have no client."

"I'm going to find out what happened to those kids, and then I'll go."

The mere mention of 'kids' sent her into a fit.

"Why do you care so much about kids you never met?"

"Because no one else seems to."

"That's a bunch of drivel. You don't know anything. Go away. Go back to Metropolis, and I'll pay you to do so."

"Why is everyone so concerned about me finding these kids or knowing what happened to them? That's what I don't get. They're not dead. I know they're here. You obviously have been in touch with them. The parents are scared. Those people at the apartment were scared.

Nothing about this makes any sense. You're running some scam that makes no sense whatsoever."

"There is no scam."

"If you say so, but I'm staying. Bye."

I got up from the bench and walked back into the library. I could hear her cursing me from under her breath.

CHAPTER 36

The Kids

I was at the library all day. It was closing time, and I hadn't even had lunch. My biological clock was still messed up from being in a different time zone, but this kind of tedious work actually went faster when I was fatigued.

I logged off the public system and headed for the main entrance like everyone else. The librarians were all gathered at the door to wish us good night.

"Is there a good place to eat that you'd recommend?" I asked one them.

"You've been here all day. Yes, make a left and go to the end of the street. The food court is there, all the food and drinks you can take."

"Thanks."

It was a nice walk, not too chilly, and I just followed the crowd. They seemed to be going to get something to eat too. We were all walking down a hill. I could already smell food, as well as hear laughter and people talking. I started to see the pubs, but there she was.

Personna was standing at the bottom of the hill, hands tucked in her coat, waiting for me. I was tempted to cross to the other side of the road, but I knew it would be pointless. She started walking toward me.

"I'm tired and hungry," I said to her to signal my complete lack of interest in her.

"Then you can grab a pint with us."

She walked to one of the pubs and I followed. As soon as I passed through the doorway and looked in, I saw them—the teen-aged kids— the ones supposedly kidnapped by Metropolis gangster child traffickers as they innocently walked out of a prestigious hotel.

It was a very large booth, and Personna slid in on their side. Both kids had blond hair and wore turtlenecks. She had on a beret; he had his off, and on the table.

"What's with the berets and turtlenecks? I've seen a lot of them, always on young people."

"Beatniks," Personna said.

"What's that?"

"It's a style, a youth culture. You Americans have cyberpunks, for instance."

I asked, "Is berets and turtlenecks all there is to this culture of yours?"

"It's more than that," the boy said.

"You do know that the berets are French," I said.

"No, they're not."

"They are. You British Beatniks have as your hallmark French gear."

"That's not true," the girl said.

"Kids, don't listen to him," Personna said. "Mr. Cruz likes to play games. He often lies to get a reaction out of people."

I smirked.

"I do have a PhD in psychology," she said to me, smugly.

"So, it's Doctor Madam Personna."

I turned my attention to the kids.

"Tell me the story."

"What?" the boy said.

"Tell me the story, and I'll go away."

"Will you?" Personna asked.

"I'll do some sightseeing while I'm here, get some pictures of landmarks, but yeah."

The kids looked at each other.

"Why do we have to tell you anything?" the boy asked. "You're not the boss of us. You're some old American fart, sticking his nose where it doesn't belong."

"Whoa," I said. "Did you just call me old?"

"Yes. An old fart," Personna said.

"I—am—not—old."

Personna laughed. "Kids, I think you found his weakness—vanity."

"I'm waiting for my story." I folded my arms and stared at them.

"We ran away," the boy said. "That's it. That's the big secret. We ran away, and our parents called your police. Someone told them about two dead bodies found in your dumb city somewhere, and suddenly, we don't know why, they were saying it was us. Our parents did that publicity and stuff, because your dumb police told them we'd been kidnapped. We only found out about it here by accident. No one cares about American news. We don't pay attention to any news."

"When we found out, we called them, and then they stopped everything. They flew back here. That's the big story," the girl added.

"That's a very good story," I said. "Very logical. Sounds truthful."

"It sounds truthful, because it's the truth."

"Two problems, though."

"Here we go," Personna said with a look of disgust.

"What are your parents so scared about?"

"They're not scared of anything," the girl said.

"Your parents are scared; so are you. I don't know what you're all afraid that I'll find out. Doctor Personna here doesn't care. She got her paycheck, but she's a street hustler too, despite her Ph.D. She knows something is up, but the lure of more money is just too much for her to ignore. She'd do all kinds of things for that money. Wouldn't you, Madam Persona?"

"That's all drivel," Personna said. She wanted to say unkinder things to me, I'm sure.

"I want you all to know that I'll find out what's going on. I always do. I've met far smarter than you with your accents, karate, and French berets. I'm like one of those killer robots. I never stop. I'll find out what's going on, and I'm not leaving London until I do. Think about that as you eat your fish and chips."

They glared at me with such menace. It's a good thing they didn't have guns.

"Are you sure you don't have anything more to add?"

It seemed like forever. I repeated my question, but none of them would utter a word.

"Good. I guess I won't be having that meal and a pint with you after all."

I got up from the booth and left. I walked past the bay window and saw the three of them watching me. I decided to get a hovertaxi back to my hotel and order take-out food, instead.

CHAPTER 37

Suits

When I told PJ that I was going to get some paying clients, I didn't mean the British couple. Metropolis was an international supercity. It didn't just have rich multi-ethnic communities. It had tons of foreign-owned businesses. Japan wasn't the only nation with major interests in Metropolis; UKT was another. I was here in London, so I was going to line up as many potential clients as humanly possible. If you wanted to do business with a British company in Metropolis, you had to talk to their bosses in London.

It was my next meeting of the day with senior management at another London megacorp. There was a big desk with the boss in the middle and two lesser senior managers. I was really surprised at how many of them knew of me, and my business card was opening doors for me left and right.

"Mr. Cruz, I must admit we are quite impressed by your summary proposal," the boss said.

"Corporate espionage is a serious problem. I've had many satisfied clients at firms of your size and greater. I've researched your company and like what I see. If you wanted a retained detective firm in Metropolis, that understands the city and its criminal element, with contacts in both law enforcement and the city government, Liquid Cool could be a nice fit for you."

The boss smiled. "We agree, and we're happy to, as they say, sign on the dotted line."

This was a good day. I was signing up one firm after another, every one of them handing me retainers in cash. I was bulging with money, literally.

"Do people really get Swiss bank accounts?" I asked the hotel doorman.

He laughed. "You have some money you want to keep from away the government?"

"The wife."

He laughed. "Yes, everyone who has money does. It's like an insurance policy for corporatists and criminals alike. I know you like the hovercabs, and they must like you too, but I'd recommend taking simple public transportation. It'll drop you right at the front doorstep."

I didn't need to hide any money from Dot, but having an off-shore bank account for Liquid Cool did make business sense to me. Run-Time had one, so I was going to have one too. It also sounded booshy in a good way. "I have a Swiss bank account."

By day's end, I had it. Walked out of the bank with a smile. I had to text PJ about the new clients to brag. She'd like that. After that, I texted the wife.

CHAPTER 38

LSHTM

I waltzed through the front doors as if I were walking into a shrine. I'd dreamed of doing so for over twenty years. It was a perfect white structure, outside and inside. I stopped at the reception counter where a receptionist sat and a security guard stood, both dressed in white.

They saw my smile and smiled too.

"Can we help you, sir?" she asked.

"I'm here for the tour," I said.

"Tour, sir? The London School of Hygiene and Tropical Medicine doesn't conduct tours for the public."

"I'm a member."

"Member?"

"Twenty years."

"Sir, you don't look old enough to be a twenty-year member of anything," the guard said.

"I am." I was looking all around, still smiling. I handed them my passport. "Look me up."

The receptionist read my name and typed on her virtual keyboard. "I don't think I've ever seen this before." She looked at the guard. "Mr. Cruz has been a member of our civilian society for twenty years. He joined as a child."

"Can I have a tour?" I asked as if I were a kid. "This is my first trip ever to London."

The two of them were almost laughing.

"Let's see what we can arrange, sir," the receptionist answered.

The man they called wore a light gray suit. He was very tall with white hair. Unlike most in the States, people here wore ties with their suits. I kind of liked the retro look of it.

"Mr. Cruz," the man walked to me and shook my hand after talking privately with the receptionist. "It is not a frequent pleasure of ours to meet a society member, especially one as old and as young as you are."

"Thank you."

"This way, please."

He took me through double doors and then down a hall.

"You probably are able to tell me about our mission better than I could. We remain Earth's leading public research university for public health and environmental medicine."

"Space as well?"

"Yes, we are a leader in health and medicine for off-world too, all the way to Mars. You've actually come at the perfect time. Most of the students are on break, so not many of the professors are here, but I can show you the research facilities."

"That's exactly what I wanted to see."

I got to see the lecture halls, where classes were held. The research facilities were in their own separate building. The director led me through security and into the hallway. We didn't go directly into the research area, where people were working—on computers, talking in groups in front of tablet boards, or conducting experiments. We were able to see through the glass wall. It was a huge space, but there weren't that many people there.

"If you don't mind me asking, how bad was your mysophobia?"

"I'm not sure I'm even a germophobe, anymore."

He laughed. "Real germophobes wouldn't be able to shake hands. Real germophobes wouldn't be on public transportation."

"It was bad, but I only have to wash my hands five times before going to bed instead of 50."

He laughed again. "Through here." He led me into another section.

He knew what I wanted. I'm sure there was a classified section, but he showed me all the 'goodies.' The room was filled with all the latest in anti-bacterials, anti-microbials, water-less cleansers, microbe scanners, UV scanners (for bodily fluid detection), etc. They were all on sale to the public. We were in London School of Hygiene and Tropical Medicine's retail store.

I came out of there with a smile as big as when I'd come out of the Swiss bank, but this time, I had a big bag of stuff. Dot had Goodwill. I had London School of Hygiene and Tropical Medicine.

CHAPTER 39

Mr. Goodstar

I stood at the platform with my big bag, waiting for the hovertrain. I was in such a good mood, and no one was going to spoil it. I had new clients, a new Swiss bank account with lots of money already, and the latest in hi-tech anti-bacterial, anti-germ wet wipes, which because they were medical, Metro police couldn't confiscate or write me up for, and more.

People were already lining up at the platforms. I didn't know anything about public transportation in Metropolis, but here, they were always on time. I wasn't right at the edge, but I was close.

He didn't know I was watching him. I was wearing one of those invisible rearview glasses—a tiny image just to the side of view of my right eye. Most people didn't wear them, because they'd confuse you with the view of what was behind you next to what was in front of you, but I had the discipline. I'd packed it in my luggage, and figured they'd be handy. I would be in a foreign country without any of my guns, and that blond Japanese maniac was still out there. I didn't want him sneaking up behind me.

Mr. Goodstar had thought he was a karate master, but I'd quickly shattered that myth in his mind. Now, he thought he was a ninja and was moving up behind me, but staying behind other people as best he could. We all heard the approaching hovertrain arriving at superspeed as it descended. Our group was at the platform near the end, which meant the hovertrain would whip by us first before it stopped about a mile up— these hovertrains were long. I stepped closer, as most people were doing. Mr. Goodstar rushed at me. I took one step to the right. He screamed as he tried to grab me and fell. The oncoming hovertrain hit him, and he disappeared as it flew by.

CHAPTER 40

DCI Fortran

People were going crazy, yelling, screaming; the overhead speakers were telling people to remain where they were. People were also looking at me. I was not staying put, because I knew what was coming. I turned around and walked back down the platform steps to the ground. People were pointing at me as I "made my getaway," or attempted to. I had seen them the very first time I came out of London International, but now they were following me—the CCTV cameras that were literally everywhere. Two drone cameras were above me.

I walked as briskly as I could, but unlike Metropolis, I knew nothing about this place and had no clue where I was going. I heard the sirens and decided that it wasn't even worth it anymore. I hadn't done anything, but it didn't matter. I was going to some foreign police station. All I wanted to do was get back to my hotel room to look at my new London School of Hygiene and Tropical Medicine goodies.

London police were not Metropolis police. We had heavy police cruisers. When I saw the London police hovercars descend from the sky, I thought I was about to be arrested by children. Their hovercars were like kiddie cars. The officer got out with their hands on their guns as they walked to me. I was just standing there holding my bag.

"Hello, sir."

"Officer."

"Did you not hear the overhead to remain where you were?"

"Sorry, I didn't."

"When there is an accident, you need to follow instructions."

The other police officer had been talking on his mobile the entire time. He flipped it closed and walked to me with a stern expression.

"Sir, you'll have to come with us to the police station," he said.

"Scotland Yard?" I asked.

"Yes, Scotland Yard."

I smiled.

The police were not amused when I asked if I could take pictures of the building for my wife. They took my bag from me, inspected it, but still wouldn't give it back. The building was not as big as Police One, but it was still a massive building. I had given them my ID, which they also didn't return.

They sat me in an interrogation room and had me wait by myself. After about five minutes, a police officer came.

"Sir, do you want anything nonalcoholic to drink?"

"Water would be fine," I answered.

"Fresh or ocean?" he asked.

I looked at him, grinning, thinking he was making a joke.

"I haven't lost the plot. Fresh is regular. Ocean is treated," he said.

"Which do you drink?"

"Ocean, of course."

"With all that salt."

"I'll bring you fresh." He left the room, but I heard him say, "American" as he closed the door.

I had my cup of fresh water that I didn't touch, and after about ten minutes, two officers came and took me out of the room, down a long hall, and into an open space that seemed to be filled with hundreds of officers in uniform or in civilian clothes. It was a similar set-up to that of Metro Police Central. They took me to an office and had me sit in a chair in front of a desk. One waited with me; the other disappeared.

A mustached man entered and he took a seat at his desk, never once looking at me. He had my ID card and passport in his hand. The second officer appeared with my goodies bag. The senior man looked up at me for the first time.

"Mr. Cruz."

"Yes."

"From Metropolis."

"Yes."

A third man came into the office. "Guv, he's never been to London, the UKT, or Europe before. Nothing in the databases," he said to the senior man.

"Mr. Cruz, my name is DCI—that's Deputy Chief Inspector—Fortran. I had the pleasure of speaking to Police Chief Hub a moment ago. He asked that we keep you here in London. I told him that we would not like that at all. He said that he was prepared to pay me."

"Chief Hub and I are good friends."

"Yes, I see that. Why are you in London, Mr. Cruz?"

"Sightseeing." I pointed to the London School of Hygiene and Tropical Medicine shopping bag. "I'm a member."

"Mr. Cruz, you don't seem to be taking seriously the fact that one of our London citizens tried to push you to your death in front of a moving hovertrain. You don't seem to be taking seriously the fact that we now have a man dead. You have only been in London a short time, and you're connected with a murder attempt and death."

"I am taking it seriously," I said. "I just choose not to be bothered by it."

"Why are you in London, Mr. Cruz?"

"Wrapping up a case."

"What case?"

"A child kidnapping case. Two children, in fact."

"Where was this case?"

"Metropolis."

"That brings you to London?"

"The parents of the kidnapped children live here in London."

"Who are those parents?"

"Well, the man who tried to push me in front of the hovertrain was the father. Being dead, it would be hard to question him, but you can talk to the wife, Mrs. Goodstar. You can even talk to the children too, since they were never really kidnapped at all."

I had one standing policeman and three sitting policemen staring at me.

DCI Fortran stood from his desk and the other men followed him. The last one closed the door. I looked at my untouched glass of water. Fresh or ocean water—I didn't even know what that meant. My Pops had always told me, "Never drink the water in foreign countries—canned or bottled beverages and drinks only."

I figured I'd be sitting for a long time in that office. I was right.

DCI Fortran opened the door and came back into the office with the three other officers.

"Mr. Cruz, here's your ID and passport back. You can have your shopping bag back. We are going to escort you out. We've already called you a cab. You will get into it, and I expect you to be on the first flight back to Metropolis. The UK is the safest country in Europe, and we do not like Americans who have a penchant for Wild Wild West antics."

"He tried to kill me. I was standing there with my bag, minding my own business."

"Yes, too bad for him. Please, stand, and let's go."

Everyone was watching me follow DCI Fortran with the three other officers behind me. They led me into an elevator and out, then out the main doors to the steps to the street.

"Have a safe trip back, Mr. Cruz."

"Oh, snaps!" I yelled, and I wasn't looking at him.

CHAPTER 41

Mrs. Goodstar

All this time, I had thought Mrs. Goldstar was a sweet ol' thing—wealthy and annoying, but I'd thought it was the husband that was the bastard.

She appeared out of nowhere; I knew exactly what was in her hand, and I was completely helpless. Only one thing could save me. I knocked DCI Fortran out of the way and dove for the ground. It was too late for the first officer, who reacted a bit too slowly and took the first volley of her laser machine-gun, sending him falling backward.

All I saw was her running at me, enraged and shooting. Then I saw her convulse, stop, drop the weapon, and collapse—DCI Fortran and the other two policemen had emptied their guns into her.

It was pandemonium. Police swarmed over the scene. Officers formed a circle around us with weapons drawn. Medics were already at the side of the fallen officer, who was still alive. Police hovercars were in the sky above us. It was a madhouse.

I picked up my shopping bag and walked to DCI Fortran.

"I just want to get back to my hotel room." I was serious now.

He nodded and pointed to a couple of officers. One of them signaled one of the police hovercars in the air, and it descended. They put me in, and it blasted off. I looked back and another one was following; both vehicles had their sirens on.

My mobile began to ring. I looked at the time. It could only be the wife. I took the call.

"Dot," I answered.

"Cruz, I have a surprise for you." Her smiling face was on the display screen.

"What?"

"Marrying me was your luckiest day, but now, you have an even luckier day. You're going to be a father."

I was speechless.

"Cruz, what are those sirens I hear in the background?" she asked. "Are you in a police-cruiser?"

CHAPTER 42

Ichi

The news was exactly what I'd needed. If it weren't for Dot's call, I probably would have stayed up all night upset at not one, but two, attempts on my life. I was not going to stay in a country that didn't allow me to carry my concealed weapons. That was just plain wrong. Instead I slept like a baby. I'd probably spend all the next day looking at baby names.

I stood on the balcony of my hotel sipping a can of sparkling water— at least it would be safe, and free of salt.

There he was!

I almost dropped the can to the floor. The only reason I'd noticed him at the side of the building was because of his blond wig and yellow jacket. I was not in the mood—not after yesterday. This maniac had followed me to London!

I set the can on the table and grabbed one of the chairs in the room. Out of the hotel room I went.

There I stood on the roof of the hotel watching him. He walked back and forth for a while, stopped, and then sat down on an atrium wall. I imagined that he thought he'd be clever and surprise me as I came out of the front entrance to catch a hovertaxi.

I had no gun, but I had the chair and gravity. Aim. Away.

The chair hit him so hard, it broke apart into pieces. His lifeless body lay on the sidewalk, chair fragments everywhere, his blond wig next to him. People were looking up at the roof and I ducked away. I ran back to the rooftop door, down the steps, and into the elevator.

This was the founding country of the CCTV. I was so angry that I hadn't even surveyed the area to look for them. The police had theirs, and I'm sure the hotel had their own. How many videos had recorded what I had done?

I reached my room and looked over the balcony. Ichi Jumper's body was gone! But not the people; they were all pointing up at me. I ducked back in.

It probably was a wise thing just to get dressed, pack up, and wait for the arrival of the police.

CHAPTER 43

The Unwelcome Committee

There was a knock on my hotel door about an hour later. I opened it and five policemen and one policewoman stood there.

"Mr. Cruz?"

"Yes."

"Are you packed?"

"Yes."

"Then we've been authorized to take you to London International and physically put you on the next jet back to Metropolis."

"But my return ticket isn't until the end of the week."

"Can I see it?"

I had it handy and pulled it from my slicker's inside pocket for him.

He pulled another ticket from his coat pocket. "This is your new return ticket. Let's go, sir."

I had my luggage and my new London School of Hygiene and Tropical Medicine bag of goodies. I didn't even have to check out when we reached the lobby. They told me that it was "taken care of" too. They loaded me into their hovervan, and we were in the air.

This was not how I'd wanted to leave London, but it was either this or back to Scotland Yard. The London police escorted me through every single checkpoint there was and boarded me on the jet—dead last, of course. They stood in the plane in the main aisle to make sure I remained in my seat. The eyes of every seated passenger were on us. When the jet prepared for its final departure, they all turned and left the plane.

At this point, I could imagine what everyone on the plane was thinking. The flight attendants were looking at me too, and the passengers sitting next to me and across from me looked as if they would pass out from fear.

An old woman was seated across from me. "Are you some kind of terrorist?" she asked out aloud.

"No, a private detective from Metropolis. I just solved a big case here. The police wanted to make sure I got on safely."

"That's not what it looked like to us," the man next to her said.

"No, it's true. You can look me up. My firm is called Liquid Cool."

At that point, everyone on the plane, including the flight attendants, took out their mobiles or mobile computers to look me up on the Net.

PART FIVE

Electric Sheep

CHAPTER 44

Flash

I was so glad to be back. The triple-decker international jet came into Metropolis air space—the dark gray skies, the ever-rain. I was smiling like a kid on Christmas Eve. My foot stepping out of the jet and touching Metropolis asphalt was all I cared about.

I came out of my departure gate expecting to see Dot. No wife. I looked around as crowds of people went in a million directions. No one. Something was not right. I found a spot against the wall as I fished my mobile out of my pocket and made sure to keep my luggage and bag close. My eyes scanned anyone who passed by. I already checked out other people who were also standing against the wall for whatever reasons, waiting, eating, talking on the phone. I even looked for anyone wearing blond wigs.

"Mr. Cruz."

That was a voice I didn't expect. It was Flash. What was my regular mobile hovercar security guy doing here? He was a light-skinned Black guy, with a ponytail and a small goatee. He was wearing his yellow jumpsuit over his suit clothes and blue eyewear.

"Follow me, Mr. Cruz," Flash said, already leaning down to help with my luggage.

"Where's my wife?"

"Oh, she's at the office. I'm taking you to them."

"Them?"

"Yes, they're waiting for you there."

"Why did they send you?"

"It's not safe out there, Mr. Cruz. All hell has broken loose."

"What's happening?"

"There's some kind of drug plague out there. People going crazy and attacking people. Glowing eyes, foaming at the mouth. It's crazy. I won't let my wife or kids go anywhere alone."

It didn't take us long to get out of the Metropolis International building to where Flash's hovercab was parked outside. Hovertaxis were the only ones, besides police, fire, and medical, that were allowed to randomly park in front of the airport. The warning lights were flashing, and he loaded my luggage and bag in the trunk. We were in the air and speeding along in the sky traffic fast lane in no time.

While he drove, I scanned the newsfeed on my mobile.

"Is this for real?" I asked.

"Metropolis has gone to hell, Mr. Cruz. You should have stayed in London Prime."

CHAPTER 45

The Peanut Gallery

When I walked into the Liquid Cool offices, with Flash right behind me, everyone was standing there, glued to the lobby TV on the wall. Dot could barely take her eyes off it, but glanced at me and gestured for me to come to her quickly. I did, and she held my hand. PJ and Phishy were there, along with a bunch of sidewalk johnnies, and others, who I had no idea who they were. Potential clients? Everyone was watching the TV like zombies.

"Look, Cruz," my wife said to me, and I looked.

On the screen were people in handcuffs being led by British police to waiting police hovervans. The broadcast was from London.

"Repeating the shocking news that rocked the supercity of London Prime this morning is the multiple arrests of what Scotland Yard is calling the largest child prostitution ring in decades," the voice said.

On the screen was the same monolith tower the Goldstars lived in. I noticed the two tennis couples being led out in handcuffs. There were the teenage Beatnik kids led away in handcuffs. Madam Personna was in handcuffs too but was putting up a hell of a fight.

"I didn't do anything! I'm American, I'm American!" she yelled.

Six female officers had to subdue her and throw her into the police hovervan.

"We asked police sources to refute the psychic Personna's claim that she was an innocent bystander. We were told, and I quote, 'She's a psychic, so she should have known her clients were running a child prostitution ring, so she's going to jail.'"

It was an almost endless parade of men and women being hauled away in handcuffs from the building and other locations.

On the screen was a reporter, who was probably London Prime's version of Holly Live. "What broke the case wide open was the investigation of the famed Metropolis private detective named Cruz." My photo flashed on the screen before returning to the reporter. "Sources have told us that the two ring leaders of the ring, Mr. and Mrs. Goldstar"—their photos flashed on the screen—"both attempted to assassinate Mr. Cruz unsuccessfully, but the famed detective killed Mr. Goldstar in the first attempt, and police gunned down Mrs. Goldstar in a hail of laser-gun fire in the second, separate attempt."

My wife was no longer holding my hand.

"Sir, you say you knew this was about to happen?" the reporter was interviewing the director from the London School of Hygiene and Tropical Medicine.

"Absolutely. Mr. Cruz has been an esteemed member of our society for twenty years. In his annual visit to our research university, he shared with me that he was in hot pursuit of these criminals."

"That lying bum," I said aloud.

"Shhh!" the entire room shushed me.

"We've also spoken to multiple passengers and attendants on the London flight to Metropolis that Mr. Cruz arrived on. They also confirmed that it was, in fact, his action that led to this stunning day of news," the reporter said.

The cameras were outside of Scotland Yard, and there was DCI Fortran trying to get into his own headquarters, only to have the media jackals blocking his way. I knew exactly what he was thinking. *Turn off your cameras and the CCTV so I can shoot you.*

"DCI Fortran! Was Scotland Yard working with Mr. Cruz to expose this child prostitution ring?" one reporter asked.

"We will be making a full statement at tomorrow's press conference."

"DCI Fortran, was this a joint operation with the Metropolis Police?"

"No comment."

"DCI Fortran, it seems that the famed detective Mr. Cruz was put on their trail when the ring leaders, Mr. and Mrs. Goldstar, were in Metropolis and hatched the grand hoax that their teenage children were kidnapped by street gangs, which was in fact a ruse for them to transport more children from Metropolis to London Prime for their illegal activities."

"No comment. All will be announced at the press conference."

DCI Fortran finally made it into his headquarters with the help of about two dozen beefy police officers, who blocked the reporters from the doors.

"Amazing!" The same Holly Live-clone, but with red hair, was back on the screen. "It seems that famed private detective Mr. Cruz is breaking big cases on both sides of the Pond."

The room erupted in applause.

"Cruz!" Phishy yelled, smiling and then broke into his chicken-dance.

"Famed private detective," PJ said. "I expect a big bonus this month. Now you have to hire an assistant for me. You're going to have stacks of messages from Metropolis and other countries now."

This was another perfect example of irony. The Goldstars had thought their kids were snatched by child traffickers, when in fact they were *all* traffickers. Now I knew why they had all been so scared.

Everyone in the office was ecstatic for me at the international publicity, all except for Dot. She was watching me with her arms folded. She was not happy with the double-assassination thing by child trafficking criminals, but I was about to work my magic.

"Ladies and gentleman," I said loudly, and everyone looked at me and got quiet. "Dot and I are going to be parents!"

"Yeah!"

Now, the party was getting started in the office. Not even Dot would be able to be mad at me now. After a million hugs and a bit of dancing, she wasn't even going to remember she had been mad at me before.

CHAPTER 46

Run-Time

The party was still going on when Run-Time arrived. Flash was still here and joined by Bugs; both worked for Run-Time. The crowd was just getting bigger and bigger. Fat Nat from Joe Blow's Smoking Emporium in Old Harlem, who I had helped in my very first major case, had arrived an hour earlier and had handed out cigars to everyone, even those who didn't know how to smoke them. He didn't mind teaching, especially if the students were female. He also came with his entire Italian cigar aficionado crew, all wearing their "smoking" gloves to handle their expensive Havanas.

There was another Run-Time employee in the Liquid Cool office, and that was The Mick, one of his VPs. In all the years I had known Run-Time, it was only the friendly female West Indian and Lebanese VPs I had ever had contact with, until becoming a detective. Then, it was his third Irish one that I seemed to have exclusive contact with.

It was all smiles, congratulations, cigars, and drinks for all—except for Dot (No alcohol for the pregnant)!

At some point, Run-Time and I managed to sneak away into my private office, with The Mick right behind us. I was not about to pull Dot into this matter; she was having too much fun.

"My business is down 30 percent," Run-Time revealed after he took a puff.

"What? Is it that bad?" I asked.

Run-Time gave me the scoop. "People are really scared. The media has been calling it the Plague, which has devastated the economy. All businesses are down. People are not going out, and if they're not going out, then they don't need private transportation or hovercar security."

"How many attacks have there been?"

"Almost a hundred," The Mick answered, "but if you listen to the media, it's more like a 100,000."

"What do we know? Someone has to know something."

"It's not a biological plague," Run-Time said.

"It's a drug. The word on the street is it's a new illegal drug on the street that makes your eyes glow. The problem is that no one knows which one." The Mick handled all Run-Time's darker matters of security.

"How can people not know which drug it is?"

"Mr. Cruz, I know you don't know anything about the drug scene, but there are tens of thousands of them out there. Addicts are creating all kinds of mixtures every day."

"If that were true, this would have happened before."

"Or someone created a super-stash, and all these people have used that same supply," he said.

"It looks as if I'm going to be driving my wife to and from work until this is solved. Dot told me someone went berserk the other day and attacked a bunch of people right outside of Eye Candy."

"I had a few drivers attacked too," Run-Time said.

"You should have stayed in London Prime," The Mick said. "You would've been safer."

"Safer? I had one guy try to push me into a moving hovertrain and then his wife tried to gun me down with a laser machine-gun right in front of Scotland Yard, surrounded by police. No, I'm staying here. I expect everyone to try to shoot me here. It's much safer here for me. Besides, I don't trust a society that doesn't allow a man to carry his own gun. I felt so naked over there. And they don't allow private hovercars, and they drink salt water. No, Metropolis is where I'm staying."

"Home Sweet Home," Run-Time added.

"You said it—and now I'm a father." This time, I was puffing the cigar.

CHAPTER 47

Cops

Dot and I stayed up most of the night making baby name lists. We had done so many times before, but we both always felt there was some more "perfect" name we were missing. Dot liked making the lists. I liked searching the Net.

My secret client was coming in early in the afternoon. PJ had scheduled them, so if they'd gotten past her, it was fine, but I didn't like secrets. PJ just said, "I know the people who referred him and they'll be here too." I had enough mysteries in my life.

The main mystery was who were the two men found dead at the River. I'd seen them when they were alive; I'd seen them dead as super-roach food. Maybe, if I found out their identity, it would still mean nothing, but I didn't think so. I also felt it was connected to that blond-wigged bald Japanese maniac after me. I had his name, but had no idea who he was. No one could help with that mystery, either.

PJ was laughing when I walked into the Liquid Cool offices, flexing her bionic arms. There were three men in the lobby, all in civilian clothes, two sitting, and one standing. The Black man standing was big and so was the brown-haired Caucasian man sitting. The Caucasian man in the center with curly blond hair was smaller, but he was as muscular as the others.

There was something about the two men sitting. They seemed familiar.

"Have we met before?" I asked.

PJ began laughing, and I looked at her.

"Let's see how long it takes him," she said.

I looked back at the men. I knew them? They hadn't said anything. I smiled and nodded. It was Ebony and Ivory! "My 'friends,'" I said.

"Don't call us that," Officer Break said, standing.

I began laughing with PJ. "All these years we've known each other, and we've never seen you out of uniform and without your helmets," I said.

"All this time, we thought you were ugly under there," PJ said to them.

"This is a milestone," I said. "I've got police visiting me on their off-hours in their civvies. How did I get so lucky?"

Officer Caps stood and pointed to the third man, who I knew now was another officer. "This is our buddy, Kabal."

"I thought I was your buddy." I said. "Hello, Officer Kabal."

PJ said, "They have a case for you."

I couldn't believe my ears. "A case? Does the Chief know you're here?"

"Kabal is here. Caps and I are not here."

The way he said the last part let me know that this was far from a social visit. I led the officers into my private office and closed the door.

Officer Break moved one of the two chairs closer to my desk, and Caps sat in the other chair.

"I'll stand," Break said.

"I can have another chair brought in."

"No, it's fine." He had already found his place against the wall near the door.

Kabal was the potential client, and he seemed in no hurry to tell me what the case was. He shifted around in his chair a bit. I sat quietly and waited. He gave a heavy sigh.

"Sorry," he said. "This is—very difficult for me. You've heard about this drug thing?"

"You mean the addicts attacking random people and dying of O.D.s."

"Yeah."

"I heard it's a sudden epidemic."

"Yeah, lots of kids, too."

"How can I help?"

"I have a daughter. She doesn't particularly like cops, especially me. But, you can't pick your children any more than you can pick your parents. Unfortunately, my daughter has been part of the drug scene for a while. Not even 19, and she has more arrests and jail stints than people twice her age, all drug related. Nothing has worked. So with this new drug madness—I have to do something. I'll never give up trying to save her, but I can't do that if she's dead.

"I can't wait until she uses again to arrest her. It may be the very drug supply that's causing this madness. I can't wait. We need to get her off of the street and into the system. It has to be done now."

"We need someone to move things along," Caps added.

I stared at them for a bit. "What are you asking? It can't be what I think it is."

"We can't do it. We have body-cams," Kabal said.

"You want me to set up your own daughter?"

"You plant it. Break and Caps will arrest her and get her off the street. This is the only daughter I have."

"There's got to be another way."

"There isn't."

I shook my head, thinking.

"We'll owe you, big-time," Kabal said.

"Let's not go there," Break said, standing at the back.

"Is this what we want to do?" I asked.

Caps nodded. He never spoke much, but if you had a shoot-out with bad guys, you could guarantee he would shoot more rounds than any other officer, including Break.

"All of us could get jacked up if this goes wrong—arrested and thrown right into prison—all of us."

"It's worth the risk," Break said.

"Today?"

"We can't wait," Kabal said.

"Okay. I don't like it, but if we're all agreed. Question: how violent is she? Don't lie. We have to be prepared."

"She's only violent with me."

"Okay. Do we know where she is?"

"We do," Caps answered.

"Shall we go then, gentlemen?" Break called out.

We all stood—one local detective and three cops going to do a "good" crime.

CHAPTER 48

Personna

It took five minutes. I timed it.

Kabal's daughter was a scary piece of work. Based on her skimpy outfit, she had probably been arrested for far more than drugs, with her raccoon-looking overuse of eye mascara. She had no hovercar and no permanent residence.

Like all dope roaches, she spent most of her time sleeping. Five minutes is all it took for me to get into the place she was staying in, plant the drugs, and go. I made sure I wouldn't be seen by anyone.

The Pony was in a nearby parking lot, and there I sat, waiting. The police cruiser descended from the sky, without any sirens. Ten minutes later, I watched Officers Break and Caps in full police battle-gear come out of the Free City apartment tower with Kabal's daughter, handcuffed. She was struggling, yelling, and spitting. They threw her into the back of the cruiser, were in the air, and gone.

Case closed.

Now it was off to Metro Penitentiary, where I hoped never to have the pleasure of being a resident. PJ had taken the call, since I'd refused to talk with her. I didn't know why I was even here. Madam Personna was exactly where she belonged—waiting for her trial to begin. This was her permanent address for the time being.

I guess I wanted to see her to gloat a bit. She'd thought she was so clever, but here she was in a red jumpsuit, shackled, being led out by two female cyborg prison guards into the visiting area. One of the guards chained her to the metal table where I was sitting. Personna took a seat. She had no make-up, and her hair was a mess.

"Madam Personna," I said.

"Stop calling me that."

"Why? Why did you call? If you were really a psychic, you wouldn't be here."

"Mr. Cruz, I've heard all the jokes already, so save your breath."

"Why did you call me?"

"Why did you come?"

"I don't know."

"You know. I remember you in that London library. You were looking at photos. It took me awhile to figure it out, but I know who you were looking for—the two bodies at the River that started all this. You didn't find them in the Metropolis database, so you were looking in the London one. I can help."

"How?"

"I'll find out who they are."

"With your psychic powers."

"Laugh all you want. You won't be laughing when I find them."

"If I can't find them, neither can you."

"This is what I want, Mr. Cruz. I want you to get me the hell out of here. You know I had nothing to do with this child prostitution ring. I knew nothing about it. Their Scotland Yard didn't even know about them until you came along."

"You were with the kids."

"Those Beatnik psychos. I didn't know. I thought they were rebelling against their parents like all teenagers."

"How would I get you out of here?"

"You're a famous detective with friends in Metropolis and London Prime. Call in a favor."

I stood from the table.

"Sure, when you identify the two men at the River."

I didn't wait or say goodbye. I left. This was her home now, not mine.

CHAPTER 49

Psycho

There was no way possible he could have known what path I would take. This was Metropolis, the largest supercity in the world. How? I was in busy sky traffic, and normally, when you're speeding along, you don't look at the ground—you're at least twenty stories up—but I did. It was so impossible that I swerved out of my lane to set down on a rooftop landing, but I didn't park. I hovered there and grabbed the binoculars from my glove box.

It was him. At the base of an all-white tower, at the top of the steps, he stood there. Through the binoculars, I saw the blond-wigged Japanese maniac. He had cuts all over his face, but he looked fine. He was looking directly at me—with his own binoculars!

This psycho was never going to let me alone, but I still had no idea why.

CHAPTER 50

Tag

Madam Personna was right when she confronted me at the pub in London Prime. Sidewalk johnnies were absolutely terrible for the secret surveillance of anyone. They were not professionals; they were street people. That was the point; I wanted her to know she was being followed. My plan was to keep her off-kilter until I'd figured out what really was going on with the "kidnapped" kids. It hadn't worked the way I'd intended, but in the end, if the bad guys were brought to justice, all was fine.

I had more in my "bag of tricks" than just sidewalk johnnies. A good private detective needed his own network of confidential informants and amateur experts on every topic under the rain-clouded sky. Two of them were crucial to me solving my previous Case of the NeuroDancer, and I needed one of them again.

He was a kid named Tag. The term cyberpunk had all kinds of meaning throughout time, but nowadays, it was used to describe the geek subculture of mostly youth, who lived most of their life in VR world. I hadn't reached out to him; Tag had called me.

Tag's special knowledge was the VR world, or as he would correct me, VL—virtual life. When not jacked-in himself, he did endless scraper jobs. With so much data garbage on the Net, people paid scrapers to sift through all of it for them.

I couldn't even remember what part of the city we were in. If you'd seen one VR parlor, you'd seen them all. The one we met in was decent. It wasn't filled with cyberpunk riffraff with their VR worlds of all sex and violence or cyberpunk geeks with their juvenile VR worlds of fighting dragons in dungeons and hunting aliens on jungle planets. It was strictly VLers (VEE-LERS). These were the people that "lived" in virtual reality. These were not arcade bars. Virtual lifers congregated in these dens, where people sat in ultra plush recliners and the plug-in interface wasn't helmets or goggles; it was a full-body capsule—or chamber. The non-initiated, like me, called them VR coffins. No rowdiness here, the only sounds heard were hundreds of conversations via each chamber's audio.

The parlor had its food dispensers in front with restrooms, a bunch of couches for people to crash on—there were sleeping bodies all over—and stools at tiny tables for people to eat. Fortunately, this wasn't one of those hardcore VLer parlors, where everyone had tubes sticking out of them, so they could eat and go to the bathroom intravenously—never having to leave their VR chamber. These were the casual, non-nasty, VR chambers. Tag was in a hoodie sitting at one of them, and waved to me when he saw me.

As I walked to him, I stopped and turned. There were about a dozen fat and skinny cyberpunks behind me. They all looked like college kids, except for the fact that their goatees and hair on the sides were going gray. I was looking at a bunch of thirty, forty, and fifty-something 'kids' who played games all day.

"It's okay, Cruz," I heard Tag call out behind me.

I walked and sat down on a stool next to him. The cyberpunks took positions around us and faced out. Tag was a thin, sandy blond kid, who wore eyeliner and whose hands up to his elbows were covered in tattoos.

"You have your own security force now?" I asked.

"I've got more guys outside," he answered.

I liked Tag, because he wasn't like the other cyberpunks. He didn't live most of his life in a VR world. He just plugged in daily. But this time, Tag looked bad, as if he hadn't slept in days. It seemed as if he were wearing his hoodie to hide that fact.

"Why did you call me, Tag?"

"I want to hire you."

"To do what?"

"To find the guy killing people."

"Tag, what are you talking about?"

"I'm talking about all these people going crazy, attacking people, and then dying."

"Yeah, from overdose—some kind of batch of tainted drugs on the streets."

"What about the glowing eyes?"

"Well, I don't know what that's about, I admit. Then again, I'm not an expert on drugs."

"It's not glowing eyes. It's residual imaging on the lens. All these people were jacked-in."

"All these people who went berserk were VL gamers?"

"They were in a synth when they went berserk."

"In a VL world? But they were all on drugs."

"People do drugs when they're in VL, too. There's even VL drugs."

"VL drugs? Virtual reality drugs? Tag, I've never heard of that."

"I'm not surprised. People jack-in and do their drugs in VL all the time. That's what all these people did when they went crazy."

"How come the police don't know this? There's a Narcotics Division that knows all about the drug scene, too."

"Narcs know non-VL drugs. Cyber-cops know cyber-hacking. Neither of them know about the underground VL drug scene. That's why I called you. You're good at uncovering conspiracies."

"Conspiracies? Tag, what are you talking about? You're all over the place. If you know something that can help stop this, then we need to go to the police. People are dying and scared to leave their homes."

"The synth is called Electric Sheep."

It was in my last major case that I'd learned some of the VR world jargon. We said VR; insiders said VL. Outsiders said VR worlds. Insiders used the term 'synth' to describe the specific virtual world that a person plugged into—or "jacked-in" to use the common slang, but these were often interchangeable terms. There were millions of synths—legal and illegal.

"The synth itself is a drug," Tag continued.

"How can a VL game be a drug?"

"VL is not games, Cruz. It's life as real as the real world. Reality is fake."

"The real world is real. A VL world is someone strapped in a VL chamber. Tag, seriously, what do you know? People are dying."

"I know people are dying. That's why I called you. That's why I've got my bodyguards. Someone is using the Electric Sheep to kill people."

"How does someone kill people with a VL game—a synth? These people are getting up out of their VL chairs, running out into the street and attacking people, then dying."

"He calls himself the Ripper. Electric Sheep is a world filled with—"

"Let me guess. Electric Sheep."

"Yeah. As you do the drug, you count these multi-colored sheep."

"Tag, you're losing me."

"The Ripper turns the electric sheep psychotic. They attack you in your mind while you're jacked-in and make you go psycho. He kills you in VL. People jumping out and attacking people is a side-effect."

"How do you know this, Tag?"

"I was plugged in myself and saw it happen to someone. A bunch of us did. I went back in to trace the code back to the break-in point and saw him."

At this point, I was listening but I had no idea what he was talking about. Most of these cyberpunks were also programmers and system architects. Some of these VL worlds were so advanced that the user could modify the experience by writing code on the fly, and the world would compensate with its own code. I had learned some of the same principles when I'd built my Pony from scratch. It was a classic hovervehicle, but it was also a sophisticated flying computer with a hoverengine.

"Saw who?"

"The Ripper."

"Who's he?"

"I don't know. He was a seven-foot-tall sheep in a black suit."

"Walking upright?"

"Yeah."

"In VL world?"

"Yeah, but let me finish. I followed him, and I saw him do it again. I know because I checked when I unplugged. I saw the guy on the news as another victim. When I was plugged in, he saw me, laughed at me, and said that he was never going to stop. I told him that I was going to stop him. Then he said he knew exactly who I was and that he was going to unplug, find me, and kill me."

Tag was getting a bit shaky. I realized that Tag was a VL addict too. He looked bad, as if his body was having withdrawals from not being plugged back into the VL for an extended period. Now, I was doubting his claim of not also being involved in the VL drug scene.

"You got to find him first, Cruz."

"Tag, you know I don't know much about the VL scene. That's why my friend put me in touch with you. You're the expert. If you can't find him, then it's unlikely I could."

"You can do it, Cruz. I know you can."

"Do you have any clues for me? How were you going to stop him?"

"I was going to plug in and find him again, since I know the synth he's using, and wait for him. I'd do a continual search of the world until he appeared, or get notified if anyone started going berserk. They always yell out when it starts to happen, then start counting sheep."

"Well, I won't be plugging into anything," I said. "Not going to happen. This is for the police, Tag. Their Cybercrime Division can go in and find this guy."

"No, they can't. They won't find him."

"Why do you say that?"

"He's a cop."

I gave him a look. "Why would you think that?"

"Not 'think.' I know. I was able to follow him for a while, while I was hacking into his code. He's a cop. I'm sure of it. The only thing I don't know is if he works for Metro Police or one of the megacorps."

"The Ripper is police?"

"Yes."

CHAPTER 51

The Far Escape Crew

Cyberpunks didn't like police, but Tag wasn't lying to me. Everything he told me was disturbing. The late NeuroDancer was going to use VL to control people. Tag was telling me that someone was using VL to literally kill people. I had PJ clear my calendar, as I had to focus on this and this alone.

However, before I could focus, I had to deal with a blond-wigged problem, once and for all.

I'd left a message on their secret voicemail days ago. I'd gotten a call the day before, and the timing couldn't have been more perfect. I figured they'd be amused at the place I'd picked for our reunion.

I stood outside the Sketchy Squirrel in the rain as their hovervan touched down near me.

"Mr. Cruz," Ms. Black said from the shotgun seat.

The doors opened, and they all came out. I was not surprised to see two new additions to their crew.

"Hello, Mr. Cruz," one of the Scorpion speedster cops said to me, the one with the ponytail.

"Well, look at this. Yesterday, enemies. Today, kissing cousins," I said.

"It was quite fortuitous for you to contact us, Mr. Cruz." The other Scorpion speedster cop walked right up to me smiling. "We have so enjoyed our partnership."

"So, they decided to share with you what they stole."

"I don't know what you're referring to, Mr. Cruz."

"Whatever. What do you want to hire me to do?"

"You're good at making introductions, Mr. Cruz." Ms. Black was standing next to me. "We want you to make an introduction to someone we can trust to get us out of Metropolis."

"In a way that doesn't attract any attention," Pius the cop added.

"You mean police attention? Sure, I'll do it."

They were all surprised by my quick answer.

"You'll do it," Ms. Black said. "Just like that—no hesitation, no grappling with moral concerns."

"Nope."

"Well, Mr. Cruz, I must say that I'm glad to see that you're becoming a real live mature adult."

"Oh, no," Mr. Pink said as he strolled up, smiling. "There's more. Mr. Cruz hasn't embraced the world of grays. He's still the black-and-white square."

"Isosceles trapezoid," I interrupted.

Pink laughed. "He wants us to do something for him. Isn't that right, Cruz Control?"

Pink made me smile. I lifted up a photo from my jacket.

"I want you to find him, beat the living daylights out of him, and get him picked up by the police, so that he gets into the system. No money. We're swapping jobs. You do this; I get you a courier out of Metropolis."

"So long as it's not the Road Courier," Ms. Blue said. "We're still throwing up after that last trip."

Black grabbed the photo. "That sounds like a deal."

"And Cruz Control," Pink began, "we'll even call you when we find him, so you can watch the 'party.'"

I was smiling now.

It took them less than an hour! I don't know how they found him so fast. I was back at my offices and had to run back out when I got their call.

I met up with them in a nicely secluded dark back alleyway. Metropolis had a million of them. I parked the Pony in a public lot and ran to them. The Far Escape crew was waiting for me in the alley next to their hovervan, and on the ground was a big sack of something moving.

I stopped where I was and leaned against the wall. They all half-laughed, seeing that I'd brought a bag of popcorn with me to eat.

Ms. Green dragged the sack to the middle of the alley and lifted one end. The man fell out and then his blond wig. Pink picked up his blond wig and put it on his own head.

"This is going to be my new hat!" Pink said to him, chuckling.

"Ichi Jumper will not tolerate this transgression!"

Ms. Green just punched him in the mouth.

The ponytailed cop took a post to watch one end of the alley; the pale, bald cop was on the other end. Then the beatdown really began. Black, Pink, Blue, and especially Green punched, kicked, slammed, beat that maniac to a pulp. When done, they stuffed him back in the sack and threw it into the back of the van.

They all loaded back in, and Black gave me a salute. Their hovervan rose into the sky and blasted off.

Now, I could work in peace.

CHAPTER 52

Personna

I got another call from Metro Penitentiary. It came in 15 minutes after another call—Police Chief Hub.

"Are you in trouble?" PJ asked me.

I had gotten back from another client call, but had to head right back out.

"I don't think so," I replied.

"That's no answer," she said. "That means you did something bad, but you're not sure if they've found out about it."

"Well—yeah."

She laughed. "They say I'm the felon, but I don't do anything bad. You're the one acting like a felon."

I didn't have a lot of time. I had a thing about being late to appointments. I'd rather be an hour early than a minute late, but I figured I'd squeeze in a visit to Madam Personna on the way to Police One.

Two female cyborg guards were leading her out to the visiting room, and she was like a ferret on drugs—hardly able to contain all that balled up energy. They chained her to the table I was sitting at and left.

"What is it, Personna?"

"Oh, you're respectful now. No Madam, anymore."

"What do you want?"

"I found them," she said, giggling.

"Okay. Anything else?"

The smile was gone from her face. "Don't you want to know who they are?"

"You're not going to tell me, so why work myself up? You can keep the information to yourself."

"I don't want to keep the information to myself. I want you to get me the hell out of here."

"Who are they?"

"Will you get me the hell out of here?"

"I'm thinking you're trying to scam me."

"You're the one with the power over me. Why would I scam you?"

"Tell me, and I'll think about it."

"No. I tell you; you get me the hell out of here."

I sat quiet for a moment.

She leaned forward with a smile. "You know that once-in-a-lifetime-trip you made to London Prime? You're going to have to go back."

CHAPTER 53

The Far Escape Crew

"Um, Mr. Cruz." It was Ms. Black's voice on my mobile—audio only.

"Where are you?" I asked.

"We're at the...the Metropolis General Hospital."

That was the conversation I'd got on the way to Police Central. I told her that I'd see her when I finished my meeting. When I hung up, I knew it would be bad news.

I wasn't at Police Central for hours and hours, like usual. The hospital's Information Booth told me where the Far Escape crew were, and I took the elevator capsule to the 63rd floor. At least it wasn't an intensive care floor. A nurse pointed me to their room down the hall.

When I walked into their hospital room, my mouth dropped open. The four of them were in adjacent beds, and they all looked as if they'd been dragged off a battlefield. There was another man in the room, who stood up from his chair, watching over them. He had red hair, and he looked really mean.

"Are you him?" he yelled.

"Him, who?" I asked. He started charging at me.

"Mr. Orange, please," Ms. Black called out from her bed.

He stopped. I kept my eye on him as I walked closer to their beds. They were all beaten badly. Pink was on the bed furthest to the end, and he sat up, wincing in pain.

"What did you do to that guy?" Pink asked.

"I didn't do anything to him. I don't even know who he is."

"That's a pack of lies," Blue yelled from her bed. She looked as if she couldn't even move.

"Mr. Cruz, we find that hard to believe," Black said. "This individual seems very *motivated* to inflict harm on you. After today, I'm sure he'll be even more motivated."

"Cruz Control, I wouldn't want to be you," Pink said, half-laughing. "He is going to get you. You can take that to the bank."

"Where are the other two?" I asked, looking around.

"They're in surgery!" Mr. Orange yelled. "He ran them over with the hovervan."

"What?" I looked at Black and then the rest of them. "You're supposed to be badass military mercenaries. He ran over your two cops with a hovervan? Are you telling me he also stole your hovervan?"

None of them answered, so the answer was "Yes."

"How could this happen?" I yelled. "How could one bald Japanese guy, who wears a blond wig, beat up all of you? How?"

I could see that Black was having a hard time getting the words out. "Well—he did."

"You had already beat the crap out of him!"

"Cruz Control, that guy ain't human," Pink said. "He must be an alien or something. He popped out of that sack, kicked, and karate chopped us before we knew what hit us."

"Don't you all know martial arts, too?"

Black struggled again. "We—do."

"I can't believe this!" I threw up my hands in the air. "It's one man! He's not an eight-foot-tall killer cyborg. One man in a stupid blond wig! How?"

"What did you do to that guy?" Mr. Orange asked.

"Nothing! He came up to me one day and gave me a card with his name, Ichi Jumper. Then he threatened me, told me to stay out of his business. What business? I never met him before, never seen him before. He followed me all the way to London Prime—and back! Who is this guy? You were supposed to be my dream team! Beat him up and hand him over to the police!"

"I wouldn't want to be you, Cruz Control." Pink let himself drop back flat on his bed. "Ow!"

"Mr. Cruz." I looked at Black as she spoke. "We did our part so we expect you to do yours. When we recover, we want to be out of Metropolis."

"What a miserable, rainy city you have here," Green finally spoke. "We'll never come back here again."

"Did your part? All you did was make this maniac angrier! I still don't even know why he's after me! You did nothing! You made it worse!"

"We—did our part, and we expect you to do your part," she repeated.

I started to pace the floor. "I can't believe this. I have to leave for London Prime again. I would say that would save me or at least buy me some time, but the maniac followed me there once, and I'm sure he'd do it again."

"Then, Mr. Cruz, we expect you to introduce us to the courier *before* you leave," Black said.

"Yeah, Cruz Control," Pink said, "while you're still breathing."

CHAPTER 54

Hub and Fortran

Dot had told me that I was spending so much time at Police Central, they should make me an auxiliary policeman. It was becoming like one endless dream, or nightmare, depending on the outcome. This time, there was no waiting. I arrived and I was led by an officer straight to Chief Hub's office. He was standing at his desk. I immediately noticed the face of DCI Fortran on the video display screen on the arm attachment of his desk.

"I believe you two have already met," Hub said.

"Hello, DCI Fortran," I said. Hub gestured for me to sit, and the officer who'd escorted me in closed the door and stood at the back.

Hub sat behind his desk. "You're causing trouble in two countries."

I smiled. "I'm a famous detective."

"You're a famous something, but we'll discuss that another time. What do you know about the drug O.D. epidemic in Metropolis?"

I leaned forward. "Now, I don't want you to be mad at me. I had to check out the new information."

I could already see his face turning red.

"You have new information?" DCI Fortran said.

"Yes."

"Well, don't keep us in suspense. Tell us what you found out," he said.

"It's not a drug. It's a VR drug."

"Yes, we know that," DCI Fortran said.

"Specifically, it's a synth called Electric Sheep."

"We know that too," Hub said. "Synth? Talking like the cyberpunks now, are we?"

"I don't do drugs, if that's what you're trying to find out," I said. "Real, or otherwise. But there's more."

"Go on."

"The overdoses aren't accidental. They're on purpose."

"Yes, they are," Hub said.

I was actually shocked by his response. They knew already.

"Mr. Cruz, this epidemic didn't begin in Metropolis," DCI Fortran said. "It began in London Prime. A large group of tech scientists did their collaborative work in one of these VL worlds. An incident happened there that Scotland Yard has dubbed the Electric Sheep Massacre."

Meetings and lab simulations in VL or "virtual life"—I was told only police and senior citizens over 80 years old said "VR" or "virtual reality"—were common practice in the business and scientific communities worldwide. This VL world was another planet—one massive continent surrounded by a calm ocean covering its surface. The land mass was filled with wooded areas, streams, waterfalls, and the ground appeared to be synthetic grass; butterflies and bird flew through the air.

The meeting structure was a glass pyramid. Spaceship after another set down on the surface and the scientists exited—much more elaborate (and fun) than simply jacking-in. It was a symposium of 300 freelance energy exploration scientists.

"Everyone, please take your seats and we'll get started," one of the scientists said from the stage. "We have a lot to cover today with our discussions and v-labs. Thank you for keeping the real agenda of this meeting secret. Many talk about changing the world to make it a better and more peaceful place. Today, we're actually going to launch the plan to do just that. People, not the governments and megacorps, will finally rule Earth!"

The inside was arranged in theater-style with the recliner seats facing the stage. People applauded and then began to sit. One of the professors at the back looked out and noticed.

"Who or what is that?" he asked.

A colleague turned and noticed the humanoid sheep in a suit standing off in the distance on the top of a hill. "I have no idea, professor. Are his eyes actually glowing red?"

"Look!" someone yelled, near the front of the auditorium.

From everywhere, outside the pyramid, sheep appeared, running at the glass pyramid. People inside began to laugh.

"What is this?" one man giggled. "We're going to be killed by killer sheep?"

"Don't worry, everyone. This must be someone's idea of a joke," the man on the center stage called out. "We've increased the building's force-field. The sheep will have to stay outside and feed on some grass instead."

"I hope they like synthetic," a woman said.

The sheep were not slowing down and as they neared, their eyes turned red. Everyone inside was on their feet. Most found the sight amusing, some were laughing, but a few were nervous.

The first sheep's body pulsed with electric charges just before it crashed through the glass wall of the pyramid—all the other sheep followed. People ran for the exits, but the sheep were right on their heels. The man on the stage tried to run but was jumped by one of the sheep. He yelled out.

The VL world looked like a WWII recreation, but it was a steampunk battle between American Civil War North and South on the beaches of Normandy. All the soldiers—different ages and ethnicities—were augmented with robotic exo-skeletons and firing laser rifles, from opposing sides. In the sky above, air armadas of blue Union and gray Confederate dirigibles faced off, firing rockets at each other.

"What's that?" one of the Union soldiers yelled.

"Who the hell is crashing into our simulation?" a Confederate soldier cried.

A vortex opened and a woman, dressed casually, jumped out. "Jack-out! We're being attacked by zombies!"

As the men disconnected from their VL pod-chambers, removing their VL soft helmets, they saw pandemonium in the bar—screaming, bar stools being thrown, patrons escaping out the back entrance. The woman who'd jacked-in to warn them was on the floor unconscious near the VL pods, a bloody hand print on the side of her face. She wasn't the only one lying on the ground, unmoving. The men, some actually dressed in either Confederate gray or Union blue uniforms, all stayed put in their pod-chambers, watching everything in shock.

They now saw the source of the violence: unknown people—not establishment regulars—running into the VL bar, enraged, screaming, attacking everyone wildly—punching, choking, and kicking. It was the scientists—tiny images flickered on their corneas, making it seem as though their eyes were glowing.

Law enforcement used VL too, for crime scene reenactments. Though they were never admissible in court, they were often incredibly accurate—Nothing was included unless there was some kind of corroborating piece of evidence. Their VL reenactment on the display screen made me feel as if I had been there.

DCI Fortran continued, "There were 300 freelance energy exploration scientists in that virtual lab simulation, some type of symposium. They were attacked by electric sheep—probably thought it was some practical joke. The scientists went psychotic, killed innocent people in the streets, nearby VR dens and bars; they tried to kill many others. The scientists all died from massive brain hemorrhages of some kind—their eyeballs were brown, as if they'd been—fried.

"Our Scotland Yard cyber-investigators suspected that it was not a freak accident. Now, we are convinced it was deliberate. Then, the same thing began happening in Metropolis on a smaller scale, but it has been increasing."

"The group in London Prime was the target?" I asked.

"Yes."

"Then why random VL addicts here in Metropolis?"

"Mr. Cruz, we believe that it may be to cover up for the original event, make people think it was a freak accident."

"The Ripper," I said.

"Excuse me?" DCI Fortran said.

"My sources said that the person doing all this calls himself the Ripper."

"Good God." DCI Fortran looked at Chief Hub. "It's as we thought. We have a serial killer loose in VR world."

Hub looked at me. "Cruz, you're going back to London Prime."

Once I had left there, I made my stop at Metro General to see the Far Escape crew, but, yes, I was heading back to the land of fish and chips again. Two psychos to deal with—Ichi Jumper and the new one, the Ripper.

Before I did, I asked how many innocent people had been killed in this 'Electric Sheep Massacre.'

Hub answered in his typical unspecific way, "A lot."

Later, I would learn—and almost fell out of my chair—that it was close to 10,000 people! All those deaths from one event in virtual reality—as if we didn't have enough murder in the real world.

PART SIX

Hiroshima Park

CHAPTER 55

Lord of the Geeks

Chief Hub and DCI Fortran hired me to poke around in the UK as a decoy, while they did their investigations. With my high-profile in the media, the attention would follow me. I was to be a consulting detective for both Metro PD and Scotland Yard—free round trip ticket, free hotel accommodations, and payment for my time—essentially to do nothing.

But I also knew that the other—and probably main—reason for this 'alliance' was to keep me under control. They wanted to keep tabs on me and monitor what I was doing. Since I kept popping up, they figured it was better to have me on a leash. They were, of course, not telling me everything—and I wasn't telling them everything. Also, Personna did come through, so my return to London Prime would involve working on more than one case.

Hub had remarked that they had planned to put me in the same hotel as before, but the management had said that, after trying to kill a pedestrian on the ground with a chair, they didn't want me ever to return. That was all fine with me, because the blond-wigged maniac was still on the loose, and that hotel would be the first place he'd check if he decided to fly to London again, too.

I was in the Infidelity Hotel. The name sounded a little risqué to me, so maybe it was Hub's idea of a joke. My room was nice, and it was in the back, so if I wanted I could use the rear elevators of the tower.

The wife also had me on a short leash. After my first international trip, she expected no more assassination attempts. She didn't care when I said that I hadn't asked for the couple to try to murder me, and she didn't want to see my name in the UK newsfeed; she was going to monitor it closely.

I arrived late, so the only thing I was going to do was sleep. I had all my London School of Hygiene and Tropical Medicine products with me and used my UV scanner for the bed. Nasty! Good hotels bio-cleaned their linens. Bad hotels washed their linens in regular water and dried with a ton of scented pads. The "new sheet smell" might fool people, but not the germs that remained. Nasty!

I had my own sheets with me. That's what one of my luggage bags was dedicated to. It was—in my mind—CDC-approved and wrapped in two distinct hermetically sealed plastic bags. First was my special bed cover, then my special sleeping bag; inside were two sheets. I was set. I was too tired to clean the room properly, so I cleaned the area around the bed, the table, desk, all the areas I would be. Once I had my anti-germ and bacterial humidifier working for a good hour in the bathroom with the door closed, it was safe to take a shower. The cleaner I used in the shower stall was strong enough to rip the first layer of your skin off. Nice! All used rags, clothes, wipes, gloves, and brushes were bagged and sealed. On my way out the next day, they would be down the trash chute.

This was the same thing I had done in the American Hotel too, but I hadn't had my new London School of Hygiene and Tropical Medicine products.

I got ready for bed, and when I was in that sleeping bag, I was in from that night straight through to the next day. My mobile was right in the bag with me so I could call the wife at my designated check-in times.

Some things were universal on this planet. The hovercab dropped me off, and the street looked like so many others that I'd been to in Metropolis. Not the seediest, but you knew you weren't in a decent neighborhood, either. It looked as if there were no one over 30 on the street, which to them meant I was a senior citizen with one foot in the grave.

British fashion was no different from in any other supercity, but with youth, it was all over the place. I had gotten used to seeing Beatnik fashion; now, I was seeing punk fashion—spiky hair, lots of black, but always with some color. Flowers on the lapel also looked to be a common part of UK kid fashion.

Here, VL was every bit as big as in the Americas, but here, even I was having a tough time figuring out where the VL scene ended and where the drug culture began.

"Where's the Refinery?" I asked a young couple wearing silver clothes and long scarves wrapped around their necks and hanging down to their knees.

They laughed at me. "Don't you know?" they said, and walked off.

I quickly learned that it was a game after asking five other people the same question and getting giggles or being outright ignored.

"Hey, can you help out an American?" I asked another.

The man almost fell over laughing. "No!"

Okay, so that was a lousy opening line.

"Where do I go to get some information?" I asked a woman cradling a robot cat in her arms.

"What kind of information?"

"I want to get to the Refinery."

"Don't you know?"

"I don't. That's why I'm asking."

"I wish I could help you, but yesterday's information is today's trash."

"What does that mean?"

"The Refinery isn't a place. It's a party. A party on the move. Only the Refinery knows where the Refinery is."

It was almost the end of the day, and it had taken half of it to find out what the Refinery was; it wasn't a place with a fixed location. Then it took me hours to find this traveling group of VL party-goers. I had a headache.

Someone had pity on me, finally, and told me to follow them. It was three of them. Two women, with cat ear attachments—I didn't know what that signified, and a guy wearing a bowler hat.

They all locked arms, the guy with me, and they skipped down the street. I wanted to die. Me, skipping down the street with a bunch of kids with cat ears. I could be blackmailed with this CCTV footage, because I knew I looked ridiculous.

Around the corner and to the end of a short street, we went. We skipped right into a crowd moving down a main street. Most of the crowd was on hoverchairs plugged into their VL helmets. Each VL chair user had people around their chair; on the edges of the crowd were muscular punks with baseball bats wearing colored shades—reds, blues, greens, purples, etc.

"Old timer," the boy said, letting my arm go, "the Refinery."

They all disappeared into the crowd, and I stood as the crowd slowly moved in front of me. I honestly could not see the end. I looked the other way, and I couldn't see the beginning. It was a sea of people; a moving town of hardcore VR users. There were also go-go bots everywhere— slim humanoid female robots, wearing neon wigs, bikinis, and knee-high boots, dancing as they walked to add to the wild party atmosphere. We didn't have anything like this in Metropolis.

I moved into the crowd and saw that there were mobile pubs moving around on hover-platforms. It was the UK. These people couldn't survive without their beer and tea, so I wasn't completely surprised. Time to work—better to start seven hours later than not at all.

For the next couple of hours, I moved up and down the Refinery to get the lay of the land. Each section was identified by its own music—either people with music belts all on the same channel or a specific DJ playing or performing. I struck up conversations, and others chatted with me—I guess there was some kind of invisible rays emanating from Americans that they could see. They all liked talking to the American.

I found what I was looking for. One of the sections was filled with more hoverchairs than any other, and the chairs were hovering from inches above the ground to many stories up. Most of the people here were on hoverboards and hoverskates. This was the section controlled by cyberpunks—the super hackers who lived in VL worlds most of their lives.

It was in this cyberpunk section that I saw my target sitting in a hoverthrone. I did a double-take. On either side were hovercouches filled with giggling girls doing shots of whatever drinks they had. When I began to walk up to him, a metallic hand was pushed into my chest. It belonged to a tall, chunky, ugly brute.

"Where do you think you're going?" the cyborg asked me.

I pointed. "To talk to him."

"No one just walks up to talk to the Geek, unless he's invited you."

"How do I get invited?"

"If you don't know, I'm not telling you. Move along, Yank."

"Listen to that hostility. People today live on Mars, and you all are still holding a grudge over that war. Aren't we friends?"

"I'm not your friend."

"America and the UKT." I put my hand on his shoulder. "Marching out into the universe, shoulder to shoulder, hand in hand, conquering the cosmos."

"You talk a lot, just like a cop."

"Cop?" I was offended. "I'll have you know I'm Cruz, the American detective of Liquid Cool."

His perpetual "I'm about to kill you" look changed to one of surprise.

"Cruz, the private eye?"

"Yes."

"From Metropolis?"

"Yes."

"Who blew the lid off that child trafficking sex ring?"

I was in unknown waters now. If he were buddies with one of the arrested members of this trafficking ring, he'd try to beat me to death with his bionic arm. If he were related to one of the victims—and there were a lot of them—I'd be given the red-carpet treatment. I had a 50-50 chance, but I was feeling lucky.

"That's me!"

The Geek was busy talking to the ladies, but noticed me in front of him. This whole moving sea of people was weird, but I was starting to like it. It meant you either had to jump on some kind of hoverplatform or you had to always keep walking.

"I know you!" the Geek said. "You're that American detective."

"That's me."

"I thought you'd left the country."

"I'm back."

"Now here you are with us. Ladies, move over and give our guest some room."

"Thanks."

The young women on one hovercouch let me jump on to sit right next to him.

"What was your name again?" he asked, extending a hand.

"Cruz."

"Cruz, of the Liquid Cool detective agency. That's it. Do you have a bunch of great detective stories to tell us to enliven the night?"

"I have a lot of them."

"Let's get our new friend a drink."

"You're American too," I said.

"I am, but I've been living here forever. If you can't be a king in the place where you were born, then move to a place where you can be. What'll you have, Mr. Cruz?"

"As long as it's not fresh or ocean water."

They laughed.

"We can do much better than that."

I don't know why it took two of the young ladies to jump off the hoverchair to get me a drink, but when they returned, the two of them were carrying the biggest martini glass I'd ever seen.

"Mr. Cruz, in the UKT, we like to drink," the Geek said.

"Can I at least have a straw?"

With my straw, I sipped as I told detective stories. I wasn't lying. I had a million of them and didn't have to make up anything. My years in the hovercar street racing scene had prepared me for this. There, at the hovercar shows and races, that was how we passed the time, with great stories about the vehicles, legendary races, and legendary collectors. Now, it was my turn to continue the tradition with stories of my cases—small and large, but all mesmerizing to the outsider. It wasn't long before I noticed that a growing audience was forming as the word got out that "Cruz, that American detective" was sitting with the Geek retelling actual cases I'd solved. Later, I heard my voice echoing throughout the Refinery crowd, and I realized I was being both video and audio-streamed.

"Are you working on a case now?" the girl sitting next to the Geek asked.

It was what I'd been waiting for. After two hours of storytelling, finally, one of them asked the question I'd wanted them to ask.

"I am, and it could be the toughest one I've ever encountered."

Everyone on the couch leaned close. There were people actually walking backwards to keep their eyes on me.

"Tell us about it," said the cyborg bodyguard, who was sitting on a hoverboard that he'd snatched from the kid next to him.

"How many of you have heard about that drug epidemic in Metropolis where the users attack innocent people before dying?"

Hands went up throughout the crowd.

"I'm about to let you in on a secret that the government doesn't want anyone to know."

There was no music playing anywhere in the Refinery. In fact, the Refinery crowd came to a halt.

"All the users were plugged into VL."

People went crazy. "I knew it!" "Didn't I say that?" "Damn government conspirators!"

"It's worse," I said, and everyone shut up.

"I think it was on purpose."

"On purpose?" one of the young women on my couch asked.

"Mr. Cruz, you can't kill a person in VL," the Geek said.

"Bad drugs kill people all the time. But can bad VL drugs kill someone?"

Everyone was looking around at each other.

"No," the Geek answered emphatically. "If that were true, then it would be happening everywhere. Here, Earth, space colonies, Mars, everywhere. VL synths are universal, and so are the VL drugs that go with them."

"That's what I thought," I said, "but then someone told me that he was in a VL world when it happened, when one of those users snapped and went on a rampage before dying."

"What did they see?" the cyborg brute asked.

"He saw another person in the VL world doing something to them."

"What?"

"Slashing them with something. He murdered them in VL, and they went psycho and died in reality."

"With what?" he asked.

"Forget that," a woman yelled from the ground. "Who was it? The murderer?"

"The Ripper," I answered.

What happened next happened so fast, that if I hadn't been sitting there and seen it directly, I would have said it was impossible. The people on the ground, the users in the hoverchairs, people on foot, people on hover-platforms scattered. All of them disappeared into the streets. It happened in probably less than a minute, and all that was left was me sitting on an empty hovercouch with my straw and humongous martini glass by myself. The Refinery was gone.

CHAPTER 56

Blue Eyes

I'll admit I was a jokester. I was good at pushing buttons and keeping people off balance. My contrarian, snarky persona worked exceptionally well for me as a private detective dealing with crazy criminals and crazier clients. That was, it worked most of the time.

I had no idea what I'd just done—not a clue. The assumption was that they all knew who the Ripper was, but I didn't know that for sure. Why did they all run away? The only thing I could do was walk until I found a hovercab and got back to my hotel. That was it for the day. The next day, I'd work on my other case.

Metropolis had Silver City, its center of its robotics industry; the UKT had Hiroshima Park. In both cases, Japanese megacorps dominated. In fact, the whole city was founded by an ancient Japanese megacorp that no longer existed, but its legacy endured. It was an entire section of London Prime that literally glowed.

Here, I was happy to take public transportation. The hovertrains and hoverbuses in London Prime were fit for royalty. The people that got on and off wore clothes and accessories of wealth and class. I took a moving sidewalk to the giant pyramid tower of the Vector Corporation. Unlike Metropolis, people weren't so anti-humanoid robot. Two doorman models opened the main glass door for me.

"Good morning, sir," they both said.

I ignored them.

The lobby was a strange set-up. There was no visible reception or information desk, no human guards. People were everywhere, going from elevator capsules, escalators, and indoor moving walkways, but there were no directories. It was a puzzle, and as the American, that meant everyone knew how to solve it except me.

"I want to see Doctor Windows," I said out loud.

"Please take Elevator 5 to Floor 120," a voice said, startling me. The voice came from the floor tile. "Please follow the lighted path."

What a place. The floor spoke to you and lit you a path.

The elevator capsule was full of people. People kept getting off until I was the only one left. It opened, and I stepped out. The hallway was massive but there were no signs, numbers, directories, or people—another puzzle.

I decided on turning right and walked. When I got to the end, the hallways went for miles in either direction. "This can't be right. They do like their puzzles here." I walked back to the front of the elevator, spun around and said, "Open, please."

The wall lifted, and several guards in suits stood there watching me. Was I in trouble?

"Is this how you greet clients?" I asked. "You hide behind walls, watching people get off the elevator. I've never been here before. No names or numbers. You hide the entrance with moving walls. What kind of business are you running here?"

"Mr. Cruz," I heard a voice, followed by a laugh, but I saw no one. I turned around but saw nothing.

"Holo-dome off," his voice said.

The guards in suits, the walls, everything I saw disappeared and was replaced by a lobby with the ceiling at least five stories up, waterfalls on the high wall, a large reception desk with three women and two men answering phones. The man who was talking walked to me. He was a Black man in a navy suit and white tie. As he came close all I noticed were his crystal blue cybernetic eyes.

"Dr. Windows at your service." He shook my hand.

"American?"

"Yes, American." He laughed. "Your secretary, Ms. Judy, said you'd most likely get here early. I had a break between meetings when they said you were here."

"What was—" I pointed.

"Oh, the holo-dome. It's an AI holo-simulation designed to screen out unauthorized people. The company feels it's a far better deterrent than security guards everywhere."

"What would have happened if I was 'unauthorized'?"

"You don't want to know."

He led me to his office. In this building, everyone must have been in the greatest shape because of the long distances they had to walk to get anywhere. It was another gigantic office, typical for any megacorp, with aquarium walls, filled with all kinds of fish swimming around.

"Can I have any refreshments brought in?"

"No, I'm fine. What's with the water thing here?"

He laughed.

"Fresh or ocean," we said in unison.

"Yes, I had to get used to it, too. Filtered ocean water is considered a more—sophisticated type of drinking water."

"Meaning more expensive."

"Of course."

"What does Vector Corp do?"

"We are at the forefront of power infrastructure manufacturing, distribution, and storage."

"More than a utilities company."

"Much more than that."

"Is it Japanese owned?"

"No, we're a multinational company; at least 16 countries make up our board of governors, but we have interests planet-wide."

"Well, I know your time is valuable." I reached into my pocket for the photo and handed it to him. "Can you tell me where these two men are?"

Windows looked at the photo. "This is Hue and his son."

"Father and son?"

"Yes, they look like brothers. I haven't seen them in weeks. They've been on their eight-week vacation."

"Eight weeks? That's long for a corporation."

"It is, but I approved it. They actually hadn't taken any vacation in about four years. What's this about, Mr. Cruz?"

"I'm sorry to tell you that both men are dead."

He looked up from the photo.

"Yes, they were found dead in Metropolis, actually."

"Dead? How?"

"Murder."

Windows dropped the photo on his desk and leaned back in his chair. He looked visibly stunned.

"Do they know who did it? I mean, was it a street crime?"

"The police don't know yet. They're still investigating."

"How did you get involved? I mean, that's in Metropolis, and you're here in London Prime. That's a long way to come, when—you could have called on vid-phone."

"I'm here on another matter, visiting clients, and in my own investigation, I learned of their identities."

"We were never notified by any police."

"We only found out recently."

"Are you working with the police?"

"Yes, I'm a consulting detective for them on a few matters."

"I see."

"Did you know where they were in Metropolis? I mean, found dead."

"Outside the main city. Were they working on something?"

"Not that I'm aware of. They were on vacation. Do you believe they were specifically targeted?"

"The police don't think so, but I feel maybe."

"Why do you think that?"

"Because no tourists would go where they were found."

"Were they dumped there?"

"No, they went there on their own."

"What do the police think?"

"They don't know much yet."

"Are you investigating this?"

"Not directly. I wanted to let you know as their employer of record and you could contact Scotland Yard, so any family or relatives can be notified."

"Yes, of course."

"If we only knew why they were there."

"I wish I could help. This is all a shock to me."

"What were their jobs here?"

"Programming. We employ thousands."

"I don't want to intrude, but would the company give their employee files to Scotland Yard to see if there might be a clue?"

"I would approve that, of course, but the company might not allow that for privacy and legal reasons. I know everything in it, what all their projects were. They were programmers, nothing unusual or exceptional. Don't get me wrong. They were good workers."

He picked up the photo from his desk.

"Can I ask you a few questions, Mr. Cruz?"

"Yes."

"Was there anything else that you do know about their deaths?"

"It was quite a gruesome scene. I don't think anyone should be left as a John or Jane Doe in the morgue."

"Yes, I agree."

"How long will you be in London?"

"I'm not sure how long it will take me to wrap up a few things, but not long. I can leave my number for you to call if you should think of anything. Right now, it's a dead case for the Metropolis police, but if there were anything new, we could get them to re-open it."

"Yes."

"Do they have family or relatives?"

"No. None. How did you know they worked for me, Mr. Cruz?"

"Metro Police."

"Metropolis Police knows the organizational rosters of foreign companies?"

"Vector Corporation has interests in Metropolis, correct?"

He looked a bit nervous. "We do."

"Maybe that's how. They keep organizational information up-to-date on all companies, domestic and foreign, doing business in Metropolis."

"Yes, that must be it."

"Oh, here's my number."

I gave him my card, and he slowly took it.

"I know it's all a shock. I don't want to take up any more of your time. I'll check in with the Metro Police when I get back, just to see if there are any new leads. Maybe something turns up. Maybe not. We have to try. For their sake."

"Yes."

I stood from my chair, and he slowly stood from his.

He walked me to the main lobby without saying another word.

"I wish it were under better circumstances, but it's always good meeting another American in London."

I shook his hand as he gave me a slight smile, and I walked to the elevator. As I walked, I glanced back. He was walking away, but was glancing back at me, too.

I reached the elevator, and it opened. Standing there was the Geek! He went pale and stood there, frozen. I reached into my jacket and gave him one of my special cards.

"That was so much fun last night," I said. "I never got to give you one of my cards. If you're ever in Metropolis and want to see the town with a real private eye, give me a call."

"Okay."

He slid out of the elevator and I stepped in. He watched me as the elevator closed.

"Oh, my God!" the Geek's voice yelled.

"Why did you come up?" Windows's voice yelled. "I told them to have you wait."

"I couldn't take it."

"He saw you!"

"He doesn't know that we're meeting. He doesn't know that we know each other."

"Are you positive about that?"

"He's a detective, but he isn't omniscient. Why did he come here?"

"He flew across the ocean to tell me personally that the police found Hue and Hue, Jr. dead."

"How did he know they worked for you?"

"Yes, how did he?"

"This is all unraveling."

"Nothing is unraveling. We'll test it at Atlantis as planned."

"He came to see me last night."

"What?"

"He was looking for me."

"Why? You didn't tell me this."

"I'm telling you now. He knows about Electric Sheep."

"So?"

"He said a person is behind it all—The Ripper!"

"That can't be. We killed him."

"He's in the VL."

"He's dead."

"I sent everyone out to warn every cyberpunk on the planet. It all makes sense. He's killing random people to cover up the massacre. He killed our entire team. He must have killed Hue and Hue, Jr. too."

"They were not supposed to test it yet!"

"It's government, I tell you."

"It could easily be the corporations."

"They'll be coming after us. They know about the juice."

"No one knows about the juice."

"They know—what are you doing?"

"My eyes are reading—what's in your pockets?"

"What?"

"Empty your pockets. Where did you get that card from?"

"It was him."

"Who?"

"Cruz. He gave it to me when we passed on the elevator."

I heard pounding and then nothing. They destroyed by business card bug. I had been standing near the elevators five floors below, pretending to read messages on my mobile, while listening to them. I pressed the button and this time, took it straight down to the ground level.

CHAPTER 57

Where's Ichi?

My trip to London Prime was over. I was woken by a call from Chief Hub telling me that the Electric Sheep VL drug epidemic had abruptly ended the night before. They didn't know if it was temporary or permanent. He wanted me on the next flight back. I wasn't even going to get a chance to see DCI Fortran in person again.

I tried to get him to let me stay at least half the day, but he was adamant and hung up on me.

It took me at least a couple of hours to get up, showered, and tidy the hotel room back to its original state. As I opened the door, four London police were waiting.

"I want breakfast!" I yelled at them.

We walked to the elevators, they put me in the police hovervan, and they took me to London International. One of them handed me my ticket, and they followed me until I went through check-in. I wanted breakfast in the hotel, not at the airport. I'd lost my appetite.

As I sat in a corner chair, I scanned the people waiting, walking by, standing, whatever. I was looking for the blond wig. Where was that maniac, Ichi?

Unfortunately, he was probably still in Metropolis, and I was about to get on an international jet back to him.

PART SEVEN

Atlantis

CHAPTER 58

China Doll and the Hell Spawn

This time, my return to Metropolis was normal. The wife was there to greet me. She told me the whole atmosphere on the street seemed upbeat—the Electric Sheep drug craze seemed to be genuinely over. Dot showed me pictures she'd taken of the baby with the home ultra-sound kit she borrowed from her parents. (Why did they have one?) It was amazing to see photos of a growing little person, and we already had the blood test. I was going to hang the picture of my son-on-the-way in the Pony.

Of course, Dot wanted to hear all about the trip. I told her most of it. She seemed to know more about the Refinery than I did, and I'd been there. "A moving, living city within a city" was what she called it. Dot zipped through hovertraffic and set her Bee down in our Concrete Mama parking space in no time. There was the Pony behind its security perimeter.

Home, Sweet Home. We were through the door and I smelled the aroma of cooking food. Dot wouldn't leave food cooking on the stove while she went to the airport. Dot let out a stream of Chinese, and my stomach dropped down through my legs to my feet. The Hell Spawn were in my place!

I heard Mrs. Wan yell back to her in Chinese. We entered the kitchen and I saw Mr. Wan sitting on *my* kitchen stool near the stove. He gave me a snarling look. Mrs. Wan just stared at me. When we were engaged and Dot was living with them, I could leave my parents-in-law-from-hell-to-be and go home, far away from them. Now, they were my parents-in-law from hell for real, and they could enter my sanctuary whenever they wanted. This was not good. Could I convince the wife to disown them so we could ban them from the premises?

"I told them you had another exciting case in London Prime," Dot said to me, looking at what her mother was cooking.

"Dot," I said. "They speak English." I looked at them. "We know you speak English, so stop with the Chinese-only act."

"We speak Chinese, because you don't," Mrs. Wan contemptuously said to me. She then rattled off more Chinese to Dot. "You can't even speak Spanish to your own parents," she added. "Useless!" She pointed a bony figure at me.

"I can speak Spanish when I want," I said.

"Liar!" she yelled.

Dot yelled something back at her in Chinese.

"You are useless. You speak only one language. We speak many," Mr. Wan said.

"Good. Speak all the languages you want."

Mr. Wan then started calling me names in Spanish. "What did I just say?"

"You said 'Mr. and Mrs. Wan are a couple of dog-eating—'"

"Cruz!" Dot yelled at me.

Mr. and Mrs. Wan started laughing.

"He can't speak any Spanish." Mr. Wan smiled.

"Useless," Mrs. Wan said. "You can't even speak to your own mother in her native tongue. You were a bad son!"

This was the hell that I found myself in. Trapped in my own place with the Hell Spawn. If Ichi Jumper had teamed up with these two, my only escape would have been to commit suicide. I ran away to my home office; at least I could successfully ban them from the room.

CHAPTER 59

Tag

Chief Hub had set up an appointment for me at Police One, but then it was canceled. I assumed that whatever the real reason was that he and DCI Fortran had wanted me in London Prime for was now complete, so they didn't see the need to continue the game playing.

They did release Personna from Metro Penitentiary, and she not only promptly disappeared, but all her psychic parlors closed down. All that meant was she'd go underground for six months and open everything back up under a new company and new name, but the same people. Maybe she'd be Empress Personna this time.

Tag was my first and only stop for the day. I needed to know what I'd done in London Prime with the Refinery and find out everything about this Geek. I found him at a new VL den; he seemed a lot more relaxed, but still had the bodyguards around. It was a new place, so I had a couple of his cyberpunks watch the Pony for a few bucks while I was inside with him.

"Cruz, you met the Geek in person!"

We sat in the booth closest to the back of the VL den and he sat with his back to the wall.

"Spread the word among your people that, if any of them see a blond-haired Japanese guy they should let you know immediately," I told Tag.

"Who is he?"

"Big trouble—but only for me, not you."

Tag sent a text, and it seemed as if everyone in the den got it.

"What was he like?"

"Who, the Geek?"

"Yeah."

"He was a guy. He was sitting on a hoverthrone, a hovercouch of women on either side."

"Yeah, he's the man."

"What is the Refinery? My wife said it's a moving, living city within in a city."

"Your wife's got it exactly. It's a never-ending street party made up of all UKT's VL cyberpunk community."

"They just walk the streets with people in VL worlds?"

"It's much more than that, but you could say that."

"Are we talking legal or illegal?"

"Both. Cyberpunks don't consider anything they do to be illegal."

"Which means mostly illegal? I need help, Tag. I said something to the Geek, and he freaked out. The entire Refinery scattered like scared mice."

"What did you say?"

"I told him what you told me—that our recent drug-induced rampage epidemic wasn't an accident. It was the work of that person you saw in Electric Sheep. I told him that the person was the Ripper. They went crazy, and all of them ran away, leaving me there by myself. Who's the Ripper?"

"The Ripper is a VL boogie man, but this one is real."

"He's a boogie man? What do you mean?"

"All the major synth creators make them and individual hackers make them. They're people who simply appear and do scary stuff in your VL world. If it's from a manufacturer, if you catch one, you can get a grand prize, lots of dollars. If it's a hacker, they try to mess up your VL world when you're not looking. Sometimes, they're strange people who appear in there, don't interact with anyone, and steal stuff or break into your place to look around."

I laughed to myself.

"It's not funny, Cruz."

"Tell me who the Ripper is."

"He's supposed to be the most dangerous boogie man around. It's like an urban legend. He never went after people, though. He hacked the megacorps."

"To do what?"

"To bring them down."

"Did he ever do it?"

"People said he did it all the time, but the megacorps would keep the media from reporting it."

"Did any megacorp do anything about it?"

"Cruz, VL worlds are filled with megacorp agents and cops."

"Yes, all your illegality. So, the Ripper is an urban myth and now is killing people with VL drugs all of a sudden."

"If the Geek says it's him, then it's him. He would know."

"Why?"

"The Geek killed him."

"Killed him?"

"Yeah."

"In a VL world?"

"Yes, and I know what you're going to say. VL worlds are not real, so how could he kill him? The Geek said he'd killed him. This was years ago. After that, no one heard about the Ripper again. Cyberpunks were saying the Geek had killed him in real life, because the Ripper wasn't trying to crash the megacorps; he was trying to crash cyberpunk currency."

I felt I was tumbling down the rabbit hole. These guys lived in their own universe. Cyberpunk currency? I didn't need to ask him what it was. The cyberpunks had their own secret cyber-money, so they couldn't be traced by law enforcement, so they could buy their drugs and other things on the Net.

Tag also told me the Geek used the collective power of Earth's cyberpunk community to delete and rewrite all the code for Electric Sheep. That's why the VL drug-induced attacks and O.D.s stopped in a day.

"Do you think this Ripper will ever be able to get back in?"

"When you're dealing with code, hackers will eventually find a way. Ripper is a great hacker, but so is the Geek. The Geek has everyone watching for him, so the Ripper won't be killing anyone else."

Tag seemed to be very angry at this point and probably knew many of the victims, personally. I could see he wanted revenge on this Ripper.

"What is Atlantis?"

"Atlantis? That's a high-end pleasure ocean colony. Only Up-Toppers can afford to go there. Why? What does that have to do with this?"

"I'm not sure. One final thing for you: does the term 'juice' or 'The Juice' mean anything to you?"

Tag shook his head. "No, why? What does it mean? Juice is slang for power."

"Yeah, I know that but another meaning."

"No."

"That's it for now—but if you hear of anything about this Ripper, or if the deaths start up again, or you hear anything new about the Geek, you tell me."

"The latest news on the Geek is that I may meet him in person after all."

"Why is that?"

"The Geek is in Metropolis."

"What? When?" I asked.

"He got here this morning."

"Really," I said.

CHAPTER 60

Run-Time

Atlantis was where I wanted to go. I didn't tell Tag about the conversation I (illegally) listened in to between the Geek and Windows. However, I needed to see this colony, because I felt that they were up to no good. If I could get there somehow, I could poke around. All I had were suspicions, nothing more.

But how was I to get there? Tag was right. Only the super-wealthy went to that place.

I made a video-call to Run-Time. He'd know what I should do.

"What are you doing tomorrow?" he asked.

"Tomorrow? I can make time if I need to."

"Clear your day then. I'll send the hoverlimo for you."

"Where am I going?"

"We're going to Atlantis."

I had absolutely the best friend in the world!

The Let It Ride hoverlimo arrived at Liquid Cool early in the morning. PJ wasn't in yet, and I couldn't bring Dot because of the particulars of where we were going, so there was no reason for her to know about it.

Their hoverlimos were unmistakable, even before seeing the neon "Let It Ride Enterprises" letters on both sides of the vehicle. I was so happy to see Run-Time's other two main VPs for a change. Mrs. Phoenicia was the Lebanese one and she was in a sharp purple suit. Mrs. Role was the West Indian VP, in a shimmering orange suit.

"Mr. Cruz," they greeted.

"Such a long time, Mr. Cruz," Mrs. Role said with a smile.

In we stepped, and Run-Time was sitting there. He greeted me with a quick handshake as the women got back in and closed the doors.

"Yes, it's been a while," I said.

The hoverlimo lifted off.

"How is this even possible?" I asked Run-Time.

He grinned. "You didn't think I could afford an entrance pass?"

"Four entrance passes!"

They laughed.

"Cruz, you need to learn that, sometimes, it's not about the money. It's about the people you know with the money."

One could not land on it, but I stood there on the port, staring at the giant hoverquadrofoil. I had seen pictures of them—a giant seacraft that looked as if it had sprouted four legs to "stand" on the surface of the water—but I had never seen one in real life. It was a high-capacity hovercraft that could fly, hover, stand on the water, and submerge underwater. As we were allowed to board, I decided it would be cool to build a small one for Dot and me. If I could build my own hovervehicle, I could learn how to make one of these too.

Beautiful, luxurious, exquisite. Whatever booshy adjective you could come up with to describe this craft, you'd be able to use legitimately. We even had our own cabin section, which was like an open hotel room for us to sit, watch TV, have food and drinks. Once settled in, Run-Time led us up to the top enclosed observation desk.

This was where everyone was gathering. I looked up at the rainy sky. We stood in a crowd of wealthy elite.

"Excuse me for a moment," Run-Time said to us. We saw him greet a group of men. Run-Time was always doing business.

The hoverquadrofoil began moving. It would skim the surface of the ocean for a little while, passing under one beautifying arch after another of their exclusive dock. This was why Dot couldn't go. Arches were too much like bridges and, because of her phobia, Dot could not go under bridges. We descended into the ocean. This was what I wanted to see— what we all wanted to see.

I expected it to be murky, but the ocean that we moved through was brighter than the surface—that's how powerful the craft's lights were. I wanted to see fish, but there weren't any. What we did see were the outer structures of the colony—antenna and slender towers at first. The entire breadth of Atlantis was visible as the captain did a hard dive and we could see the underwater city in full splendor in front of us. There were smiles and gasps. We leveled off, and the craft sailed in. It was about another half hour until we reached the city and began to dock. Atlantis was beyond huge.

"How many people can it hold?" I asked Run-Time.

"Two hundred thousand at any given time, staff and visitors included."

Our tour guide was a young Brazilian woman with green eyes. All the staff wore white outfits, and she was no different. The first stop was the docking bay, which had a fleet of smaller hoverquadrofoils, and an assorted array of submersibles. Atlantic Pleasure Colony wasn't just a resort; it was a major marine research facility.

The next stop was a closer look at the research facilities. They might have been scientists with advanced degrees, but even in white, they all looked like a bunch of cyberpunks to me. Our guide walked us past the large glass bay wall, where we were able to watch them work. They were talking, eating, and typing—not much excitement there. The guide stopped in front of a dolphin robot hanging in the air on cables. She said it was being retrofitted. I saw it as just a gimmick for tourism, and bet that the same robot had been hanging there for years.

We took the elevators down to the aquarium observation bay. It got colder every level that we went down. We all filed out, and the guide stood in the center, directing us to find any spot to look out. The bay was so large that I was nervous that the water would crush the glass and drown all of us. I'd wanted to see fish; I had fish. I'd thought fish were small, but all the fish we saw through the observation windows, in multiple colors and lengths, were at least twice the size of a human being. Fish eat well at Atlantis!

Now, we were taken back up to the main level to see the hotels. We couldn't walk on the hotel grounds—we weren't guests—but we could observe from behind our glass section. Everybody was in bikinis, even the staff; their bikinis were white. All the non-staff women were wearing their body weight in jewelry. They had swimming pools with crystalline water, holo-tennis courts, indoor skiing, indoor boating, indoor racing—basically, any sport they wanted to play, they could play—masseuses everywhere, roving bartenders everywhere. Play, play, play. Boring.

Run-Time was watching me.

"What?"

"I know you didn't come here for the tour, Cruz."

I smiled.

"All I ask is that, when you do your solo exploring, you don't go anywhere or do anything that will get you in trouble. Atlantis does have its own police force."

"The police and I are good friends."

"I'll remember you said that when they lock you up."

Moments later, I left the tour group and was walking around on my own. The Geek and Windows were coming here to "test" something. What? Why here? Atlantis had a map directory on one of the atrium walls. It was interactive by touch or voice. I played around with it to see all the sections of Atlantis. Clearly, we wouldn't be given the tour of the staff living section or police section. What else did Atlantis have to offer?

"Can we be of assistance?"

"Oh, snaps!" I jumped back from the two men, who both looked as if they were grown from a petri dish—they looked too perfect. "Your hands!"

The men had webbed hands! They laughed.

"It's not real. It's an appliance," one said.

I stepped closer to them and looked more closely.

"Your feet too."

"You can buy both in the Atlantis Pleasure Colony Retail Store. Matching fins, personal underwater lung."

"I want one of those. Where's the store?"

They pointed me to one of the hallways.

"Great. Oh, while you're here. What is this section?"

"Sir, you cannot go there. It's restricted. Those are the power generators for the colony."

"Oh."

"Seriously, sir. Don't go there."

"I won't. I'm going to the store."

"Sir, we know who you are."

"Me?"

"Cruz, the detective."

"You do know me. Who are you?"

"Atlantis Police."

I smiled and, this time, shook their webbed hands. "The police and I are friends."

"Good. Then you won't mind then if we follow you—as friends—to make sure you don't go any place you're not supposed to go. We see you broke away from your tour group. You're not supposed to do that, Mr. Cruz."

"I'm not?"

"Mr. Cruz, shall we skip to the chase?" he asked.

"What does that mean?"

"Do you want to come down to the Atlantis Police Station and keep us company, since you're obviously not here for any tour, and you surely can't afford to stay in the hotel?"

"Hmm, let me think about that offer. How about I go to the retail store first, buy a lot of stuff, including the webbed appliances for myself and the wife, rejoin my tour group, and leave."

"Mr. Cruz, they say Atlanteans are telepathic, but you, sir, could be one of us."

I briskly walked away from them to the Atlantis retail store.

CHAPTER 61

Tag's Friend

Dot loved the Atlantis gear. She wasn't big into swimming, like me, but couldn't wait to dive into a pool and try out her pull-on webbed hand appliances.

"I'll race you!" she said to me.

She didn't need webbed hands and feet to beat me in a pool, for the simple reason that I wasn't going into any public pool. Public pools were nothing but big, teeming vats of nastiness! Unless I were in a fully enclosed diving suit and could get immediately to a CDC-approved anti-contaminant gel pool, I wasn't going in.

I got every bit of information on Atlantis Pleasure Colony that I could find. There was nothing unusual about it. Why would a scientist for a utility megacorporation and cyberpunk guru be interested in that resort? "Test" what? Nothing fit.

Where was Ichi?

It was like that feeling in your gut that just outside the corner of your eye something was lurking. I didn't, for a second, believe that he was gone for good. I knew he was out there, so I had Phishy circulate his photo on the street. I offered a high reward for the first sidewalk johnny that spotted him.

PJ patched an urgent call into the Pony, and I had to pull out of sky traffic to take it.

"What's wrong?" I asked the frantic cyberpunk on my dashboard screen.

"He's gone!"

"Who?"

"Tag. The Ripper got him!"

"What are you talking about? Tag was surrounded by security."

"I know. I was one of them."

"Then how could the Ripper get him? How do you know?"

"Tag is gone! The Ripper got him!"

"How do you know? What did you see?"

"He's gone."

I realized that I was talking to someone who was no mental giant. I was going to start praying today that my son wasn't going to grow up to be a moron. I needed a different approach.

"What's your name?"

"What?"

"What's your name?"

"Chip."

"Okay, Chip. I don't know what you know. I'm a private detective. I need details. Do you want me to help Tag? I know you do, because that's why you called. Tell me the last thing that happened with Tag—before he was gone."

"He was in the den—the same place you met him. He wasn't even plugged in. He was on his mobile. Everything seemed fine, then he went to the bathroom and we all heard him scream. We all ran in there—all of us—and he was gone. We ran outside, and all the guys watching the back were on the ground."

"Dead?"

"They were unconscious—stunned. It took them a while to wake up."

"No one saw anything? No hovercars?"

"One of the guys said a black hovercar was there and flew away, but he didn't see anyone or Tag. It was the Ripper! He said he would get Tag."

"Chip, how are the guys who were stunned?"

"They're fine. What about Tag?"

"Okay, let me get on it. Call PJ immediately if something else comes up or you have some news for me."

"Are you going to find Tag?"

"I'm going to try."

"He's probably dead already!"

"No. Don't say that, because I don't believe he's dead at all."

"How do you know?"

"Based on what you told me. Let me poke around and see what I can see. Chip, one more thing—the Ripper. Did the Geek ever tell anyone who he was?"

"No. But he's here in Metropolis."

"I know. Tag told me."

"He could have helped you, but he's gone too."

"What do you mean?"

"It's a complete End of Times. The Geek is gone. Tag is gone. It's the Ripper!"

"Where was the Geek supposed to be?"

"He disappeared at the airport."

"How? Metro International is a major air and spaceport with its own police. How could he disappear?"

"His tribe was waiting for him. He landed, but he never came out of the gate. The Ripper got him!"

This kid had a real one-track mind. The Ripper was everywhere!

"Was the Geek with anyone on the jet?"

"He was with the Mad Scientist."

"The Mad Scientist? Does he have blue eyes?"

"That's him. The Mad Scientist."

"Why do they call him the Mad Scientist?"

"The same reason they call the Geek, the geek. He's a mad scientist."

"Scientist of what?"

"I don't know."

"I want you to get with your people and find out why."

"Hold on."

He was talking to someone off-screen. They sounded as if they were arguing, and I heard him say "The Ripper got him!" several times. He came back.

"The Mad Scientist is an energy scientist. He works on power. He invented the Holo-Core."

"What's that?"

"A VL power-pack, so you can play your synth anywhere you want without having to be plugged into a power grid. How do you think everyone jacks into VL worlds on the street?"

"Chip, it's not a question I ever thought of."

"How are you going to find them? That's what everyone here wants to know."

"By getting off this video-call and going to find them."

"Watch out for the Ripper. He'll kill you."

CHAPTER 62

Officer Break and Caps

Criminals don't stun people; they shoot them. DCI Fortran had referred to the Ripper as a serial killer. If the Ripper had wanted to kill Tag, he would have done it and gone. Maybe he'd stun him, if he'd wanted to capture him, but I didn't think so. He wouldn't stun a bunch of bodyguards, ball up Tag, and make a hovercar getaway. Only one group stuns people and leaves them alive. That would be the police. The third eye on my third foot was tingling and telling me something was going on.

I saw the sirens in my rearview mirror and began to slow down. The police cruiser flew along my left side and a policeman inside waved for me to follow them. It looked like Officer Caps. I followed them for a few minutes in hovertraffic and then they signaled they were descending. We parked on a tower parking lot, and as I landed, the cruiser flew in reverse to set down right next to mine.

It was Officer Caps, and with the window rolled down, he was looking right at me. Officer Break was in the driver's seat.

"The only reason we're here is because you helped our friend," Officer Break said.

"How is his daughter doing?"

"She's in rehab and alive," he answered. "Cruz, do you have some kind of genetic defect that prevents you from keeping out of trouble?"

"My Ma and Pops always thought so."

"We were never here, but you have a Federal surveillance warrant on you."

"What? That's for psychos, crime bosses, and terrorists."

"I don't know what you did, but you did something."

"I didn't do anything. I just got back from London. How could I have done anything?"

"Listen to me, Cruz. You did something. Innocent people don't get Federal surveillance warrants," Caps said, "but you know that."

"Look up something for me," I said.

"So, you know what you did?" I heard Officer Break's voice.

"Just look it up. I have a theory. Look up a cyberpunk kid, named Tag, with low level cyberhacking beefs."

Officer Break typed into his dashboard keyboard. Something flashed on the screen.

"Your friend is in Federal custody," he said.

At that point, I knew I was in trouble.

"There has to be some kind of clue in the notes," I said. "Something."

"It's so high up not even we can read it—but it has something to do with the Trash Division," Officer Break said.

"I've had nothing to do with the Trash Division for months and months."

"What about those bodies at the River?" Officer Caps asked. "You and a couple of employees of the Trash Division reported it."

"Yeah, it was our civic duty to report it to the police."

"Cruz, you are so full of it."

"But I didn't do anything!"

Caps pointed at me. "You did do something."

Their police cruiser rose in the air and blasted off.

CHAPTER 63

The Trash Boss

Trash Services was in Nil Point—way out, away from the major parts of Metropolis. It was where all the garbage hovertrucks were always flying to and from. The skies around their building headquarters were thick with their vehicles, almost like swarming bees. Trash Headquarters was the center of a huge ground public parking lot with hovershuttles buzzing to get people to and from the main building.

I made it through security and to his offices—seven full-time secretaries—for what? Finally, they let me into the waiting area. I was not in a good mood. A door opened, and the Trash Boss's Chief of Staff came out. I still didn't know why a trashman, who sat behind a desk all day needed a chief of staff. He didn't look as if he were in a good mood either.

"Mr. Cruz, why are you here?"

"I'm here to see Mr. Pyle."

"Why?"

"I'll tell him."

"You'll tell me, and I'll tell him."

"No, I'll tell him and ignore you."

"No, I'll leave you here and ignore you."

"Good, I'll sit in the lobby and wait, and I don't care how long I have to wait."

"How about I call the police? Or maybe the Feds?"

"What's that supposed to mean? Good, you call the Feds. I'll call the police. The police are my friends, so let's see what chaos we can create. I'll call my wife too and have her get the media down here."

"No one cares about—"

When I pulled out my mobile and started dialing, he turned around and ran back through the door.

"Who are you calling?" a voice yelled, startling everyone within earshot. It was the Trash Boss. "Get in here."

Mr. Pyle was the Director of Trash Services. He was an important man in the government; everyone knew it, and he made sure that those who didn't, knew it too. I never liked him.

I closed my mobile and walked his way. He led me through the hall, past all his secretaries, and into his office. His enraged chief of staff was standing near his desk.

"Why are you here? You can't be here."

"Why are you jacking me up with the Feds?"

"You did that yourself!" he yelled at me.

"I've done nothing. I was in London Prime solving cases and saving lives. The only thing I'm doing is following leads—"

"Stop your investigating," he yelled. "That's why you're in Federal trouble."

"I'm a private investigator. I'm supposed to investigate."

"You go do that. The Feds will get you."

"So you won't tell me what I supposedly did?"

"Ask the Feds."

"I will. Maybe I'll suddenly remember a few things while I'm talking with them about you."

"What does that mean?"
"You'll have to ask the Feds."
I stormed out of his office.

CHAPTER 64

Punch Judy

I flew out of Nil Point like a rocket. In less than an hour I was at Let It Ride Enterprises and threw the Pony's keys to Flash to put it into storage. If the Feds were watching or coming after me, then it would be wise to go underground. I had investigation work to do.

I started to wonder if the reason Chief Hub had canceled our meeting was so that I wouldn't stroll into the arms of the Feds. I needed facts, not more speculation.

PJ called me, and I realized that I could be traced by my mobile phone too.

"PJ," I answered.

"Boss, you need to take notes."

"Notes on what?"

"On what I'm about to tell you."

"Tell me then."

"We're on a party line."

"Oh, no. Code talk."

"In a flash."

She hung up.

Wow, now I was acting like gangsters and felons. Being able to talk in code on the fly, so possible eavesdropping Feds wouldn't know what we were talking about.

"Mr. Cruz." Flash ran back to me waving his mobile. "It's your office."

He handed it to me and PJ's face was on the screen.

"Hurry."

"Atlantis in not only a resort colony. There's another Atlantis."

"What? What other Atlantis? Where are you getting this from?"

"It was a tip left for us on the machine. I'll text you the information."

Maybe the Feds did have a legitimate reason to think I was doing something wrong.

"Thanks, PJ."

"Bye."

CHAPTER 65

Road Courier

Tag was a scraper. He would have dissected our conversation and then gone onto the Net to do searches. He would have found this other Atlantis, and that's what would have flagged the Feds. What was Atlantis besides an underwater resort colony?

The hovercab dropped me off at the shore. There weren't any real beaches along the outer Metropolis shoreline because of the constant rain. It had been all washed away eons ago. Between the land and water, all that remained were jagged rocks. Being here was nothing to take lightly. There was the land and directly next to it was a Great Ocean. To look out across it was to be terrified.

I had been waiting for hours in the pouring rain, and I wasn't happy about it. I never used umbrellas, but today, I wished I had one, because I was way beyond being drenched; I was made of water at that point. A yellow light appeared under the dark water. The sky above the ocean made it too dark to see in the distance, but I heard it—the violence of the waves. I was told that the waves of the ocean could be seventy to one hundred feet high. I had flown over it four times in a jet to and from

London Prime but—with my seats always in the inner aisles—never had the chance to look out the windows to see.

A submersible rose from the water and then glided to me. A door opened and I leaned forward to look in. It was blacker than the sky. A flashlight turned on inside, and I saw it was the Road Courier. I got in.

He wasn't wearing his mask this time. There he sat, looking at me. I reached into my jacket.

"I'm soaking wet," I said.

"Ever heard of umbrellas?"

"Next time." I pulled out the plastic pack and handed it to him.

"At least you were bright enough to properly seal up the money." He threw it into his glove box. "Before we go, I need you to be sure that you want to go. Once we leave, there is no refund and I won't stop until I get to the destination and back."

"I understand."

"Are you sure?"

"Before I answer your question, what do you think I should say?"

"I think you're crazy as a bag of mongooses but it's not my money."

"What is Atlantis, since you know what it is?"

"Atlantis is the central hydropower utility plant for Metropolis. It supplies 50 percent of your great city's power. The government isn't smart about most things, but it has genius-level IQ intellect when it takes full advantage of all this rain."

"Hydropower. What's the big deal?"

"Much more than that—millions of turbines everywhere, but no one knows they exist. There are small ones in the drainage vents, larger ones in the water overflow tunnels, and the colossal ones along the coasts and in the ocean itself. There's turbine energy powered by water flow, the rain, and ocean wave motion. It's hydropower that has tapped Earth's rain and the very energy of the Great Ocean—more powerful than a hundred atomic bombs—and it never stops. Metropolis is powered by water.

The Road Courier had given me the proper analogies; I understood now.

He continued. "What's the big deal about everyone knowing about the city's primary source of power for 50 million people and another 50 million people in the surrounding areas? I don't know—maybe that someone could blow it up. That's why it's top-secret. You could get life imprisonment for simply knowing about it, and you want to go there for sightseeing. I ask you again, are you sure?"

I gave a heavy sigh. "The second I contacted you I was committed. I can't back out now. You're the Road Courier. Nothing can happen when you're driving."

"This isn't a road. This is the ocean. When you go into the ocean, police are the least of your worries—and I'm not talking about roving bands of cannibalistic gang members, either. You have one last chance."

"We go," I said.

We learned in school that Metropolis power came from nuclear. Everyone knew that; the power plants were in the Hinterlands. If this were true, then according to the Road Courier, that was a grand ruse for national security reasons.

The submersible had dived fast. He put on some glowing glasses and kept driving. Outside was pitch black. He flicked a switch as he took off the glasses. Now, there was a strange bubble of light around us. It wasn't black waters anymore, but a ghostly light-blue glow.

"How long will it take?"

"A long time," he answered.

The Road Courier was right. We were three hours in, but I wasn't about to fall asleep on this mission. There was no music, no TV entertainment. If he could drive, the least I could do was keep alert.

"What was that?" I asked.

My head turned to look out my passenger window. I had seen what looked like a giant tail of something pass along my side.

"You don't think the oceans are empty, do you?"

"Was that a fish? A shark?"

"Something."

I kept myself from yelling. The "fish" had razor teeth in its mouth and was so large I thought we were about to be eaten. It raced past us on the driver's side, bumping the submersible. He jerked the steering wheel to compensate and keep us on course.

More giant fish swam past. They were not like what I had seen at the Atlantis Pleasure Colony. Those fish looked "nice." These fish were much, much bigger and looked very dangerous. Also, those fish didn't have teeth; these did, which meant they ate flesh.

"These are some big fish. I didn't know fish grew this big in the open ocean. Why are there so many of them? Are they attracted to the light?"

"They like the heat of the water around Atlantis."

"Oh, we're here."

"Not yet."

He slowed down, and we were moving on inertia alone.

"We'll let the river take us by it," he said.

"River?"

"There are undersea rivers, currents in the ocean. We're riding one, so they don't pick up our engine."

He reached into his glove box and handed me the biggest binoculars I'd ever seen. They were heavy, but I knew they were the best tech. He pointed me to where I needed to look out my passenger side.

Atlantis Power Facility. It was a series of gigantic sphere structures hanging in the middle of the ocean. I didn't know how far down we were, but it must have been deep. I saw cables and tubes coming from the surface and the same descending downward. There were giant fish everywhere.

This was what the Geek and Windows had been talking about. But "test" what and how?

We drifted along them, and there were more and larger spheres.

"People live down here?"

"Lots of people do. There are more people here than in the other Atlantis—most of them security."

The Road Courier seemed to know everything.

"Have you ever heard of Vector Corporation?"

"They run the research center at Atlantis—this Atlantis."

That's how they were going to test whatever they were going to test. We drifted past the last structure and thirty minutes later, the Road Courier started driving again. I jumped.

"Was that a human head?" I said.

He chuckled. "That was a dead fish. Your mind is playing with you."

A red light started to flash on his submersible. He kept driving, ignoring it. It was impossible for me to do so.

"What's wrong?"

He didn't answer. I felt our velocity increase more and more. He put on his glasses and flipped off the ghost light. The indicator kept flashing red. I grabbed my seat as he sideswiped a giant fish.

Suddenly, we were rising, and fast—very fast. The submersible broke through the surface, went up, and then crashed down on top of the water. The Road Courier reached under his dashboard. I heard a noise above my head. I looked up and rain was pouring down on me.

A second later, I yelled, as I was blasted out of my passenger seat. I screamed as I went flying through the air into the rain and darkness. I hit the wet pavement with a thud. I was dazed, lying flat at first, then I sat up. I touched my head and my fedora was still there, somehow. I looked around and at the edge of my feet were the jagged rocks. The Road

Courier had ejected me out of his submersible like a sack of potatoes. I stood up slowly and realized that I was at exactly the spot where I was waiting for him.

The trip back was a lot shorter than the trip there. My hands were still shaking. I'd thought I was going to land in the water. The current would have swept me out, the fish would have swallowed me up, and my body would never have been seen again.

My hands grabbed my thighs as I leaned down. Although, I was still shaking, I had to snap out of it and get out of here. I turned and saw them. There were like a million red and blue lights flashing about five miles away down the shore. I wasn't going to wait to see if they were looking for me.

A hovertaxi flew overhead. I jumped up and ran to it. He saw me, stopped, and began to descend. I was out of breath, probably from the cold and fright, but reached it. The driver's side opened.

"I'm glad to see you," I said.

A figure jumped out and attacked me.

"Ichi Jumper has you now!"

PART EIGHT

Mercury-Laced Electric Sheep Buried in My Brain

CHAPTER 66

The Man With the Spoon

This was bad!

The blond-wigged Japanese maniac had captured me at the precise time when I was most vulnerable. I awoke sitting in a chair, looking up at a sunny, cloud-free, blue sky. The streets were packed with happy pedestrians. The skies were filled with hovertraffic. It was Metropolis. I was in a VL World.

This was worse than bad!

He'd set me up. The tip about a second Atlantis had been his doing. All he had to do was follow and wait. He probably had been circling and circling in his hovercab, waiting for me to appear. He'd gambled I'd come back up from the ocean, and I did.

But who was he? How did he know so much about my cases? How did he know about the top-secret Atlantis facility? Who was he?

"Ichi Jumper has your gun. Ichi Jumper has your wrist-gun."

His voice came from the clouds like a deity. I felt my wrist, and the pop-gun was gone, and my shoulder holster was empty.

This was virtual reality! It was not real!

My brain was going to believe everything I was seeing was real when it wasn't. I jumped up from the chair.

"Ichi Jumper has smashed your mobile." Now, there was no way for me to be traced.

"Ichi Jumper warned you, and you did not listen." I began running down the street through the crowd.

"Now, you must die." This was not what I wanted to hear.

I ran at a good pace, looking at the signs—not a neon one anywhere. There was a general market, and I ran into it and down the aisles. They had nothing I was looking for. I went to the counter and made a motion to the counter person for something to write with. He looked at me funny. I pointed to my mouth and shook my head. He smiled, but gave me a stylus pen. I made the gesture to write on something. He pulled an electric notebook from under the counter. I grabbed both and ran out of the store.

I wrote something on the electric notepad and put it in front of every person I saw. I was in a live VL world, all right. They all read what I wrote, but no one acknowledged it. I was running forever.

Finally one said, "I know him."

I wrote "WHERE?" on the pad.

"Can't you talk?" the guy asked me.

I shook my head.

"What are you doing?" Ichi's voice boomed from the sky.

He wrote an address on the pad. I read it and nodded to thank him.

Mr. Ichi hadn't realized that I wasn't some doofus. He could hear me and even see me, but not close enough to see what I was writing on a simple electric notepad. I wasn't a VL world genius, like Tag, but I did know enough.

I kept waving at one after another, but no one would stop. A pink convertible hovercar descended with a bunch of college kids.

"Where are you going?" one girl asked.

I showed them the pad and pointed to the address.

"We can take you there," the girl said. "Hop in."

"Why can't you talk?" a boy asked me.

I wrote: I lost a bet.

They all laughed. "One of those. Why are you going to see him?" he asked.

"Is it a scavenger hunt?" another asked.

I pointed to her and nodded.

"That's fun. We could do that," the driver said.

"Look down there," a girl said.

On the ground, we saw a herd of multi-colored sheep coming down the street.

Is Ichi the Ripper?

The thought popped into my mind. I don't know why I hadn't thought of it earlier, but I could only handle one thing at a time.

We arrived at the dojo and I jumped out and ran inside. The kids were right behind me. There was a crowd gathered, encircling a bald-headed man in a toga, holding a bent spoon. People were chanting and levitating in the air.

I pushed through them and stood before the man.

"How can I help you, my son?"

"A crazy maniac has jacked me into a VL chamber, and I can't get out," I blurted out.

He smiled. "All you need to do is close your eyes."

Electric sheep crashed through the walls from all sides—a stampede! People pulled guns from their robes and started firing lasers at them.

The man put a hand on my shoulder. "You have to have faith, my son. Close your eyes and set yourself free." I noticed the spoon in his hand wasn't bent anymore.

"But I'm plugged in."

"Not there," he said. "Here."

I closed my eyes in the VL world.

There was noise of gun-fire, hooves scraping the hardwood floors, rumbling, falling concrete. I sensed my wrists in the real world. I wiggled my toes in the real world. I clenched both fists. I could perceive the straps restraining my wrists.

"Ichi Jumper will administer the dose!"

I ignored him. I perceived the straps restraining my ankles. I could feel the weight of the VL helmet on my head. I strained to stretch my wrist straps as much as I could, relaxed, then did so again.

"Ichi Jumper will not be ignored." I pulled my arms out of the straps and grabbed for the helmet.

"Ichi Jumper will not allow that!"

His hands were on mine, fighting me. I punched in his direction, but hit nothing. He was jamming the helmet back onto me. I grabbed his wrists, instead, with all my might. He got the helmet back on me but was trying to pull free from me.

I felt a sharp kick to my chest and his hands were free. I yanked the helmet off and yelled as the eye sealant ripped off some of my skin. I caught the next kick in the mouth. My head snapped back, but I managed to open my eyes.

Ichi Jumper was running in place. Why? What kind of violence was he about to unleash on me? I threw the helmet at him, but he slapped it away.

"Ichi Jumper will beat you to death."

I didn't even care why he was after me anymore as the blood dripped down my mouth. I glared at him with my eyes squinted.

"I'm going to hunt you down and kill you, you maniac."

"No. Ichi Jumper will beat you to death now."

I didn't even have a chance to react as he kicked me in the head so hard I thought that my head was going to come off. The entire VL chair tilted over and I crashed to the ground.

He jumped up in the air to come down on my head. I managed to knock him somewhat off target, but he landed on my side, and I yelled again. Then he just started kicking me—quick kicks, kicks that did cumulative damage.

The door was blown open. Ichi stopped and instinctively jumped out of the window as if he were diving into a swimming pool. Feds swarmed in.

They got me out of the chair and got me to a sitting position. All my ears locked on was what one of them said to the other.

"Sir, he got away."

PART NINE

Frenergy

CHAPTER 67

The Feds

I had never been beaten up before; I had beaten people up before. I'd defended myself, but never had the stuffing kicked out of me like that. I didn't like it.

This time, I was in Metro General. I was hurting too much to worry about the sea of germs I was lying on in the bio bed. Worse was the unfashionable white hospital gown they had me in. They had better not have damaged my hat.

I was hooked to all kinds of wires going to monitors on the bed. The nurse had been in earlier; I'd told her to turn off the TV on the wall, and I didn't want to hear any music either. I hurt too much for any entertainment. Peace and quiet was what I needed.

Two Feds strolled into the room, wearing their black suits. I turned my head away and closed my eyes. I was not in any mood for them.

"Mr. Cruz, is that any way to treat the people who saved your life?" one of them said.

I turned my head back to them and opened my eyes. "Go away."

"Mr. Cruz, we have a lot of questions for you."

"Mr. Cruz, we didn't like the fact that you were trying to hide from us. Lucky for you, we're better at tracking than you are at hiding," said the other Fed.

"Give me your mailing address, and I'll send you a cookie."

"Mr. Cruz, you've got a smart mouth. Too bad your friend didn't do more damage to it."

"How could you have let him get away?" I asked.

"We were after you, not him. We didn't even know he was there or that you were being held captive."

"Where is he? You're the great trackers. Why can't you track him? He's a suspect."

"Suspect in what?"

"The Electric Sheep Massacre case."

"Mr. Cruz, Chief Hub and DCI Fortran told us you might try that. Your friend isn't the Ripper. We're not going to be your personal bounty hunters."

"Fine. Tell me where he is, and I'll get him myself."

"You don't look like you're going anywhere for a while, and we know you like to shoot people."

"People like to shoot me."

"Mr. Cruz, this is now a police matter. If you shoot an unarmed person, that's called a felony. You don't get to pick and choose which laws you want to follow and when to follow them."

"Go away." I closed my eyes again.

"Why were you at Atlantis, Mr. Cruz?"

"I was invited by my best friend to see what a high-class underwater resort was like."

"Mr. Cruz, we're not going to play games with you. You know that's not what we mean."

"That's the only Atlantis I know."

"We know you know which Atlantis we mean, which, we remind you, is classified and can't be shared with anyone, including your wife. We also remind you that we were waiting for you."

"Yeah, Mr. Cruz, you know, the hundred and one police sirens."

"Lucky for you we saw that hovertaxi, Mr. Cruz, or you'd be dead right now."

"I told you. Give me the mailing address, and I'll send each of you a cookie."

"Mr. Cruz, knowledge of that Atlantis facility can mean an automatic trip to Federal headquarters on an indefinite hold. Trespassing into waters of the Atlantis isn't merely a felony. It's treason."

"I've noticed that you haven't thrown on the handcuffs yet. What about Tag? How did that indefinite interrogation work out for you? Have you released him yet?"

"He's been released," a Fed answered.

"So, you're harassing me, now? You've got nothing. I only know about one Atlantis. I don't know anything else. If you've got the proof of something else, then arrest me. Otherwise, go away. I had some crazy maniac try to kill me, and you aren't part of any solution I need. Go away."

"Mr. Cruz, we're going to let you rest a bit, but we'll be back. You're not going to talk your way out of this, and we have no problem putting you in indefinite hold, just out of spite."

"Good. Go away until then."

I pressed the nurse call button on the bio-bed.

The Feds were still standing there when the nurse appeared.

"Are you okay, sir?" she asked.

"Nurse, these men are bothering me. They won't let me rest after my near-death ordeal. I'm suffering from post-traumatic stress, and they're causing me more psychological distress."

"Gentlemen," she said to them, "I must insist you leave at once."

The Feds shook their heads, smiling, and walked out of the room.
"Do you need anything?"
"No, just peace and quiet."
"Call me if you need anything."

CHAPTER 68

China Doll

Dot was mad, but once she saw how badly I'd been beaten up, all was forgotten.

I was finally going home. The doctors and nurses wanted me to stay in the hospital longer, but I wanted to go. Dot got them to put all my things in a bag and a nurse had gotten a hoverchair for me. I could walk, but barely.

"Did you get my phone too from PJ?" I sat on the edge of the bio-bed, wincing. It even hurt to talk.

Dot handed me my mobile. I opened it and opened the picture files. I lifted up the phone to show the picture of Ichi Jumper.

"He's dead," I said. "I'm just warning you now. There's going to be some serious violence."

She studied the photo then looked up. "That's fine with me."

A male nurse helped her get me in the hoverchair and helped us to the parking bay. I couldn't wait to get home and hit my man-couch. I was too weak and tired for a full-course shower, so my man-couch was where I would be sleeping—so long as the Hell Spawn weren't around. I expected to sleep for days.

I couldn't sleep. After only a few hours, I just got up. My brain wouldn't rest. There was too much to do. I hobbled to my home office in the apartment and called PJ.

"It was a set-up?" she asked. "He gave you the tip? How did he know?"

"I don't know. I still don't know who he is. No one does, but you have his picture. Make sure to watch for him, and you have my permission to knock his head off if you see him."

"Oh, yes, I'll punch his skull in, this Ichi Jumper."

"Get that client in the office today."

"What time?"

"Whenever he can get there. Then call me and let me know."

"Okay. How bad did he beat you?"

"Bad."

"You need to soak in the tub with healing salts in the water. It works."

"Is it a remedy from your Enfantes Terribles gang days?"

"No. It's from my grandma. Do it. It works."

CHAPTER 69

PJ

I couldn't sleep. After only a few hours, I just got up. My brain wouldn't rest. There was too much to do. I hobbled to my home office in the apartment and called PJ.

"It was a set-up?" she asked. "He gave you the tip? How did he know?"

"I don't know. I still don't know who he is. No one does, but you have his picture. Make sure to watch for him, and you have my permission to knock his head off if you see him."

"Oh, yes, I'll punch his skull in, this Ichi Jumper."

"Get that client in the office today."

"What time?"

"Whenever he can get there. Then call me and let me know."

"Okay. How bad did he beat you?"

"Bad."

"You need to soak in the tub with healing salts in the water. It works."

"Is it a remedy from your Enfantes Terribles gang days?"

"No. It's from my grandma. Do it. It works."

CHAPTER 70

Run-Time

"**I** hear you got quite a beating," Run-Time said. His face looked concerned from my video screen on the side-table phone.

"I'll live. Is Bugs around?"

"He's on site today."

"Can you spare him to pop over to my office sometime today?"

"Absolutely. Bug is a free agent. He goes where he wants."

"I'll have PJ call him."

"What's this I hear about you and the Feds?"

"I'll work it out. It's another misunderstanding, but I'll work it out. Have there been any more drug-induced attacks?"

"Not a one. My son plays those VL games, so he's the authority in my house. He says that the entire VL community is unified. Anyone who goes into a VL world is to enter armed with a laser weapon, and any electric sheep you see, no matter how cute, you're to gun them down."

I couldn't help but laugh a bit, despite the pain.

"Yes, I know. You can't go into a VL game unarmed and you have to watch out for fluffy electric sheep. We had banned my son from all VL when this madness first started, but he pleaded with us once the crisis was supposedly over and, get this, presented his mother and me an 'entertainment safety proposal.' I read it, and he changed my mind. He can go into his VL games, and I send in a few armed bodyguards to watch over him. Cruz, you can't make this stuff up."

CHAPTER 71

Phishy

Next on the video-call list was Phishy.

"Cruz, you look like you fell out of a hovercar while it was flying."

"Thanks for that, Phishy. I have a job for you."

Whenever I said those words to him, he lit up and smiled.

"Sure, Cruz. What's the job? Are we going to get that guy for you?"

"Phishy, you and the sidewalk johnnies are not to go anywhere near him, if you see him. They are to report in, and that's it. I sent a team of military mercs after him, and he put all of them in the hospital, too. Stay away from him. Hear me, Phishy?"

"I hear you, Cruz."

"If he's too dangerous for us, then he's too dangerous for you."

"Okay, Cruz."

"What I need from you are weapons."

"Weapons?"

"He took my pop-gun, so I need another one."

"He didn't get the omega-gun, did he?"

"Fortunately not, but I need a pop-gun replacement and need to borrow a bit more."

"More?"

"When he attacks me again—and he will—I'm not going to be strapped to any VL chair, so I'm going to need a lot more than the pop-gun and my regular piece."

"You want to be a walking arsenal." Phishy was laughing.

I nodded. "I have the wife's permission."

He laughed. "This guy is so dead!"

CHAPTER 72

Hub

"Mr. Cruz." Chief Hub took my call right away, which I didn't expect. "When are you going to finish your questioning with the Feds?"

"Soon."

"How soon?"

"When I'm able to walk and don't need a straw to eat my food."

"You seem to be up and around to me."

"Who is this bald Japanese guy with the blond wig? Why can't anyone tell me who he is?"

"Because he's not in the criminal databases. Not even the Federal ones."

"What about Up-Top?"

"What about them? Up-Top does its own thing."

"Can you send the photo to them to run?"

"I'm working for you now, am I?"

"Why did you tell the Feds that he's not the Ripper? How do you know that?"

"Because we know."

"You don't know who he is."

"True, but we know he isn't the Ripper because we know who the Ripper is."

"Who?"

"Mr. Cruz, you are not a law enforcement officer. You're a civilian, but you keep forgetting that."

"Will you send the photo to Up-Top to ID this maniac?"

"I will. I'll even call you back if we get a hit. However, you'd better finish your questioning with the Feds sooner rather than later. They don't like you the way I do, and they're likely to haul you in at the most inconvenient time they can think of."

"I'll call them."

"Do that. Bye."

CHAPTER 73

Ma, Pops and Hell Spawn

Chief Hub was right. The Feds probably had both the Concrete Mama and Liquid Cool offices staked out, and if any of their agents spotted me and it wasn't in the direction of the Federal HQ, I would be scooped up faster than the speed of light. I was too injured to drive, and I wasn't going near another hovercab for the foreseeable future, so I looked through my mobile Rolodex.

I heard noise in the apartment. Dot was at work, and Ichi wasn't *that* good, so it could only be the Hell Spawn.

There was a knock on my closed home office door.

"Cruz."

That was Ma's voice!

"It's open."

My Ma and Pops came in. My mother ran to me. She held my face and looked me up and down.

"What bad man did this to my boy?" she asked in her heavy Spanish accent.

"A very bad man."

My Pops walked with a wood-sheathed sword wherever he went. It wasn't until my first major case that I'd learned what I'd never knew growing up; he actually could use that sword—he was a Kendo master! These days, he liked to wear a dark fedora similar to mine.

"What are the cops doing to catch this man?"

"Nothing."

They were surprised by my answer.

"What does this *cabron* look like?" he asked.

My parents had come at the perfect time. I printed up a stack of photos to hand out. I gave Pops one, and I gave Ma one. They looked at it, while speaking Spanish to each other. My Ma folded it up and put it in her purse. I saw something shiny in there.

"Ma, are we still carrying guns in purses? I thought we weren't going to be doing that anymore."

She grinned. "No hablo Ingles."

"No hablo Ingles, huh?" I said, smiling.

My parents-in-law appeared behind them and reached out their hands for photos. I gave the Hell Spawn one each, and they studied it. Mrs. Wan turned to someone behind her and let loose a bunch of Chinese. Behind her was a five-foot Chinese woman, who looked to be one hundred years old.

"Give her one too," Mrs. Wan directed.

"Who is she? Your mother?"

"Ha." Mrs. Wan took another photo. "This is my grandmother. Wans live a long time, very long life like the dragon."

Good grief. I was going to have to deal with the Hell Spawn until my dying day.

Mr. Wan held up the photo. "I see him, I cut him!"

"This man is very dangerous. I sent a whole team of military mercenaries after him and he put them all in the hospital. If you see him, stay away from him. Call the police immediately. Call me. Stay away from him."

They all completely ignored me.

My Pops unsheathed his sword and sliced the air. My Ma pretended to quick-draw an invisible gun and even added the sound-effects "Pow-pow!"

"Cut!" That was Mr. Wan's favorite saying. "Cut him!"

Mrs. Wan pulled a big-ass gun from behind her back. She was packing guns in her back waistband, now?

"We dangerous people, too," she said.

Even her grandmother was holding a tiny gun in her bony hand.

I needed to get away from all these crazy people immediately.

CHAPTER 74

Space Visitor

I got a call and Dot arranged my transportation for the day, courtesy of Run-Time. I'd have my own hoverlimo to take me wherever I needed. That was music to my ears.

My first stop, after escaping my apartment filled with the parents and the Hell Spawn, was to Federal HQ. It was time to get the whole thing over. I wasn't going to tell them anything; they knew it, but they'd keep me in there all day, anyway.

That's exactly what they did. I sat in the same interrogation room from morning to evening, and all that changed was the team of Fed interrogators. They asked. I answered. I lied. They knew I was lying. They couldn't do anything about it. I couldn't leave until they were bored of asking the same questions over and over again.

When the marathon session was over, an agent led me to a Metro police officer.

"Where am I going now?" I asked the male officer.

"Police Central. Where else?"

"Chief Hub?"

"Chief Hub is off-duty. Someone from Interpol."

We were able to use a general-purpose conference room, where the pale brunette spacewoman waited. She was an Interpol agent on rotation duty on Earth to liaise with both local and Federal police forces.

"Your man wasn't in the Interpol criminal database, but he was in the general space population directory. He was born in space. The probable reason you've had so much trouble capturing him is that he is a GMH, as with virtually all off-worlders."

"Genetically modified human," I said. "What else do you know about him?"

"That's all we have. He left with his parents to live on Earth as a child, we assume to Japan."

"That was almost 40 years ago. Your GMH maniac has been running around my planet all that time."

"Since he's not in any Earth criminal database, he's been an upstanding citizen until he met you. What did you do to him?"

"I didn't do anything to him. I'd never met him before he started stalking me and trying to kill me."

"Yes, all that sounds very plausible. He woke up one day and decided to kill you for no reason."

"Are you going to do something about him? He's one of your GMHs."

"You say GMH as if he's some kind of super human. He's not and neither is any other GMH. They're not from the planet Krypton. No superpowers. Maybe the reason you've been unable to capture him is because you all are not that competent."

"I'm quite competent. You're not going to help us get him?"

"*Get* him? He's an Earth citizen. We have no jurisdiction."

I wasn't at all pleased.

She smiled. "Your planet is quite interesting. You don't like humanoid robots, but you have no issues with swapping out your organic body parts for robotic ones to turn yourself into cyborgs. You have this irrational fear of anything genetically modified when, in fact, your whole planet's population is. Do you all really still believe your food is unmodified? Or that your increasing 'natural' life expectancy is because of normal evolution? No wonder your planet is ravaged by crime and depression."

"We should be perfect like Up-Toppers?"

"You said it, not me."

"There's no crime Up-Top?"

"I didn't say that, but nowhere near the levels here."

"Because no one lives up in space. We have elementary schools with more people than your space colonies, the moon, and Mars populations combined. What are you going to do about this maniac?"

"The person you're referring to is an Earth citizen, so nothing."

"Exactly the answer I expected."

"You enjoy your wonderful planet, Mr. Cruz."

"If your Up-Top paradise is so perfect, why do you have so many suicides?"

"That is not true. That's Earth propaganda, created by your own psychological community."

"We may not be perfect Up-Toppers, but we have purpose, however miserable. Humans weren't meant to sit around all day and only do yoga and finger paint sunsets all day the way you all do. I like my planet fine."

"Your planet is happy to have you. You are the perfect couple. I'll go back to my Up-Top and leave you two together."

CHAPTER 75

Windows and The Geek

Now that I was done with all people and places law enforcement, I could have my life back. The plan was to swing by a retail store. I wanted to get something for Tag, who was still traumatized from getting scooped up by the Feds. I told him, better them than the Ripper. But I wanted to buy him something. What do you get a cyberpunk who spends more time in a VL world than the real world? Snacks. They're either always eating or doing drugs. I wasn't buying drugs.

PJ called me again. What she told me made me sit up straight.

"When?"

"He said he'll call back."

"I'll be ready."

"Are you sure you're comfortable going back into VL after the last time?"

"If that's where he wants to meet, that's where I'll meet him."

"Oh, Bugs and the client finished all the work."

"Good. Call me when he calls back."

As the hour approached, I was getting nervous. It seemed I *was* getting a bit scared about going back into a VL world after my Ichi ordeal. I arrived at Tag's new "command center" in the basement of another VL den with dozens of boxes of snacks for VLers. Not only did I win him over, but everyone else in his little VL den, once the boxes started getting opened. I expected the snacks to last only a day.

Tag allowed me to use one of his VL chambers—no more helmets and eye plugs. No more of that low-tech nonsense. More importantly—for my comfort—Tag was going to go in, too.

It was the surface of a barren moon—a large spaceship had crashed, buried in the ground in the distance. "Blue Eyes" and the Geek watched me approach. I was riding a horse to them. I stopped and got down. In addition to my normal outfit, I had both a portable laser cannon and a sword strapped to my back.

"No chance of any electric sheep here," I said.

"It's not a very nice thing to give people business cards with listening devices," Windows said. His bionic eyes seemed even bluer in VL.

"I know I have terrible manners. I'll have to have my Ma retrain me, or my wife can do it."

"Was that you?" the Geek asked. "Was that you in that submersible the other night? That was incredibly stupid."

"I've never seen the real Atlantis before, so I went to see it."

"Why?" he asked. "What were you going to do? What was the purpose?"

"I wanted to see where you and Blue Eyes were going to test your weapon."

"Weapon? We don't have a weapon."

Window put a hand on the Geek's arm. "He's just trying to bait you. He doesn't know anything." Windows looked at the horse. "You ride horses, too, Mr. Cruz?"

"Yeah."

"What's his name?"

"Tag."

"Well, at least you're capable of telling the truth some of the time," the Geek said. "Hi, Tag," he said to my horse.

"Why don't you tell me the truth about everything?" I said. "Who killed the two guys at the River?"

"The Ripper did that," the Geek said.

"Why?"

"He was trying to steal the device," he answered.

"We can't tell him anything," Windows said to him.

"Then why did you call me here, Mad Scientist?" I asked.

"Because, Mr. Cruz, you're going to help us get out from all this. We hear you have friends in high places."

"Me?"

"You've done it before. You can do it again. We can pay."

"I'm not doing anything until I know everything."

"Why did you say weapon?" the Geek asked. "What are you thinking—that we're terrorists about to blow up Atlantis?"

"I don't know you. Why not?"

"We're dedicated to peace for all humanity."

"Please stop. My horse and I will start to gag."

"You can laugh if you want," Windows said, "but it's true. This is all for humanity."

"What was the Electric Sheep Massacre about?" I asked. "Let's start there."

"The Ripper was getting revenge."

"Revenge?"

"The three of us invented the device."

"Then you killed him," I said. "But you didn't kill him."

"He wanted to use the device for pure greed, sell it to the highest bidder."

"So, you two peace lovers murdered your partner for the good of humanity? Listen to yourselves. You sound like every criminal crew out there."

They both were not happy being called criminals.

"What's the device?" I asked. "What is this all about?"

"Free energy," the Geek said.

"We've invented a way for anyone, all the people of Earth, to have access to free energy," Windows told me.

"What are you talking about?"

"The device converts water to pure energy. All you need is water, and you can power anything forever," he said. "No more energy grids or production and distribution facilities, no more turbines or dams. We cut out the government middleman between the people and energy—forever."

I had to stand there thinking for a moment. The implications of what they revealed were so monumental I didn't think my brain fully grasped it all.

"How did you kill the Ripper before?" I asked.

"I—drowned him," the Geek said. "He was getting more erratic. We think there might have been radiation poisoning involved in the initial tests years ago."

"Radiation? Your device is nuclear?"

"It's a portable fusion device," Windows replied.

"Fusion is nuclear, isn't it?"

"It's not what you're thinking at all. It's completely harmless, and the fail-safes are 'fool'-proof."

"The guys at the River were testing it there? Why?"

"We couldn't run the final tests at Atlantis, but we needed a large secure water supply," the Geek said. "The tunnels near the River were perfect—secluded, underground, and we knew the backwash schedules."

"How do you know it was the Ripper?"

"He called us," Windows said.

"He called you?"

"Yes. He was torturing them to get the access code to the device. He didn't know we could remotely detonate it, and that's exactly what I did. He killed them while we watched. He used a knife."

"Why did he kill all those innocent people?"

"He's insane," Windows answered. "We don't know why—cover-up the original massacre, make people think it was a freak accident, or show us what he could do in VL. Think of all the power he has now that he's back from the dead."

"He went after my community," the Geek said. "They were targets."

"The original Massacre was of your people?"

"Yes," Windows answered. "We secretly put the meeting together—handpicked everyone who was there. It was sold as a 'new energy' symposium to talk about alternative energy sources, terrestrial and in space, but it was really to prepare for the release of the device. Besides us, only he would know the significance of that gathering."

"Maybe you didn't drown him," I said to the Geek.

"He was dead. I was sure of it."

"But here he is. Will he be able to do it again," I asked, "kill any more people in VL?"

"No," the Geek answered. "No one will be able to do what he did ever again."

"But how did he do it? How do you kill someone in VL?"

Windows replied, "Mr. Cruz, he's not killing them in VL. That impossibility hasn't changed. He's *finding* them in VL. The impossibility he changed is the impossibility of hacking into their VL interface devices—chairs, chambers, and helmets."

"He was killing them with the hardware, not the software," the Geek chimed in.

"VL devices can't fry your brains and eyes," I countered.

"They can if you tell the power grid to send thousands of volts to a specific outlet node."

"Will he, or anyone be able to do it again?"

"No one will be able to do what he did ever again," the Geek repeated.

He said it with such unshakable certainty, and because of that, I was certain. He was the VL guru, a genius, so he would know. He probably had already made sure every cyberpunk on the planet and Up-Top knew how to prevent the Ripper's homicidal abilities in VL and those of any other future Ripper-wannabes permanently.

"What's the plan for this device?"

"We'll hand it off to the Refinery," the Geek answered.

"Not as dramatic or orderly as the original plan," Windows added, "but the effect will be the same."

"The Refinery is in London Prime."

"The Refinery is everywhere," the Geek corrected me. "We'll give it to them and they will give it to the people of Earth."

"Then it will be Paradise on Earth?"

"That, Mr. Cruz, is exactly what will happen," Windows said. "The people have never had free energy. We will be able to transcend all economies and truly be free to each live up to our unique and full potential."

"We'll end the power of world governments and world megacorporations forever," the Geek added.

"What does any of that mean? Why does this topic keep coming up with me? People will be free to live up to their potential? People will be free to sit in their legacy housing all day, doing yoga, finger-painting, drugs, sex, booze, and VL all day. What's wrong with you two?"

"We obviously have a higher view of humanity than you do," Windows said. "Hey, maybe we're wrong, but let's find out. How much to get us out of Metropolis after the digital hand-off?"

"What about the Ripper?"

"Don't worry about him," the Geek answered. "He'll be disappeared, and this time, he'll never return."

These two were very violent for a couple of peaceniks who wanted to "liberate" Earth's humanity.

CHAPTER 76

The Ripper

The only thing Tag was thinking about was the notion that the world would have free energy. The fact that the Ripper would be dead also added to his euphoria. He promised not tell anyone, but he was jumping around as if his legs were perpetual pogo sticks.

I still felt that I didn't completely understand the full implications of what Windows and the Geek wanted to unleash. I had to get educated fast!

Before I went anywhere, I needed to gear up. Phishy arrived in a hovercar, driven by a couple of his crazy friends (literally, two of them were sitting in the driver's seat). He was the man I was waiting for, with a large black briefcase in each hand.

First, I took my tan slicker coat off and put on my bulletproof vest, then my shoulder holster. Phishy fitted me with my new pop-gun on the left arm, after rolling down my sleeve. He gave me a new ammo belt with its bullet clips, laser pellet clips, and anti-personnel chemical sprays, then strapped on a new girdle pouch, filled with stun sticks. Phishy helped me put my slicker back on. My omega-gun went in the holster, and another smaller gun was clipped on my belt.

"Cruz, you're set."

The entire VL den of kids, including Tag, was watching the whole time. I noticed the nervousness in their faces.

"I'm going to avenge all the cyberpunks in the world and kill the Ripper!"

Everyone yelled, "Yeah!"

The place was not in VL. Windows and the Geek were waiting by the real Valves, and they heard the Ripper coming before he'd even appeared. The smirking man walked to them with his hands in his pockets. He had dirty-blond, shoulder-length hair and wore a long tan brown jacket with oversized combat boots.

"Look at this," he said to them.

"The murderer," Windows said.

"I hope you two aren't going to try to kill me again," the Ripper said.

"You killed our friends!" the Geek yelled.

"Did you think I'd let you kill me and steal the device that I co-invented? If I had to come back from the grave and kill all of you, then that's what I'd do."

Windows stepped to him, unafraid. "You didn't only kill all our colleagues in the VL lab. You killed innocent young people, who had nothing to do with this."

"There's no such thing as the innocent. Are you two going to give me what you owe me?"

"All you are is about the profit and greed!" the Geek yelled.

"So says the two men who are part of the one percent. You've never had to starve, never had to go without."

"That justifies what you did?" Windows asked.

"What *I* did? *You* were the ones who tried to kill *me.*"

"Because you were going to kill us," Windows said.

The Ripper smiled and then laughed. "Well, you do have a point there. Where's what you owe me?"

"We'll give you the device—" Windows said.

"—but after we give it to everyone else too," the Geek added.

"Yes, the new world order," the Ripper said, "where there is no money or desire, no class distinctions. Well, sorry, I'm not interested in such a world. I want to be filthy rich, first. After I die, then I don't care what you do."

The Geek was pointing a gun at him.

"No drowning this time, I see," the Ripper said.

"You killed Hue and Jr.," Windows said. "It only seems fairs that you join them at the very place you did it."

Windows and the Geek felt it, then heard the growing rumble.

"What's that noise?" the Ripper asked.

The Geek watched him closely, his fingers getting twitchy on the gun's trigger. "It's our friends—your enemies."

The Ripper laughed. "The unwashed masses, who can't help me get to Up-Top to become one of the uber-rich—but it's okay."

They began to appear. The Refinery was here! Hundreds of thousands of people—on hoverplatforms or by jetpack—running, flying, and driving—heading to them.

Ripper watched them, laughing. "You're killing me in front of a crowd?"

"No one is going to miss you," the Geek said.

"Did you think I'd let you kill me again and steal my invention again?"

"What did you do?" Windows asked.

"I told a *few* people about the device."

"Who?"

"Everyone in this who matters!"

CHAPTER 77

Everyone Who Matters

The Ripper suddenly grabbed Windows, using him as a shield, while he drew his own concealed weapon.

"Hey, Geek. Look at this. A high-stakes shootout in front of an audience. Reality VTV! Who says reality is fake?"

"Let him go!" the Geek yelled.

"Drop the gun, or I'll kill him."

"No!"

"Either shoot through him and kill me, or I'll shoot through him and kill you," the Ripper said to Geek. "Windows, baby, you're dead either way."

I blasted a hole through his head, and the Ripper fell face-first to the ground. Windows was startled, and the Geek lowered his gun with a shocked expression. I came out of the main tunnel of the Valves, where I was watching them, my omega-gun in hand.

The full Refinery crowd had reached them. Tag was one of them and he ran up and started kicking the Ripper's corpse. Soon, all kinds of cyberpunks jumped in to join in on the fun.

Tag smiled and pointed at me. "That's my friend, everyone! I told you he'd kill the Ripper!"

From the applause, it was as if I were some rock star. That's when I pointed my gun at Windows and the Geek. The applause stopped.

"What are you doing?" Windows asked.

"Give me the device."

"Why would we do that?" the Geek asked.

"When you all told me what you told me, I sensed it was incredibly dangerous, but I couldn't grasp all the implications. When you don't know something, ask. That's what I did. I asked a lot of people I trust, and I can articulate it, now. You can't give it out."

"Why?" Windows asked. "It's better to give it to one of the megacorps? We wouldn't give it to ours; why would we give it to any other? That's not why we invented it."

"We're making a better world," the Geek said.

"A better world. What do you think the megacorps will do? The world governments?"

"The entire world will have free power," the Geek said. "That's the point. Empowerment for everyone."

"You two can't be so naive. The planet is run by the governments on one side and the megacorps on the other. It's a stalemate. Neither is stronger than the other. Neither one can overpower the other. That's what keeps us all free. You put this device out there, then the megacorps will take over the planet."

"That's not true."

"Yes, it is, and you know it. You'll tip the scales to their favor."

"The government would have free power, too," the Geek countered.

"The government controls infrastructure and power. If they don't control the power, they have no leverage over the megacorps. You two idiots will start a war. That's a war the megacorps could win."

"The government has the police. They'll maintain—"

"I've been a detective for a relatively short time, but you know I'm friends with police and know quite a lot about the megacorps, most of which I will never be able to reveal publicly. If there was a war between government police and corporate samurai soldiers and all the other mercenaries they have, I am not convinced, for a second, that the police would win outright. Even if they did, what would be left would be too weak to fend off the crime world. I'm not risking that war, and neither are you. Give me the device."

"The people must be empowered," the Geek said.

"Have you ever been to a municipal town hall meeting, or watched the citizen-on-the-street interview segment of the news? We don't want *the people* empowered; we want the *right* people empowered. People who will actually sit down, roll up their sleeves, get informed—not endlessly rattle off platitudes 'let's make the world a better place' or 'empower the people'—and do the work. You two are purposely ignoring the fact that 'empowering the people' empowers the megacorps too. That's the problem. We don't want wars. Were you two not paying attention in history class? Why do we all live in monolith towers with nuclear shields still and it rains all the time? Give me the device."

"No," the Geek said.

"Since you won't listen to reason, then I'll appeal to your innate desire for self-preservation. What do you think the Ripper meant when he said, 'I told everyone who matters?'" I asked them. "You two have already started the war."

"What are you talking about?" the Geek asked.

"Two armadas are approaching us—one is the Metropolis government and the other is the Council of Corporations."

"You're trying to trick us." Windows looked off in the distance, and I knew he was focusing his bionic eyes.

"Look at the geo satellites. That's what I'm doing." I handed them my mobile, and they looked at the screen. "They're going to put you two in a lab, strap you in a VL chair, and strip your mad scientist skills right out of your brains. One, or both of them, are going to kill all your people,"—that caused quite a reaction of fear from the crowd—"kill both of you and me, and then start killing each other and the war begins. All idiots, like you, say you want Paradise, but how many millions have been killed on this planet by people offering Paradise?"

"There's nothing wrong with wanting Paradise, Mr. Cruz," Windows said.

"True, but let's get there without killing everyone. Humanity hasn't evolved to that point, yet. Give me the device, and I'll make sure neither one of them gets it. You two need to disappear and make sure no one ever finds you. I'm sure you can get your cyberpunks to make sure every trail points back to the Ripper as the sole inventor of the device."

The three of us looked at his corpse on the ground.

"They're almost here!" someone yelled.

The Geek pressed the top of his left arm, and it opened.

"Everyone is a cyborg these days," I remarked.

He pulled out the device, a nine-inch cylindrical tube.

"This is the last prototype," he said and handed it to me.

"You have the remote detonator?" I asked Windows.

"I do." He smirked and handed it to me.

"You two better get out of here."

"One day, the planet will be ready," the Geek said.

"Yeah, it will, but not in our lifetime."

Windows and the Geek walked into the Refinery crowd, sat on a hovercouch and then the entire mass of people and machines began to do a U-turn. I watched the Refinery's "living city" fly away. However, another growing rumble was approaching, more formidable than anything any of us had ever seen in our lives.

It was just the corpse and me in front of the Valves when they arrived. I had beheld a sight that no other Metropolis dweller had seen—the supercity's entire 500,000 jetpacked police force in one place. That was during my first major case, when the former criminal organization, known as the Animal Farm Syndicate, thought they could take over the city. They thought wrong.

This was that, squared to the nth degree. A larger police hovercruiser, a model that I had never seen before, landed, and Chief Hub exited not in uniform, but in military battle armor flanked by lines of other fully armored police troopers. The sky was black with police hovercruisers.

Opposite them were hovercraft to fill the other half of the sky. One craft descended, and a Caucasian woman in a kimono-style slicker exited with two suits, a male and female, and dozens of helmeted samurai soldiers, swords strapped to the back and laser machine-guns in hand.

There were three forces of nature in the universe in Metropolis—the government, megacorporations, and crime. Two of those forces were about to face off, and should they come to blows, no one—including me—would be left unscathed.

The woman walked forward to where Hub waited.

"Police Chief Hub, it's an honor to meet you again."

"Madam President," he said, "I don't think I've ever seen the President of the Council of Corporations outside of her tower headquarters."

She smiled. "Even I venture out into the field when necessary for business."

"Do you always go to such meetings with your personal air-armada?" he asked.

"Is it the practice of the Metropolis Police Department to interfere in legal business matters between clients, in military gear? Are we at war, Police Chief Hub?"

"No, Madam President, but I was about to ask you the same thing."

The woman looked at the corpse at my feet. She looked at me and sighed.

"Our client seems to be dead," she said.

"Oh, no," I said. "He's dead. There's nothing 'seeming' about it."

"Did you kill him?" she asked.

"Yes, I did."

"Do private detectives often murder citizens?"

"When they try to shoot someone, yes—and that's called self-defense. Besides, he's the multiple murderer responsible for deaths here in Metropolis and in London Prime."

"It's too bad there won't be a trial to prove your conjecture or feeble attempt to link us with those crimes. The client came to us. Before that, he was completely unknown to us."

Her eyes focused on the device in my hand. I raised it in the air to give her a better look.

"That belongs to me," she said.

"That belongs to the city of Metropolis," Hub interjected.

She raised a finger, and her male aide stepped forward with his mobile computer screen. "We have the signed documents transferring ownership of the device to us—"

Hub drew and blasted the aide's computer out of his hands. Every samurai soldier aimed their weapons. Metro Police aimed theirs. Even I was shocked by what Hub had done. That man had some steel balls.

"I don't see any signed documents," he said.

The aide's mouth was still hanging open, as was the female aide. The Council of Corporations President was unfazed.

"We, of course, have copies," she said to Hub. "We purchased a legal product, and we will not leave this place until that product is in our possession."

"That device is stolen national security property and will be taken into possession by the Metropolis Police Department," Hub said.

"It's so predictable for the government to invoke state security, when it has nothing else. Police Chief Hub, please know that I will use all the force necessary to obtain that legally purchased product. We will not be bullied by a government paper pusher, who has today decided to play soldier. We employ real soldiers, and they are standing with me."

"Since we're only paper pushers, and not the best police on the planet, having dealt with criminals far more dangerous than you, whenever you want to start, say the word."

I began to get their attention by throwing the device in the air a bit and catching it. Then I threw it from one hand to another. Then I began shaking it and tried to see if I could break it in half. I looked up and Hub and the CC President were watching me like frozen statues. Everyone was watching me. I'm sure snipers on both sides were moving into position.

I walked to the spot equidistant between both of them and set the device on the ground and then took several steps back and then folded my hands and waited.

It was funny to watch them. Hub looked at me, then at her. She looked at him, then at me. They were both deciding if they should just dive on it like a little kid, yelling "Mine!" I saved them the trouble.

The device exploded. Hub jumped back, and so did she. Police and soldiers re-trained their weapons on each other. After they calmed themselves, Hub was glaring at me. The CC President looked as if she were going to run up to me and claw my eyes out. I stood with the remote detonator in my hand, showing them. I tossed it to the ground.

"Neither one of you will have it." I walked through them both and away from all of them.

I would have to walk more than two miles to my waiting vehicle, the same hoverlimo on loan from Run-Time's company. I heard the CC

President yell to one of her aides, "Scan the fragments to verify it was not a dummy."

She and Hub would realize that it was the real thing and that it was forever out of their grasp.

CHAPTER 78

Ichi Jumper

I came out of the elevator, and I could see my Liquid Cool office door was open. I walked in and there was The Shocker waiting, with Bugs and PJ next to him. She pointed.

There, at the threshold of my private office, was the crispy-critter body of Ichi Jumper. I had no doubt that he'd planned to hide somewhere in my office and wait for me. He didn't know that I had all kinds of friends, including those very good at rigging booby-traps for maniacs.

A loud sigh of relief came out. It was over. I didn't know who he was, why he was after me, and never would. It was a mystery I could live with (though I would find out the reason in my next case). Ichi Jumper wouldn't be hunting me anymore.

My posthumous mentor, Wilford G., had said in his book, *How to be a Great Detective with 100 Rules:* One of the simpler things that you had to accept, being a street detective, was that everything wasn't always going to be tied up in a nice, little red bow at the end. Sometimes, the bad guy would get away. Sometimes the case wouldn't get solved. Sometimes, every question wouldn't get answered. That was life, and it existed long before you came into the universe, and that's how it would be long after you exited. So be a grown up, accept it, and move on to your next case.

I did that happily and moved on to my next case—and my next cases. The Electric Sheep Massacre Case was filed away, and the war between the uber-governments and the megacorporations would never come to be, and neither would free energy, because nothing ever was truly "free" in this universe.

Speaking of cosmic events, Dot and I would welcome that cool baby, known as Cruz Jr., into the world. Up until then, I had dealt with all kinds of psychos—humans, cyborgs and robots—and even crazier clients.

However, I had never, ever dealt with—extraterrestrials.

PROLOGUE IN THE EPILOGUE

Hoverhotels. Metropolis had many of them for the society's eccentric—but super-wealthy—leisure class, all different sizes and configurations. They were mobile, floating residences that slowly circled the supercity in an endless loop. The course of one—a pink domed hoverhotel—took a month, high above the normal hovertraffic sky lanes. There was never much of a view for the occupants—dark, rainy skies all around.

In a middle suite, a well-dressed man sat in his living room in the dark, waiting. The shades for the large bay windows were pulled back on either side, but any illumination was minimal—only an occasional passenger jet in the distance with blinking indicator lights. The plush chair he sat in almost swallowed him whole, his forearms resting on its arms. The call came in—a slight ringing in both ears. He waved his fingers in the air to connect.

He looked at his wrist and neon numbers flashed. "You are late by five minutes, two seconds."

Another man's voice on the other end cleared his throat. "Sorry, sir."

"Good news for me?"

There was a long pause on the other end. "Sir, we have a problem."

"Yes?"

"The London Prime sellers are dead—both of them."

"Explain to me slowly—and carefully—what happened."

"We tailed them from their arrival at the airport, to their hotel and wherever they went in the city, as instructed. We never let them out of our sight, and they never knew we were tailing them. They got some hovertrash truck drivers to take them to the River—that's outside of—"

"I know what and where the River is."

"Well, they were dropped off. They were waiting, so we assumed it was for other buyers. They were carrying a silver briefcase. We planned to come up, stick them up, and steal the device, but—"

"Yes?"

"Someone else showed."

"Who?"

"We got a good picture of him for ID."

"And? So who is he?"

"The database said he's—dead. He was a scientist—renewable energy scientist—specializing in nuclear fission power—from London Prime, UKT, too. He didn't look like a scientist, though. He looked like someone you wouldn't want to run into in a bad dream."

There was a long pause. "What did this supposed dead scientist do?"

"There was a terrible fight. They went into the Valves and—he killed them and took the device—the silver briefcase."

"What did you do, besides watch?"

"We tried to get there, sir. We were going to stick him up and take the device from him."

"Or you could have just shot him since he was a murderer and a thief."

"That too, sir, but—well—we got there and—he just disappeared. We don't know where he went. There was no place for him to go. We would have done an exhaustive search, but he was gone, and we didn't want to be seen, so we got out of there."

"Yes."

"But we stayed in the sector, sir, to keep watch. See if we could spot him again, or if someone else showed up. We never left—day and night we waited."

"And?"

"The trashmen came back with a third man."

"Who was the third man?"

"We IDed him, sir—a Metropolis detective by the name of Cruz."

"Cruz!"

"Yes, sir. What's wrong?"

"The one who solved that City Hall scandal case and the Blade Gunner situation."

"Oh, yeah. Yes, sir, and the Movie-Town scandals too."

"This changes everything."

"It does, sir?"

"This detective has a reputation for finding things out. We can't have him meddling in our plans."

"Maybe he can lead us to the dead man and we can get the device."

"If only that could be so. Are the police involved now?"

"Yes, sir. They called them in soon after. They showed up in force. The entire area is cordoned off."

"We have to continue as if we'll never get the device. What is of paramount importance is keeping this Cruz character out of our business. He must not learn of us. He has connections with Metropolis PD, the Feds, even Up-Top police."

"Really, sir?"

"He pretends to be small-time, but he isn't. Who do we have here now in the city?"

"Um—Ichi—"

"Ichi Jumper?"

"Yes, sir, but using him is like using a machine-gun to dust your house."

"He gets results—a true agent of chaos."

"But, sir, he walks up to his targets and gives them his business card with his name on it. What professional does that?"

"This one does. He's untraceable, so what does it matter? Contact him and get him after this Cruz. Ichi will have no problem dealing with him. He has never failed."

"What are the instructions for Ichi?"

"Get this Cruz off the case."

"What if Cruz won't go away?"

"Kill him, of course."

"Yes, sir."

The man on the other end hung up. Immediately, another call came in and the man waved his fingers again to connect.

"Did you hear all that?" he asked.

A new male voice answered, much deeper, with a faint echo in the background, as if he were calling from a tunnel. "Yes."

"We have to assume the device is gone. Even if we can obtain it, it will be too late. The launch is in two days."

"The device was the answer to some key problems."

"It simply means we go back to the original plan. What of the freighter?"

"They will soon arrive on Mars with the object, make the final preparations, then depart. So you have a year for them to get to Earth."

"I'll be waiting."

Extraterrestrials, Martian freighters, secret objects, and mystery men—Oh my! The new case explodes in *I, Alien Hunter (Liquid Cool, Book 5)*!

Thank you for reading!

Dear Reader,

I hope you enjoyed my **Liquid Cool** cyberpunk detective novel, ***The Electric Sheep Massacre***.

<u>Can You Write Me a Review?</u>

If you enjoyed ***The Electric Sheep Massacre*** *(Liquid Cool, Book 4)*, I'd greatly appreciate an honest review on one or more of the following sites:

Reviews are the best way for readers to discover good books. My writer's motto is simple: "Readers Rule!" Thanks so much.

Always writing,

Austin Dragon

CONTINUE THE ADVENTURE

Get Your Next *Liquid Cool* Books!

- ***These Mean Streets, Darkly*** *(Liquid Cool Prequel Short)*
- ***Liquid Cool*** *(Liquid Cool: The Cyberpunk Detective Series, Book 1)*
- ***Blade Gunner*** *(Liquid Cool, Book 2)*
- ***NeuroDancer*** *(Liquid Cool, Book 3)*
- ***The Electric Sheep Massacre*** *(Liquid Cool, Book 4)*
- ***I, Alien Hunter*** *(Liquid Cool, Book 5)*
- ***A.I. Confidential*** *(Liquid Cool, Book 6)*

- ***Liquid Cool Box Set*** *(Liquid Cool Prequel and Books 1-3)*
- ***Liquid Cool Box Set 2*** *(Liquid Cool: Books 4-6)*

Also by Austin Dragon

See all my books in science fiction, horror, and fantasy at: http://www.austindragon.com/books

ABOUT THE AUTHOR

Austin Dragon is the author of the ***After Eden Series***, including the mini-series, ***After Eden: Tek-Fall***, the classic ***Sleepy Hollow Horrors***, the new epic fantasy adventure ***Fabled Quest Chronicles***, and the cyberpunk detective series, ***Liquid Cool***. He is a native New Yorker, but has called Los Angeles, California home for the last twenty years. Words to describe him, in no particular order: U.S. Army, English teacher, one-time resident of Paris, political junkie, movie buff, Fortune 500 corporate recruiter, renaissance man, dreamer.

He is currently working on new books and series in science fiction, fantasy, and classic horror!

Connect with Austin on social media at:

Website and blog: http://www.austindragon.com

Twitter: https://twitter.com/Austin_Dragon

Pinterest: http://www.pinterest.com/austindragon

Google+: https://google.com/+AustinDragonAuthor

Goodreads: https://www.goodreads.com/ADragon

Other books by Austin Dragon
See all my books at: **http://www.austindragon.com/books**